NATURE'S FURY

DENNIS LUKE

NATURE'S FURY

BY
DENNIS LUKE
With Adrian Tame

In amongst all this chaos comes an unexpected
real-life hero

A publication of Wild Dreams Publishing
Traralgon, Vic
© 2019 by Dennis Luke
All rights reserved, including the right of reproduction in whole or in part
in any form.
Wild Dreams Publishing is a registered trademark of Wild Dreams
Publishing.
Manufactured in Australia.
All rights reserved.

Graphic Artist Lime
Editing© Adrian Tame and Katie Nash

ACKNOWLEDGEMENT

I'm grateful and humbled for the support and help from my trouble and strife wife, Margaret, and my two tin lids kids, Elliott and Bellinda, Ell and Bell, for putting up with me for so long. Lord Cardigan (Adrian), for your help in editing and advice throughout this journey.

And Kerry the English tutor, who tried valiantly to help me with the grammar side bar stuff.

Last but not least Katie and Yvette from Wild Dreams Publishing, who are to blame for this venture.

Keep on fighting Melissa.

1

PROLOUGE

Death is inevitable. The problem is no one knows when, where or how. You could be in a plane or train crash, or even as you're walking the dog one sunny afternoon, when a car suddenly careers out of control.

Sometimes victims are aware of the approaching danger, and are powerless to stop it. But every so often we don't know what our next move will be, or what driving force is guiding our fate.

Life can be inextricably linked to the many and varied forces. It's only when you find yourself facing death that you sometimes find the will to live - or not. Take Mother Nature's Fury for instance...

∼

HIGH ABOVE THE earth there are hundreds if not thousands of floating satellites, with their lenses fixed below on a monolithic clouded formation, which has come to be known as Cyclone Yasi. It is currently heading west towards the North Queensland Coastline. Meanwhile zooming in you can see a small diminutive figure, on a bright sunny morning in North Queensland. A reporter is preparing for a live broadcast. With the stunning beach setting around her, she is about to take her listeners into her world of impending doom. There she begins to portray to the world what some will thrust aside as typical media hype... but is it?

"G'day Australia, this is Wendy Sinclair here on A.B.C. Radio. I'm talking to you live from Mission Beach in far North Queensland.

It's nestled in between Cairns and Townsville, a beautiful two-hour drive south from Cairns, along a winding and sometimes treacherous coast road. It's the middle of the morning, and what I can tell you is there's got to be over a hundred people here, strolling casually along this wonderful golden beach. They are all mesmerised while looking out across the calm water – which is not making much of a disturbance at this time – along the shoreline. In the face of an approaching dark and gloomy looking cyclone in the distance. There are people here of all ages, including a mum holding her baby son, while she takes snapshots of her family. There are young teenagers, who have never been exposed to a threat of this nature before, and older people, who've seen it all in the past. It's an eerie feeling - the palm trees are swaying gently, all unprepared for what's coming.

As she steps off the pavement her eyes are also transfixed on the darkness out to sea, as her feet gently sink slightly into the golden sand, as if she is walking on a spongelike substance. She is on the golden shoreline of the Porter Promenade, and you can just see Dunk Island in the distance. They will certainly feel the full force of this cyclone, as it continues on its predicted course. Finally she walks over to her first interview, with an unassuming young couple, who are affectionately holding hands in a romantic embrace.

"Graham and his wife, Joy, are here from Tully, located just south of Mission Beach, and I'm speaking with them live." Placing the microphone in front of them both, she awaits their individual replies with her first probing question. "What's going through your mind right now, Graham?"

In his younger days, he played as a front rower for his local rugby club. But his career ended early when his right knee collapsed with a badly damaged cartilage. After finally receiving some reasonable compensation, they decided to get away for a while, and reflect on their past together, and unwind, so to speak. Before looking ahead to figure out what capacity of work Graham can do with his health, especially his troublesome knee, and now life with type 2 diabetes, and the ramifications of trying to lose weight.

At one hundred and ten kilos, and over six foot tall, Graham speaks to Wendy as his large form towers over her. "I was on this coast... gee must be twenty years ago now, before Cyclone Larry roared through, but this one's much more threatening." He shrugs his massive shoulders and finishes by saying, "I'm older now and perhaps a bit wiser."

Joy interrupts her husband's introduction and she is a diminutive figure like Wendy. "He's a big bear on the outside, and a big sook, all soft and cuddly on the inside, and I wouldn't have him any other way though." Joy's hands struggle to touch each other around the back of his wide girthed belly.

Wendy smiles at the attempted affection. "I see the romance is still there. Now, when are you two planning on leaving? Are you going back to Tully, or have you made other arrangements?"

Graham nods. "Now that we know more or less where the cyclone's heading, we're going south for a few weeks, down to our family in Melbourne. We'll stay with them until we decide to come back."

As he began to become slightly emotional, he struggles to get the rest of his words out. His voice is choking up to the point of embarrassment, and he has to turn away to keep his pride intact, as Joy attempts to hug him again and says, "If we have anything to come back to, that is."

Finishing their interview before moving onto the next person, Wendy adds, "thanks for talking with me and I hope your home survives. Wendy turns around, and as if she organised these interviews beforehand, as the next person is waiting for her. "Now I'm talking with Casey. I've been watching you taking snapshots with your family, and your son... what's his name?"

Casey smiles, "its Preston."

"What brings you to Mission Beach this morning, and shouldn't you be getting out of here?"

"We're up here on holidays from Melbourne and in a few minutes, we're off home as we're not waiting for the cyclone. We've had a great time here, and we were planning to leave tomorrow anyway, but we've moved that forward." There is tension in Casey's voice as she talks about the extreme danger that everyone can see, currently building offshore.

"You must be wondering why people are finding this so attention-grabbing."

Casey nods. "We've only ever seen cyclones on television. We have storms in Melbourne and they're scary enough, thank you very much." She declares with a touch of sarcasm in her voice, followed by a playful smile, which indicates that they will be glad to be gone from here, sooner rather than later.

"Thanks Casey and I hope you and your family get home safely." Wendy shows a wry smile in return, fully understanding Casey being in two minds as to getting out of here. It's hard to imagine just how much things could change within a few hours for the picturesque holiday spot.

"Now I'm with Bellinda and Elliott who are also from Melbourne. Seems half of Melbourne is up here. Can you explain why that might be?"

Bellinda begins, "Elliott and I are here for a Scout conference, and we were hoping to get some down time on the beach for a few days. But I guess we'll have to ride out the cyclone, like some of the other guests, and help with the clean up afterwards."

Elliott continues, "We didn't realise that it's so cheap to stay up here, whether you're on your own as a family or group, and that's one of the reasons why we came. Also, the Scout philosophy is to help other people, and it is second nature to us."

Bellinda adds, "I'm not sure how it's going to affect the conference, so we'll just ride out the cyclone, and entertain the kids like we do on Scout camps."

Elliott follows up, "If Bellinda and I were not in scouting, then we wouldn't have learnt some of the life skills that we are about to face. So we urge anyone listening that has kids, do yourself and them a favour, and join scouting, it's an adventure they'll never forget." Wendy is slightly taken aback by the maturity shown by Elliott and Bellinda, wondering why she missed out on all that adventuress spirit, as they are showing enthusiasm while calmly standing before her.

"Good luck riding out the cyclone, and I hope the conference goes well. And finally, I'm talking with Chef Jasmine here at the Castaways Resort & Spa, at Mission Beach. Hello Jasmine, how have the guests responded this week to the news of the impending cyclone?"

"Well, we have well over a hundred guests who have decided to stay and ride out the cyclone, others though, who were not terribly impressed by its timing, have already left. Those guests that have chosen to stay know their safety is up to them."

"What about supplies for the residents in the community at large?"

"Over the years, most communities along this coastline have stuck to one simple saying: 'Stock up and shut up.' Everyone knows it's vital to be ready."

Wendy observes the busy area still teeming with holidaymakers. "I'm surprised to see so many people on the beach. Aren't they concerned?"

"Most of them will probably enjoy the day, and some will stay into the evening, and then come inside around dusk. Then we'll all get together to support each other to get through the night, especially some of the older guests, and children."

"Does anything out of the ordinary happen along the coastline before a cyclone, I'm guessing you have experienced or heard of a few strange things over the years?"

Jasmine nods. "Yes, at a place called Bingil Bay, it's just five minutes up the road. That's where all the action is when a cyclone is about to arrive.

You can bet many surfers, windsurfers, kite boarders and kayakers will be out in the giant swells until the last moment, riding for as long as possible."

Wendy wraps up her interview. "Gee thanks for that great insight, Jasmine, as we head back for my late breakfast, and then I'm outta here too. This is Wendy Sinclair, reporting live on A.B.C. Radio, from Mission Beach, up here in North Queensland."

As Wendy and Jasmine stroll quickly back to the resort, everyone happily enjoys the morning sunshine. But their eyes cannot dismiss the increasing dark and ominous clouds out to sea.

2

THE NORTH QUEENSLANDER

As the story breaks around the four corners of the globe, the media frenzy is unleashed on a few billion people, of the destructive forces of cyclone Yasi that has hit with a vengeance in far north Queensland. As one reporter explains through the people he has just interviewed, the cyclone sent shivers down their spines, when they saw it in the distance.

The rotating cyclone advanced towards them, a clouded monster exposing nature at its most threatening.

Children, too young to realise the enormity of what was coming their way, continued running rings around their worried parents. They insisted their children stop playing around, as this was neither the time, nor the place, conscious of what others might think of their parenting, when in reality few could care less.

But, most children only showed bewildered looks upon their faces. Instead of obeying their parents, they continued laughing happily in the shallow surf, running away from the advancing waves to avoid getting their feet wet.

Before long, they were whisked away to a safer place, or

so their parents thought. Once inside their safe havens, they hoped would protect them from disaster, they became frightened by the unfamiliar sights and sounds assaulting their senses.

The children couldn't grasp the scale of this advancing catastrophe, until they heard houses shattering and buildings being ripped apart piece by piece, like limb from limb as if it were an animal, or possibly a human being, in this raging environment.

Someone was heard saying, "It was bad enough that we lost our house to a fire more than a decade ago, and now this? I thought it couldn't any get worse. This is too devastating even to think of a future. Will there be anything to go back to?"

The aftermath brought with it a certain feeling of numbness. A feeling as if life was over and they would have to begin again, completely.

As the days went by, news filtered through of houses, lives and friends to the sudden realisation of those that had survived, that everything had changed.

Nothing remained as it was.

This massive category five cyclone had roared ashore, with meteorologists suggesting that soon the warnings will be a category six, or even seven, with the severity getting worse.

Yasi destroyed homes, shredded crops, uprooted trees, decimated marinas and resorts, bringing powerlines down, and worst of all, left people missing.

Not knowing about one's house, their family and friends, or life after this catastrophe. People felt numb. That last part, (trophe) is interesting, like someone or something achieving success while it destroyed everything in its path.

The Red Cross described how one of its workers in the

town of Tully, moved a group of elderly people from one shelter to another. She was concerned the first location was unsafe. Her instinct saved their lives as the first shelter was completely destroyed. Was this woman commended for her efforts, or were they overlooked in the chaos? Maybe it was because the first shelter was a timber building, but the second was made of brick. The story about the three little pigs and the big bad wolf that came huffing and puffing... all came flooding back.

Margaret and her husband were huddled together in their bathroom, petrified by the cyclone's menacing roar. "The noise... it was like a train coming, it was absolutely terrifying and unbelievable when the windows popped, with glass flying everywhere, Cyclone Larry and all the other cyclones? They were nothing compared to Cyclone Yasi," they said.

Tully was decimated, it was estimated that up to half the town's homes lost their rooves to the 140-knot winds. The landscape looked like a war zone. Only there were no bombs, just Mother Nature's fury.

6 PM, THURSDAY, FEBRUARY 3, 2011.

S omewhere in a north-western country town in Victoria, Australia, a young handsome radio host is preparing to read the evening news of the day. This news is all he will broadcast, for reasons that will become apparent to all the local listeners within the district, who rely on regular updates in their secluded community.

"G'day, this is Michael Scanlon here on your outback's own radio station, A.B.C. Crazy FM, and here is the latest news. Cyclone Yasi arrived late last night, just before midnight, in North Queensland. It crossed the east coast of Australia between Innisfail and Cardwell, hitting areas from Ingham to Cairns. Residents experienced unforgiving winds of up to three-hundred kilometres per hour. It lasted three to four hours over a five-hundred-kilometre radius. The eye of the cyclone crossed the coastline at Mission Beach just after midnight, passing over the town of Tully sometime after.

The prospects of it continuing as a large and intense system are high. Astonishingly Cyclone Yasi has maintained its intensity further inland more so than what is considered normal, before it decreased slightly to a category three system near Georgetown, 450 kilometres further inland. It also affected the mining town of Mount Isa.

On the phone in Tully is A.B.C. reporter Wendy Sinclair. Good afternoon Wendy, can you update us about the damage?"

"Hello Michael, the conditions are quite devastating around me, as you can imagine, with debris strewn across roads that are impassable. It will be some time before any reasonable amount of traffic will be allowed on most of the roads... especially in the short term. Even as I'm talking to you, I am still receiving reports of fifty-foot waves crashing into the North Queensland coastline of Innisfail last night. Huge rainfalls have brought to a standstill an area hundreds of kilometres to the north, west and south of Innisfail. The howling winds uprooted one-hundred-year-old trees as though they were sticks of wood. According to reports, all types of vehicles were being tossed around in the air like paper. Some vehicles have finished up in trees, a couple on rooftops, and due to the enormous strength of cyclone Yasi, a bus is sitting precariously in someone's swimming pool.

I was here only yesterday after leaving Mission Beach in North Queensland, and these pools were filled with happy families enjoying the hot sunshine, oblivious to the approaching holocaust.

Many families, who were hiding and cowering from the overnight destruction, have woken this morning to complete devastation. Some residents who spoke with me earlier said they felt powerless and numb. Several others spoke to me as they were coming out of their unaffected homes, saying over time they had lost confidence in the government and weather services. So mostly they'd ignored the weather warnings, as they kept changing when and where it would hit."

"Were many of those one-hundred-year-old trees still intact? Or do you think they were infected in some way?"

"Funny you should ask me that, Michael. It was only a couple of weeks ago that some of the residents and a couple of representatives from the local council were discussing this very thing. They were going to get someone to inspect the trees for infections. But now I guess they will have to rethink it and cut them down, that's what's left of them, of course."

"I heard your podcast talking with Jasmine, the chef, at the Castaway Resort on Mission Beach. What did she have to say?"

"I asked her what went through her mind when she saw the devastation this morning. She didn't say anything for a few moments until she replied, 'Raw and broken.' I thought that was chilling, she nailed it."

"Wow, that's some awesome words there, Thanks Wendy. We now go to Cardwell and talk to Roger Aldridge. Hello Roger, tell us what can about last night's cyclone. I'm guessing that you're seeing the same as Wendy has?"

"Good evening Michael. Yes much the same here. It's a mess alright. Reports have been coming in throughout the day about wild seas and damaged boats. Many of the large and small boats moored along the jetties or offshore were tossed about like paper, landing on top of one another, creating numerous heaps of boats looking all squashed and mangled wrecks. I've never seen anything like this before. These once pristine sandy beaches are now cluttered with pieces of broken boats, and with heaps of rubbish scattered all along the shoreline.

They're alongside remnants of kitchens, and other fittings like outboard engines, canopies, eskies... and even food. Discarded clothing sat scattered on the sand, giving the impression that someone has washed up on the shoreline, or drowned. Driving rain has flooded the low-lying areas along the coastline. It continued its devastation into other towns on its way to Mount Isa last night, before it turned south this afternoon.

Authorities have received calls today from many residents who were terrorised by the howling winds while they cowered inside their houses. Some people told me it was just pure luck they are still alive. Their children were too frightened to sleep... unsure if they would survive the night. Waves higher than ten meters covered and destroyed some of the smaller buildings along the coastline. Areas further inland that is located at the bottom of the many deep valleys, which have continued to flood over the past twelve hours."

"Thanks, Roger, I've seen some of the photos on your station's website, and it looks like you have a long clean-up ahead also, especially along those pristine beaches you spoke about."

"Yes, thanks Michael, and I'd like to add that there are probably journalists older than I am, that have seen this devastation before. But for a newbie like me... this is just overwhelming and I can say without any fear, I'm feeling quite a bit emotional about all this. The reactions from most of the community at large who are not dillydallying around, they are focused on getting on with this large clean-up operation."

The interview winds up as a more emotional Roger finishes off with, "take care with what's coming your way, Michael."

IN AN OUTBACK AREA of the Australian bush, events are

unfolding that will have a catastrophic effect on the lives of thousands. Particularly those in the small community town called Steering.

With the ever-increasing pace of life now, compared to years ago, the changing weather patterns will mean that things are a quicker tempo now. Are you in that much of a hurry... to die?

4

(A BATTLE OF WILLS)

Yesterday, February 2nd, 2011.

IT's the early afternoon hours of the day before the cyclone, Jay, a stockman, leans on a cattle stockade gazing out across the parched landscape. With his left foot resting on the bottom fence railing, and with his arms folded on the top railing, he is squinting against the hot sun beating down on him. A small group of people are also standing close by.

Jay recalls the recent death of his parents to a reckless driver. Sorrow clouds his vision as he frowns and purses his lips hard together from his anger, at the callous way they were taken from him. They were too young to die like that, as they were both only in their early fifties, and still full of life. He and his brothers will not forget them... ever.

The little group is dwarfed by the flat and dusty property, brought to its knees by the prolonged drought. Jay and his brothers, John and Sean, are preparing a stock transfer in a far North Eastern part of South Australia. The flies are annoying at best, having been brought in by the weathered animals. Most of the people are reverting to the great Aussie salute, as they attempt to wave away the annoying flies. It's currently 42 degrees Celsius in the shade, as a clash of wills is about to take place... man, beast and nature are the protagonists.

Jay is from a family of rugged tough stockmen. He is in his late twenties, six foot four, broad shouldered and tanned. His brothers share his strong build and handsome, smiling, sharp, eye-catching, suntanned legs, arms and facial features, complete with a chiselled chin and blue eyes. But, only Sean has the dimple in his chin.

They all wear wide-brimmed Akubra hats and on hot days like these, hardened but light shirts and shorts with heavy duty boots. The three brothers had left the family property after their parents' sudden deaths. Roaming the country and working where and when it suited them, for money and for pure pleasure.

Robyn Hunt produces a regional A.B.C. radio program for a station called Crazy FM, and is at the cattle property to interview these three stockmen.

Robyn is smartly dressed in a light blue t-shirt and long shorts, with dark flowing hair down to the middle of her back. She is wearing comfortable shoes in this unpredictable rough environment.

Robyn is unprepared for their handsomeness.

As she turns on her recorder to start the interview, she looks up and is struck by Sean's stunning good looks, and piercing blue eyes. She has seen many good-looking men in her job before... but not like Sean.

Maybe it is the partly closed deep set piercing blue eyes, that are closed by the sun and with his smouldering presence that melts her into the...

Jay puts a hand on her arm, snapping her out of her trance, while Sean is all charm, distracting Robyn.

Robyn is about to begin her introduction but is still taken aback by Sean's charms, and stuffs up her first interview attempt. Finally, she opens her mouth, but it takes a few words before she settles into her familiar rhythm. Clearing her throat, she finally begins her interview with a deeper, more confident tone.

"The role of a stockman has often been celebrated in various forms of media, for their ability to bring down a bull, or is it for their cheeky, sharp wit?" She turns to them and smiles at the brothers... especially Sean.

John chimes in, "Early stockmen were carefully selected, and highly regarded men. This was because of the value and importance, in those early days during the last century, of livestock. They needed to be able to handle animals with confidence and patience, and to make accurate observations about them, while they are able to still enjoy the great life outdoors."

Jay moves away as John and Sean continue with the interview. He watches from a short distance as a semi-trailer reverses up to the old wooden loading dock, where Texas longhorn bulls stand motionless inside the fenced-off area, their flicking tails their only sign of life in this withering heat.

THE SEMI DRIVER, Ron Williams, is just shy of forty, and it's something he's not looking forward to.

He is large of frame, and is used to winning life's confrontations, whether with man or beast, but he is exhausted after the long drive in this unbearable heat, regardless of the air conditioning.

A strong looking rugged type, presumably younger than one might guess, he begrudgingly steps down from the cab.

Sweat forms on his forehead and trickles down the front of his face, almost as if he was crying. He is dressed in the customary dark blue singlet, dark blue shorts and heavy boots. His portly belly also gives the impression he likes a beer... or two.

Up until a couple of years ago, after he was pestered by his wife to stop, he would often have a few beers. Now he doesn't touch a drop unless he's not driving for more than a couple of days.

Dianne orders him to stop, before she throws him his big straw brimmed hat. He ruefully puts his hat on his head. In his younger days, he would never wear one, but after Dianne pestered him about the implications of Melanoma, he tries to wear it.

She had lost her father last year because he hadn't covered up in his younger years, simply because it wasn't understood like it is now, or spoken about back then, and she worries about Ron out there in the heat.

He stubbornly thinks that he might not be affected by it now. But, it's the cancer which comes out anywhere on your body later in life. It's about not wearing a hat on his slightly balding head... especially in this heat.

The effect of this overwhelming heat is accentuated by the air conditioning he has left behind in the cab. He has been given to understanding the horrors of little or no instruction into personal hygiene. He has been told in no uncertain terms by the missus to put on deodorant, especially in this heat. *'Do not be like other people who don't use any sort of deodorant, especially in any hot climate in western civilisation,'* she has continually nagged him about it.

With the blast of the heat, he begins to make whinging sounds that reflect his demeanour, as he walks back to the loading area with an awkward gait.

A glassy-eyed but somewhat menacing gaze from one of the longhorn bulls, waiting in a separate holding area brings an unexpected shiver down his spine as he passes it. After all these years of moving large beasts, it's something a little new to him. Ron has never dealt with Texas longhorns before today, and gets the feeling that this could be a little bit more than an average run to the abattoir. He takes an awkward step backwards, frowning and eyeing down this one particular bull.

"First time with longhorns, mate?" says Jay, pleasantly, but with the rough tone born of years outside in dusty surrounds.

Ron turns and nods awkwardly putting out his right hand. Jay does likewise, and they exchange names.

Jay explains, "Well at least ya only have to take 'em to the abattoir, mate. You don't need to lay a hand on 'em, compared to the rest of us, so relax, mate, and enjoy the show." Jay puts his tongue in his cheek to let Ron know he is having a bit of fun at Ron's expense, even though Jay knows things can quickly turn bad, especially when one of these types of bull is on its own and agitated.

Ron asks in his deep and commanding voice, "Brought the wife and kids along for the trip. Ok if I get 'em to stand somewhere so they can watch, as you say, the show?"

"Yeah, sure, Ron," says Jay, pointing to Mrs. Wilson the wife of the farmer who owns the beasts. She is standing by Jay's wife, both of them ready to watch the loading. "Stand over there near the shed and out of harm's way, as I'm about to go back to a radio interview."

JAY and his brothers have been helping the Wilsons sell up and move on after fifty years of hard labour, and all because of the drought.

Over the last decade, a severe drought has affected the continent of Australia, due to the prolonged effect from the weather phenomenon known as El Nino (the dry).

The long drought has affected the supply of natural grass. Vast lands across the world, not just in Australia, have become dried up, so much so that some cracks in the earth are quite deep.

This situation has brought about the need to sell the Wilson farm, or it would have broken their spirits.

Texas longhorn bulls and other varieties are getting loaded into semi-trailers to be sent to other farms or abattoirs, located across various parts of the country.

Robyn had already spoken with the Wilsons and found out some facts from their experiences once they'd come to their farm. They love the open air and beautiful country, where they have made so much of their life. But, they had finally realised the toll that it has taken on them both, with no public holidays, working over Christmas, no rostered days off, weekends or a decent holiday.

Jay and his brothers were asked to help as the new owners will do other things instead of running cattle or sheep. The Wilsons, who are now well into their seventies, will be heading to a small cottage in a couple of weeks, and this will allow them to be closer to their children, and grandchildren.

The Wilsons had made the commitment to the farm from the beginning, unaware of the toll it would take on their life.

But, how would anyone know what the future would bring?

The decision to sell up had been just demoralising. But, walking for both of them over the last few years has become somewhat laboured, with Mrs. Wilson faring the worst – a diagnosed hip condition in need of urgent replacement.

Medication also helps Mr. Wilson have some good quality of life, but they aren't helping his wife, an operation the only fix. By the time surgery will happen they would have settled into their new home.

The opportunity was to get out now while they have a buyer, without being distracted by pride or selfishness. They are getting out now because they can, not because they want to.

BACK AT THE LOADING DOCK, Ron turns to Jay. "Thanks Jay, will do." Ron turns around and strolls to his recently purchased Kenworth cab where his wife, Dianne, is watching their two twin girls, who are fraternal in their looks, as they bounce up and down on the double bed, located in the sleeping compartment in the back of the prime mover.

Dianne is a bold, thirty something eye-catching women, with olive skin and long blond hair tied up for the journey.

She hasn't a care in the world, or at least that's the

impression that she seeks to get across. She's devoted to her twin eight-year-old girls, and top to bottom in love with her man Ron. Dianne is dressed in a casual, light coloured red dress with light pink sandals, and a not-too-large wide-brimmed hat, with a couple of small feathers protruding from a one-centimetre white band.

Bridgette is more like her father, dressed in a t-shirt and shorts, with a baseball cap and a band holding her hair in a ponytail.

Her hard-wearing sneakers complete the impression of a tomboy. She has a stockier build than her sister Stephanie.

Stephanie is smartly dressed like her mother, with a smaller hat. She has some freckles like Bridgette with her flowing long blonde hair, and smoother features. Apart from that of her tomboy sister, she has a small beauty spot to the left of her well formed petite nose.

Ron has some stern words for the twins. Ron says, while trying very hard to keep a straight face, "Don't you know this is where your mother and I sleep? I don't think your mother would appreciate all those lumps, and you dirtying the sheets on her side of the bed, do you?"

The girls stop, and drop their heads, thinking they are in trouble.

"I thought *that's* where *you* were sleeping," Dianne remarks, pointing at the driver's seat as they both try to keep a straight face.

Ron turns back to look at Dianne. "Ha-ha funny, c'mon, got something for you all to see."

Once the girls had put their footwear back on their feet, they scramble out of the prime mover, the girls skip along the dusty path together, causing the dust to rise up onto Stephanie's nice clean clothes, but not Bridgette's. Dianne calls out to Stephanie to stop getting her clothes dirty.

Stephanie stops as Ron walks past shaking his head. A smiling Bridgette on the other hand continues on without a care in the world as they pass Robyn along the way. As Ron hears Robyn continue her interview with the stockmen, he takes the family to the viewing area located next to a large shed.

ROBYN ASKS. "Do you have many problems getting the bulls with the wider horns into the trailer?"

Jay answers cautiously. "Well they pretty much have that figured out for themselves and most go in without any help from us. Mind you, those three over there could be trouble." Jay points to the offending trio, then to another bull on its own. "But that big one we'll have to leave 'til last. He'll need a little bit more persuading than the rest of the herd." He raises his voice in the bull's direction so the bull can hear him.

"ESPECIALLY HIM", he shouts sarcastically with a smile.

The large, unpredictable bull snorts, and completely ignores Jay.

Robyn asks, "Some of these yearling longhorn bulls still have their horns. Is there a reason for that?"

"The owners can't always afford to have them removed. Plus there's money to be made for a complete set of horns." John's voice reflects his sympathy for the many farmers grappling with selling and moving on to somewhere else.

"Surely the majority of farmers through recent generations, have experienced hardships on a similar scale, at one point in their lives?"

Jay nods, "Sure, but nothing could have prepared even

the real smart ones for this drought. I've seen the insecurity throughout the country. Even ends in suicide sometimes. There are quite a lot of other farmers in the same boat who are grappling with selling and moving on to somewhere else.

Sean agrees with what Jay says, and with his demeanour reflecting not only the hardships, but also what some farmers have had to deal with, when it comes to unruly bulls.

"The prized yearling weighs in at around one ton, and as you can see, he continues to eye off the rest of the herd. He has been separated from this group since his birth, to protect them from his volatile nature. Longhorns are regarded as docile, especially during their quiet periods and in between mating season. But there's always that one farmer intent on breeding feisty cattle."

Robyn nods and is aroused by his husky tone. She listens and looks closely as Sean continues. "For the most part, they're incredibly unassuming animals. They're even calm enough to make great pet cows, I guess."

This brings a surprised expression to Robyn's face and he nods in confirmation. "Seriously, they can be trained like dogs. But you'll never put 'em in an environment they aren't familiar with, as they can't cope with too many distractions."

"What do you mean? Even in a controlled environment with crowds standing around?" Robyn looks at him, surprised.

Jay nods. "Yes, like a cattle sale or the local showgrounds, anything can spook them, even a balloon."

Suddenly and nervously Robyn points at the pen nearby. "But these ones have been penned overnight, haven't they? Most of them look quite placid to me from here."

Jay smiles, "Sure, but someone like you looking at them

for the first time can get the wrong impression. They're not always what they seem. Also their horns can grow in different shapes. Some curl up and back, or even forward, while some are straight as can be, making them seemingly hostile to the untrained eye, like yours Robyn."

Sean adds, "It's often this prized Longhorn that will cause trouble. It can be likened to the monsoon season as their whole mood can suddenly change from quite placid, to uncontrollable."

John removes his hat to have a short scratch of his head, and then turns back to Robyn with a more serious look on his face, and with a more rigid stance.

"There is now proof it's not just the colour red that attracts the bull, or the sight of the moving cape, but maybe it's the challenge against a matador itself." His tall handsome demeanour enhances his narrative.

Robyn nods with interest, "I've watched the running of the bulls in Spain on TV. It shows how scary they can be, with hundreds of blokes and the occasional woman all trying to come on all macho-like to achieve bulletproof status."

John grimaces, "Most years it's a lottery for death. So if your number's up... it's a terrible way to go."

Jay interrupts the monologue and talks about how the award-winning longhorn became so nasty.

"The Longhorn's mother died after giving birth. He was thrashing about when his legs began to appear. Nobody realised the damage he was causing his mother. Robyn felt sad for the bull's mother. She could not imagine having to give birth to a beast like that.

"A few days later even the vet found it hard to hold him still. He kicked the poor vet in the groin region, and in doing so the vet dropped like a sack of potatoes, onto the hard ground and nearly knocked himself out. The newborn landed squarely on its feet, and took off as fast as he could... nothing was going to hold him back." He gave a chuckle.

John joined in the laughter. "Not being able to see well enough being a newborn, he stumbled through the grass and tripped on some rough ground, finally collapsing outside the barn where he was born. He got smart and his owners found him hard to pin down."

John continued. "He grew into a tough, fierce beast. One flick from his horns could make a mess of anything, or *anyone* that got in his way."

Sean smiles as he looks down on a melting Robyn. "Rage is in us all, animals and humans alike. All it takes are the right circumstances mixed with an overwhelming affliction to do harm, to whomever or whatever. And then it can be quite unexpected if the right situation presented itself to those that are unfamiliar. So you have to have your wits about you when you're around *any* animal and not just bulls."

Robyn attempts to remain professional by looking at her notes instead of the stockmen, especially Sean. Then she raises her head slightly and without making any eye contact with him, continues her questions.

"With rage, in your opinion, do you believe there is a distinction between both animal species and humans that can be attributed to genes, hormones, testosterone or even D.N.A.? Or are there more environmental factors like heat or surroundings? Can we learn to understand how to live together?"

Robyn looks up into Sean's beautiful, piercing blue eyes as he listens to her... and she would love to say 'yes, we can live together.'

John spoils the moment of her desire and explains to

Robyn, "yes, some factors do, and there are many ways animals and humans can live together. But it all comes down to understanding, acceptance, patience, love and respect of animals, regardless of what type they are."

∽

A FEW MOMENTS LATER, back at the loading dock, Jay is guiding the bulls calmly up the ramp and into the trailer, while John and Sean use plastic ribbons to move the animals around.

Robyn continues her interview. "What are the ribbons for?"

John responds, "Working cattle this way is the preferred method nowadays, having taken over from electric prods." He explains that small deliberate movements of the ribbon alongside an animal's head will turn and guide it.

"Wildly waving a stick is not a good idea and children are taught at a very young age how to work all animals, especially bulls."

Robyn nods with interest. "I read somewhere that most pens or stockades go in a circular clockwise direction. Why's that?"

Jay answers this time. "Holding the bulls closer together keeps 'em calm with less chance of piercing one another. Calm animals are easier to guide than agitated ones and it helps us move 'em without causing stress or pain."

"How do you know which animal to put in first... then next?"

"When a particular animal is selected we open a side gate to allow the animal to head straight up the ramp, and into the trailer. Most can go in at any time, but some are left till last, depending on their character. Like that one over there." Sean explains.

John adds, "That big young Longhorn had a nose ring put in at birth. That decision was crucial that one be placed on him at birth after his behaviour on that day. Much too wound up for a newborn... maybe he has ADHD?"

It is now time to put the biggest Longhorn bull in. The other bulls that have been loaded are kept in separate holding sections away from the other Longhorn bulls. Some of which have had their horns caught on wire, or gaps in the timbers. The boys have to make sure none of the other bulls receive any accidental damage, especially to their hides, or cut themselves thus causing infection.

John and Sean use prodders that have a slight electrical charge in them, to coerce the more resistant ones if needed. Today most go in without any trouble.

Jay will lead the prized Longhorn towards the back of the trailer, with a nose ring connected to a rope to temper its aggression.

The trailer is backed up to a run that extends out into a paddock, where the prized longhorn had roamed and enjoyed himself recently, with the last group of fertile longhorns from a neighbouring property.

"By this time tomorrow, Robyn," says Jay, "the prized longhorn will most likely be in pieces of steak. I hope for his sake someone might take him off the abattoir's hands, and use him for stud."

"Why is this breed of bull so different from others?" Robyn asks.

"These days Texas Longhorns are a registered breed. They're good cattle for many reasons, their meat is good and lean for eating, and they don't need antibiotics or added hormones. Then there are their beautiful colours and unique horns. Farmers like Mr. and Mrs. Wilson often appreciate the history and qualities of the breed." Jay answers.

"Do they breed like other bulls?" She asks with a hint of suggestion in her voice, wondering if Sean would partake in her subtle hint.

Sean responds this time, ignoring her expressions.

"They're often used as service sires on other breeds of cattle, because they tend to have fewer birthing difficulties. Quick growing calves have fewer health problems, and that's partly due to their fitness. Also they live longer and they're disease resistant. All this helps them survive harsh conditions."

"Cattle that rarely see humans can grow wild and wary, yes?" Robyn questions.

Jay nods in agreement. "Yes absolutely, and Texas longhorn bulls reach about twenty five percent of their eventual tip-to-tip horn measurement, at about one year of age on average. By four years of age they have reached approximately ninety-five percent of their maximum length. That's why that big one is standing there motionless and ready for anything. He has slightly longer horns than those of the same age which is partly due to his unique nature. Plus you would have to be a bloody idiot not respecting something as cunning as that one."

Robyn smiles, I'll hang around and watch you and your brothers do your stuff if that's okay? And thanks for talking with me today."

John nods, "Not a prob, Rob. Just in case something goes wrong, I'll get you to head over there with Ron and the rest of the onlookers."

Robyn thanks them all, but has a special kiss on the

cheek for Sean, who covers his embarrassment by hurrying off with John and Jay to load the bulls.

CLOSING IN ON THE TRAILER, the prized bull shows he is more than a match for the brothers, who soon realise they could be in for a bit more than trouble.

As he struggles with the rope, Jay slips on a mound of bullshit while leading the huge longhorn into the back of the trailer, allowing the rope to slacken enough for the nose ring to loosen.

Taking his chance, the longhorn rears up using his weight and strength to halt his progress, as he walked casually up the metre and a half wide ramp.

Jay has landed on the trailer floor in front of the bull. He lies deliberately quiet and motionless. He is acutely aware of the half a metre long horns waving dangerously close to his head. Luckily, the longhorn is distracted for a moment by Ron's wife, Dianne, and her flapping red dress.

It billows around her in the breeze near the side of the rear of the trailer, giving Jay just enough time to regain his footing, and strengthen his hold on the rope that is loosely connected to the bull's nose ring.

DIANNE WAS FEELING SOMEWHAT bored by the show and the intense heat as she headed back to the truck, oblivious as to the consequences of her boredom.

Robyn is seen talking into her microphone, commenting on what is happening in front of her.

No one has noticed that Dianne had moved away from behind her children and Mrs. Wilson.

Mrs. Wilson is also more interested in how the children were reacting while watching the bull than she is about the show, as she had seen it all before.

The eyes from the longhorn bull show a familiar steely gaze, which fills him with something a little like Testosterone.

John and Sean force the creature back up the ramp, ramming him repeatedly on his rump with the electric prodders. Without warning, the bull surges backwards and catches the brothers off guard. And for a split second, it seems Jay will be trampled to death, but at the last second the bull switches his attention to John and Sean.

Together they leap clear over opposite sides of the ramp, falling hard on the ground, yelling curses at the beast to disguise their dented pride.

The bull storms back down the already unstable ramp into the holding area where he breaks through a weakened part of the fence like it was made of paper, and turns back around in the direction of Dianne.

Terrified at what she sees in front of her, she scrambles behind a sturdy looking part of the fence. Her flowing red dress further enrages the bull. Dianne is frozen on the spot as the bull builds up speed and continues to charge towards her.

Upon hearing the commotion, Mrs. Wilson, and especially the children, sees the large bull heading towards their mother. They begin frantically crying and screaming to encourage their mother to get out of the way, or run as fast as she can.

Their calls of distress are not received by Dianne, as the bull closes in on her.

5

(THE BROTHERS)

Early evening
        In a neglected northern part of the town of Steering, five young men are preparing to leave their home, for a night of drinking at the local pub.

Luke is the youngest of the five and is not a big drinker like his four brothers. He is about to celebrate his eighteenth birthday, and has no idea of what his siblings have in store for him.

Luke is scrawny, but at 180cm, is growing fast. His life has been changing recently since he started full time work, introducing maturity to a mind and body.

He suffers and continues to work through various ailments like a heart murmur, epilepsy, no Achilles and an Autism spectrum disorder known as Asperger's. But looking at him both now, and in the past, he is no different than anyone else his age, as some ailments are managed through medication.

It is only the brain that is different to, well, most normal people. Nothing has stopped him though, compared to a few years ago, when he'd almost given up on any hope for the future.

He doesn't care too much about his diet, but struggles to find the room for food sometimes, as his metabolism is excellent, and the lack of energy to do the least menial task is gradually improving.

Nick is twenty-eight, and is the hardest and oldest of the brothers. He has assumed seniority over the family since the death of their father. He's not sure where their mother has disappeared to.

This, alongside his shortness of stature, leaves him in a state of permanent anger, punctuated by regular outbursts of foul temper, rage, nonstop drinking, or undiagnosed bipolar.

He lies across the dilapidated old sofa in the lounge room, thinking about another beer. Finally, he stands up and goes into the kitchen and grabbing the handle, aggressively flings open the fridge door, taking the last can off a shelf. His brothers know not to touch anything on that particular shelf, or they risk a flogging.

He flicks open the can and sculls it down in one long gulp. He turns around so everyone can hear him belch loudly, as he addresses the second eldest brother, Rick, who has just entered the room.

Rick is twenty-four and is dressed very differently from Nick. He wears an ironed white shirt, neat blue shorts, and black shoes. Nick is dressed in a tattered t-shirt and shorts, so he can reveal various tatts on the upper and lower parts of his body.

"Go and get..." Nick suddenly belches again, "... that little shit from his room and let's get this party... farted."

Nick laughs, realising what he has just said. "Shit, I

meant started... no... I like farted," He corrects himself and continues laughing again.

Nick had started drinking a few hours ago, and over the years, his body has come to accept copious amounts of liquor. Consumed over a short period, it has little effect on his senses, or so he thinks.

The twenty-two-year-old twins, Ryan and Brian, dressed remarkably like Nick, enter the lounge room. The pair of them will do anything for Nick, but not out of sibling affection. They are both only too well aware of his temper and will go to any lengths to avoid ending up on the wrong side of it.

Nick flings his empty beer can with a resounding crash into the rubbish bin, receiving a high five from Rick for landing it without touching the sides.

Rick, a few years younger and sightly taller than Nick, is every bit as habitually foul tempered, but something reserved in his nature serves to keep Nick off-balance.

Rick is an accomplished athlete.

In fact he is a long-distance runner with a good chance of representing Australia in next year's 2012 Olympics in London.

Luke, almost as elegantly dressed as Rick, is escorted out of the house, into the claustrophobic, humid atmosphere of the early evening. Nobody says much, apart from Nick, as they'd all just as soon be back in the air-conditioned house.

Nick just wants to get legless. That, and take out his frustrations on Luke. Nick believes that everyone in the family is lucky to be more like him, and not like Luke, who had gotten off easy. Why shouldn't he get the same treatment, like the oldest four had had meted out to them on a daily basis, by their alcoholic father?

Unfortunately some men, and to a lesser extent, some

DENNIS LUKE

women, will do intolerable things when they're drunk, that always shows a lack of level headedness, especially compared to when they're sober.

The old man's been dead now for a little over a year now, and he had mellowed before he died, thus sparing Luke the worst of his drunken rages.

The other four never quite understood this and felt like they somehow owed Luke, for what he was lucky enough to have missed.

Luke would learn later on in life that some people don't know how to, or have the courage to remove themselves from violent family situations, or to seek help.

Nick opens the electronic garage door, revealing his new metallic black SUV with its dazzling red and orange flames along each side. He climbs in behind the stainless-steel steering wheel, he recently made with a small silver skull glowing in its centre. Rick climbs in next to him, as Ryan and Brian sandwich Luke between them in the back.

Nick, Rick and Ryan work at the abattoir with Nick in the killing room, and Rick and Ryan in the boning room. Nick gets top whack and has been employed there for close to a decade.

Management have long turned a blind eye to his vicious treatment of the animals, partly because he's productive, and partly because no-one else wants his job.

Nick indulges the dark side of his nature by tormenting animals as they attempt to flee back down the ramp, which leads to the gun he is holding.

He is able to take full advantage of Australia's typically complex rules and regulations, covering the treatment of animals in abattoirs. Those suspected of having diseases or being injured are screened out for isolation slaughter, providing Nick with ample opportunity to indulge in his more sadistic leanings.

This particular meat is used separately for other animals like dogs and cats.

Standing at the top of the ramp, he places the device just above and in between the eyes, enjoying the power as he watches the lifeless animal drop. This is done at the end of the current stock, so as not to contaminate the good meat.

Earlier that day, a fifty-three-year-old called Rex spent his first day on the job under Nick's supervision. Dressed in protective clothing, he had watched an animal drop down a chute, where he shackled the beast by its left hind leg, making sure it didn't flinch while being stunned with the special gun wielded by Nick.

Rex had pulled a lever hoisting the animal onto an overhead conveyor railing where a cut in the neck split a group of blood vessels, including the jugular veins. It bled profusely as it passed slowly over a draining trough. Then the head, legs and tail were removed from the carcass.

Rex then placed the tail and legs into a plastic bag to prevent contamination of the carcass. The head was hung up for inspection, while Nick congratulated Rex on his handiwork.

The hide had been chained and pulled off at the flank by a hide puller, "some guy from Sweden, he doesn't talk much," Nick said.

The brisket was cut by an electric saw from the breast, and offal was then taken out and dropped onto a large moving table, before the carcass was split down the middle.

Nick had shown Rex how to use the electric saw to cut the animals into two precise halves. At this stage inspectors had checked the carcass and offal.

"They'll officially stamp the inspected carcass and offal which are fit for human consumption." Nick had explained.

"What's offal?"

"It's the internal organs and entrails of a butchered animal. They can be used for many other dishes like intestines, which are traditionally used for sausages. Makes you wonder what you're eating at a B.B.Q, doesn't it?"

Both chuckled as the nerdy inspectors looked on in disgust, and didn't say anything awkward.

Nick clearly held these men in contempt and Rex soon realised, he intimidated them ruthlessly.

Nick babbled, "When I first got here years ago someone read out an article in the abattoir newsletter. In earlier times it said that mobs of people sometimes threw offal and other rubbish at condemned criminals, as a show of public disapproval."

Rex had cringed at the thought of having all that sticky stuff all over him.

"Some even tried to pretend it didn't affect them, and soon shown to be the prime undesirables they were."

"Come with me and I'll introduce you to my brothers," Nick said, ignoring Rex's response.

"They'll show you the rest of the caper and when we're through, you can join us at the pub for dinner tonight, and a few beers."

Left alone with Rick and Ryan, after Nick had made introductions, Rex casually remarked, "Nick showed me some interesting ways for killing animals."

He missed the glance that passed between the two brothers. Rick motioned Rex over to the area where the basic cutting is done, and began to explain to Rex how it is done.

"Each side of the beef carcass is cut into two quarters,

between the fifth and sixth ribs, by mechanical scissors in the quartering area. Feel down here to get the right spot and make sure you count correctly, as the inspectors go ape shit when someone stuffs up. You've got to be quick. Roughly one thousand head of cattle, sheep or other animals are slaughtered here in a day."

Rick continued to explain. "It all depends on what's waiting in the holding yards or if the semi-trailers arrive."

At this point, the twins' brother, Brian, had turned up and was introduced to Rex, who was told that *'you know what'* would be the main attraction at the pub that night. Rex just looked mystified, but hadn't said anything for fear of poking his nose into what seemed to be their personal family business.

Brian is in his final year as an apprentice electrician and is a regular at the abattoir with his boss, repairing broken down machinery and performing maintenance checks.

LUKE IS the only one of the five brothers intent on using his head rather than his hands, to earn a crust. He's in his final year at high school with a secret ambition to work in law. He's been dreading this night out for months, knowing some form of embarrassment and humiliation that Nick has carefully planned, without letting anyone else in on the details, is not forthcoming, and that will be his focus.

That evening, Nick drives the SUV out of the garage and onto a dirt road, to arrive at the local pub a few minutes later. Luke doesn't have the suicidal or bulletproof tendencies like that of his older brothers. First item on the agenda is getting Luke drunk as quickly as possible. Then the plan is to get him laid for the first time, in some misguided initiation ceremony.

Had he known anything of this, Luke wouldn't have wanted it, preferring to fall in love first with someone of his own choosing.

Then a son would be good to continue the family line. That would happen when he was ready for the responsibility. One way or another, being younger doesn't really help him understand the power others have over us. We feel helpless until one day, if at all, we stand up against this barbaric treatment, and don't allow this sort of bullying to take place any more.

When Luke was sixteen he went off to do some work experience, and he didn't want any help from his four brothers.

He went to a few places during his school holidays and met up with an old school friend. The friend told him about how he continually got bullied at work. One day he'd had enough and strung up five of the bastards as he called them... with ropes... naked. He'd left them there to suffer in full view of the public. They'd all thought he was on holidays in another state and they never touched him again after that. Only because they thought it was an ex-employee who had left a note that was spray painted on their naked bodies.

It was done to all new young employees as a form of initiation back then. It was done to them and they thought it was just the way it was... but not anymore. Luke often has visions of payback against his controlling brothers. He often felt he could do so if he had the chance... only to realise later he wouldn't have the strength or the guts to do anything like that.

It's not in his nature, but only for a moment it reinvigorated him to feel... strong.

He wondered if the time for retribution would ever raise its ugly head in another less involved form, so he praised his friend for his courage that showed no remorse for what he had done.

Had Luke felt compelled, or was he just being supportive to an old friend?

He felt obliged not too upset him, but only to go along with his friend's conquest.

INCESSANT RAIN IS DISPELLING the torment of the recent hot dry spell, as they drive through the humid night air. Nick is wondering what it will be like inside the pub. He wants the night to go smoothly and has high expectations of having as much fun at Luke's expense. Given the amount of time he's spent organising the entire sordid business, he will be less than happy if it goes wide of the mark.

Arriving at the pub, Nick sees the carpark is nearly full, and is frustrated at having to park a hundred metres from the building. So he parks in the disabled spot. After all, he's more important than any cripple.

Nobody inside tonight would give a shit either. And he can't remember anyone ever parking in that spot... *ever*.

They climb out of his SUV. Nick glances skyward as rain hits his face, and as he looks down at the hard but wet ground, he is annoyed that his precious vehicle will get wet and dirty.

On seeing his brother's concern, Ryan comments, "Forget the rain, all you need to worry about is the lightning."

But, Nick runs for the door trying to keep himself dry, and he misses Ryan's comment, or so Ryan thinks. Luckily Ryan was far enough behind Nick as not to receive any possible belting. And as he continues on towards the doors with a slight grin of satisfaction on his face, thinking Nick didn't hear what he said. He is cautiously aware he could get double that, if he steps out of line again tonight.

The brothers enter into the main bar and the entrance brings its normal combination of anxiety and contempt from those already there. Conversation dies out as every eye is on the brothers. The braver patrons express their disgust with a stream of obscene abuse, but not quite loud enough for its source to be readily identified. Nick and his brothers search above the resounding disharmony of voices for the culprits.

The brothers elbow their way across the room to their favourite corner, where Rex is waiting.

On his way to the corner, Rick orders a jug and five pots, and tells the barman, "I'll start a tab. Stick the grog up the end of the bar," he demands like he owns the place as he hands over a hundred dollar note.

Rex interrupts, "The first shout's on me, mate, so you keep your money for the next round."

Nick would have handled it differently.

He'd probably spend more than that before the night was over. But when the beer arrives, he thanks Rex, grabs the closest pot, and sculls it down, then immediately pours himself another from the jug. He leans on Luke's shoulder and drops a none too subtle hint about what's in store.

"What do I care what happens to you tonight?" Nick sneers. "I won't remember it in the morning anyway." Then he sculls his third pot.

A cringing Luke struggles to turn away, not only from Nick's bad breath, but his contempt for Nick as well.

Luke eyes the crowded room.

Fear of the unknown fills his mind, as Nick leaves him alone... for now.

6

(A DYSFUNCTIONAL FAMILY)

Every member of the Lockwood family is looking out their respective car windows, as they drive across the drought-ridden rolling hills, which are scattered throughout the district.

They are heading to a beautiful, timber house set on twenty acres, home to Pearl's father, Jack, who is eighty-eight years young.

After a two-week holiday in Melbourne, their car is jammed to the rafters, so much so that the driver can't even see out the back window. They are visiting Jack on their way home, as a welcome break on their long journey back from Melbourne.

Pearl's husband, David, has just turned thirty-eight, and is a transport manager for an interstate trucking company.

He works both at home and on the road throughout the year, and is looking forward to a break from his dysfunctional family. It's been, in all reality, a miserable holiday. He won't be doing it again in a hurry. He loves his wife dearly, but the kids, or as he – just like his father-in-law

Jack – calls them, the 'little shits,' have been intolerable during their time away.

The newborn, Stephen, is the only one to behave only because he's too little to be like his siblings. David is wearing a tight fitted short sleeve shirt – trying to give the impression that he is fit, not fat – dark blue shorts, and ancient runners. He suddenly bursts into song to break the monotony of the journey. "Alone on a hill, da-da-da-da," he sings absently, pretending to remember the words.

Pearl turns to him angrily, with a probing look on her face. "Why are you singing *that*?"

"Oh it just came into my head, when I looked up at where your father is right now."

Tiffany responds angrily from the back seat, "Dad, that's not a very nice thing to say about Grandfather."

Rhys, her brother, is in rare agreement with his sister. "Yeah Dad, that's not called for."

Pearl chimes in, "What on Earth possessed you to come up with that? You *know* he's up there all alone."

"I didn't say it to be cruel, like, it just popped into my head, you know, like stuff does from time to time. You know I just say stuff without thinking. I'm sorry, OK? Jeeze, I *know* he's all alone on that hill."

And then he adds as an afterthought, "It's so fine-looking with fantastic views and all that. Building it with those windows going all the way around, gives the place... you know, something special, trendy."

Inside the car it has gone unusually quiet as David turns into the tree-lined driveway. The sun is just setting on the property, throwing shadows in front of them. He parks the car in front of the weatherboard house while glancing up at the veranda that goes all the way around, for walking, and as a great cover if it's raining.

Intent on being the first to find her grandfather Tiffany bolts onto the veranda ahead of Rhys. She is disappointed Jack is not there with his normal, welcoming hug.

Meanwhile Pearl takes baby Stephen out of the insert of the child restraint and carries him inside with David.

Pearl has been wearing on and off for the last year, the same one piece floral dress that goes all the way down to her ankles, as though she thinks it is the early nineteen hundreds, and has no reason to wear much else.

It's comfortable and that's all that counts.

Pearl is a year older than David and was considerably anxious about her pregnancy, and as a consequence, began putting on weight, especially in the latter months, even before Stephen's birth.

David, being David, has obviously not realised with Grace's two previous pregnancies, most women can put on between ten to twenty kilograms. But he still believes she is letting herself go, both mentally and physically.

They find Jack in the kitchen preparing their dinner. Pearl had rung him earlier to let him know they were coming, and not to fuss about dinner. Annoyed, she tells him, grumpily, to go somewhere else and sit down, and that she would take care of the meal.

SHE ANNOYINGLY GREETS Jack with a kiss on the cheek and a dutiful hug. David shakes his hand but senses coldness from Jack, who excuses himself, leaving Pearl to get on with the evening meal.

Before he goes, Jack gives her a loving smile and then retreats to another room for some peace and quiet, so that he can listen to a program on poetry that was occupying him, before the family's arrival.

He's happy to be away from his visitors. He doesn't have much time for them, apart from Pearl.

Outside on the veranda, Tiffany is running, as her feet loudly bang along the veranda, when she hears the radio coming from the lounge. She enters through the back door wanting to change the station to something she can dance too.

Tiffany enjoys the freedom to go anywhere she likes in this big house, giving her the opportunity to completely shut off from anything that is troubling her, in her miserable life.

Sounds of verse are heard around the house.

I love a sunburnt country, a land of sweeping plains, of ragged mountain ranges, of droughts and flooding rains. I love her far horizons; I love her jewelled-sea, her beauty and her terror...

Tiffany, not noticing her grandfather spreadeagled across the couch with his eyes closed, turns the dial to look for a music channel.

Jack feels inspired by the verse, as he experiences visions of this breathtaking land of Australia, when the raucous notes of a pop song interrupt his daydream.

He comes around to see Tiffany dancing around the lounge. Then she notices her grandfather in his laborious state, creakily attempting to raise himself angrily up from the settee. A somewhat delayed reaction makes it evident that he is awake. He is lucid enough to realise that he is not where he thinks he is, but at home on the couch.

"Oh," he says, feeling stupid. Jack mumbles, "I was listening to that poem you..." But before he finishes talking,

Tiffany quickly leaves the room, embarrassed and upset at disturbing her grandfather who she adores.

Jack moves to the radio, but before Jack had time to switch the channel back to the program of verse, an editorial comes on the radio, delivered by Michael Scanlon, a twenty-five-year-old local radio personality.

MICHAEL SCANLON HAS RECENTLY RETURNED to his hometown after twelve months in the city, where he'd embraced a culture of those that work in trades and surf nuts, having grown his dreadlocks down to his middle back.

It all started a couple of years ago as a $50 bet between eight friends. Even though he has collected his winnings long ago, he has grown to love his dreadlocks, and has no plans to remove them.

As he prepares his editorial, Robbie, his attractive producer, glances across at him admiringly. Like most women in the district, she is acutely aware of what a good catch he would be as a prospective husband, completely forgetting her aroused state from the cattle property yesterday morning with Sean.

Due to the humid conditions both inside and out, Robbie is five eleven, and her slender form is comfortably dressed in a light blue, short-sleeve top with buttons and straps at the end of the sleeves, and a light coloured floral dress just above her knees, with comfortable slip-ons that she only wears at the station.

Standing six feet two inches tall, Michael has draped his slender form in a t-shirt bearing a picture of Mother Goose on the front, beneath a wrinkled denim jacket with pockets and holes in his denim jeans.

But he has nothing on his feet, as he left the runners he wore at the front door.

～

"G'DAY, Michael Scanlon here on Crazy F.M. and it's ten past six on this wet, balmy Friday evening. It's currently twenty-two degrees with humidity at 100%. I can't stand this humid stuff as it makes you drip all over. Do you know someone who doesn't use deodorant because they haven't been told about personal hygiene, phew?"

Back at the house, Jack lifts up his right arm while sitting there on the couch, and wrinkles his nose at the smell wafting from his armpit.

Even in this heat and without the air conditioning on, he still chooses to wear long pants and an ironed long sleeve shirt, complete with armpit stains. It is something his generation have done all their lives, and it is all they know and are comfortable with, regardless of what others say.

"Looks like a very uncomfortable evening both inside and out. Hope you're lucky enough to have that magical air conditioning. Imagine living like those who suffered over a hundred years ago without it."

Jack mumbles to himself, "We just got on with it, not like these wimps today."

"Some of you could have missed the continued warnings from the weather services about impending doom. WE'RE ALL GOING TO DIE!"

"Fool," says Jack sarcastically.

"Now, those weather service people need to understand how the general public misinterpret their warnings, as most people don't have a clue what they're on about. I sure as hell don't. They need to use simple language."

"Right, they've got no idea," agrees Jack.

"The weather needs to be presented in layman's terms, and yes I'm one of them, like most people who have difficulty making any sense of their riddles."

"Riddles, more like a bloody Jigsaw puzzle, and they never get it right," Jack chimes in.

"Like most things, nature feeds off something. Cyclones are just one of nature's bad moods, feeding off warm water, bringing sudden flows to rivers and creeks that have been dry for over a decade."

Jack screams, "**A decade, where have you been living... Bloody hell mate!**"

"If the weather services don't warn us that something's about to happen, people can be very down on them."

"Bloody oath we are," says Jack.

"Beware of animals at times like this. They're out there sheltering, or looking for food. Their eyes are on you."

"This is ridiculous you stupid man, what are you on about?" Jack mutters as Tiffany and Rhys enter the room. The old man squirms in his seat, taking up as much of the settee as he can, so they don't come and sit next to him.

Tiffany whines at him, hoping he doesn't get upset at her changing the station. "What are you listening to, Grandad?"

"It's something to do with the weather. You wouldn't understand. Leave me be, and go and play outside with the trucks."

"You *always* say that, Grandad. It's not very nice."

"You wouldn't want us to get run over, would you?" Rhys looking annoyed is feeling hurt that his grandfather apparently doesn't want them around.

TIFFANY TEASES Rhys by pulling down his loose-fitting shorts, something she knows Rhys doesn't like and something she has done to him for as long as she can remember, and is shocked, like Jack, to find he's not wearing any jocks. Rhys grabs his shorts and pulls them back up to cover his assumed embarrassment.

Rhys believes it's more comfortable this way in the hot weather. He fires back at Tiffany as they leave through the side door, saying he likes the freedom and not the constraints of most of the tight-fitting jocks.

"Little shits," mutters Jack. At least that's one thing he and David agree on, but he would never admit it.

He turns his attention back to the radio. For some reason there is eerie, ghostly music coming from the speakers. Jack yells out, "David, can you come in here please?"

David gets up from the kitchen table, muttering his impatience with his father-in-law.

Pearl smiles and tuts, "Just humour him, please; you know what he's like."

"Yes... Dear." He says in a not too familiar mocking tone, smiling.

"Don't you 'yes dear' me," she says sarcastically.

As David walks into the lounge room, Jack motions him to sit. "Ssshhh, be quiet. Listen to the radio for a minute."

"Roads are being closed unexpectedly, causing people and livestock to be trapped for days or potentially for weeks, leaving them to survive without the most basic of supplies, often with no power or phone coverage."

"Is this a radio story you used to listen to when you were younger, Jack?" asks David naively.

Jack's only response is a stern glance and an even sterner order. "Listen to the message on the radio."

"Will you be rescued alive, or found dead? No matter how long it takes... it's waiting for you."

Sarcastic laughter can be heard as Michael intentionally doesn't turn of his microphone.

David perks up, "This is good stuff, Jack. Why didn't you call me earlier?"

"Be quiet. It's for real, you... it's not something from the past."

"As it diminishes from a Category 5 Cyclone, it's weakening into a tropical storm as I speak to you. It was heading inland towards Mt. Isa, but over the last hour, it's turned south and it's heading along the New South Wales, Northern Territory and South Australian borders. And tonight it will be in North Western Victoria, leaving in its wake untold devastation from the flooding rains. We've seen nothing like this locally for years. Is it too late to find shelter? Has your luck run out tonight?"

On hearing this and realising that he wasn't joking, David decides they should leave soon after dinner, so they can be home before the storm hits. He listens intently hoping to finding out if and when it's arriving locally.

"Humans can have a rush of blood. Animals can have a rush of blood. Mother Nature, on the other hand, mixes blood with adrenaline. Suddenly it brings our unsuspecting minds together in the same place, and time, forcing us to panic uncontrollably in an unknown torment. Can you guarantee your own safety between now, and the morning light? We'll be back after this break to talk with listeners who have called in about their near death experiences."

"Bloody Hell, is he for real, Jack? Or is he having a lend of us, the cheeky bastard."

"Let's go and have a look on the computer to see where it is. That should give you an idea how much time you have after dinner."

Pearl calls to them to come and eat, and asks David to go and find the kids. Jack thinks, or maybe he hopes, they are both under a truck. Finishing dinner can't come quickly enough for Jack, even though he loves his only daughter dearly. As for the rest of them, the sooner they leave... the better.

After dinner, Jack and David check the computer again to try to establish where the storm is currently located.

David yells to his family, "Get a move on. We're leaving right now. I don't want to get stuck in this storm."

They set off in their new car for the short trip home. David plants his foot on the accelerator, much to Pearl's dislike, as she grabs onto the door trying to restrain her sudden movement sideways. Tiffany and Rhys simultaneously and unusually yell together loudly, "Go Dad!"

The car disappears down into a valley on the other side of the river, and through the town of Steering towards Mackenzie's bridge, and then finally, towards home.

A nice normal comfortable bed, a decent night's sleep... well, one can only hope.

7

(NO BULL)

F *ebruary 2nd, 2011.*
The previous afternoon, on the Wilson farm around four p.m., the longhorn is within striking distance of Dianne when a rifle shot rings out.

The shot is heard by everyone watching the terrifying events unfold, as it brings down the longhorn just after it smashes through the sturdy wooden fence.

The lumbering beast suddenly drops to the ground, sliding to within a few feet of Dianne.

Paralysed with fear, she has been unable to respond to the cries from her family to run for her life, and is standing stock still as the longhorn crashes to the ground in a cloud of dust, just inches before her.

As the dust clears, a stunned form emerges. Suddenly Dianne's knees buckle, and she too, slowly crumples to the ground in a dead faint.

Ron rushes to her side and is cradling her head in his arms when she starts to come 'round. It dawns on them all that the unthinkable would have happened, if Mr. Wilson had missed his shot.

Meanwhile Jay is congratulating Mr. Wilson on his sharp shooting.

Mr. Wilson had shot the bull with a tranquiliser dart in the neck region, stopping him dead in his tracks.

The farmer brushes away the compliment with his arm, explaining he learned the deadly art in the Army. Embarrassed by all the fuss, Mr. Wilson changes the subject and points to the large bull's strewn form, spreadeagled on the dusty ground.

"By the time he wakes up, he'll be as mad as hell and with a sore head to match. We need to get him safely in the back of the trailer before then."

Everyone gathers around the beast, taking advantage of this unique opportunity to have a close-up look, without feeling threatened.

"I'll have to get the tractor, there's no way in hell we can move this big lump without it," Mr. Wilson says.

Robyn asks him how he dropped the bull so quickly.

Mr. Wilson explains the different methods of bringing down a very large charging animal. "This is the most effective area to drop a bull. You have to know how long the drug takes to cause anaesthesia."

"What's 'ana'-'sthesa'?" asks Bridgette.

Mr. Wilson looks at her and smiles, as does everyone else at her attempt at saying a not too common word for an eight-year-old.

"It means putting something, in this case the bull, to sleep. Now where was I? Some drugs increase body temperature more than others, and this can give the animal an 'excitable' phase, before it falls over. Over the years, I've learnt there are several drugs you can use for the very large animals, like Bob here. It's a bit of an art as different people use different drug combinations in similar situations."

Stephanie asks, "Why would it work quicker?"

Everyone else nods as if they were thinking the same thing.

"Good question. The effect it had is because it's closer to the brain and because of the rush of blood the bull had at the time he was heading for your mum. One to two seconds is all it took for me to paralyse the bull, and watch it collapse to the ground." He says ruefully, scratching his chin. "I must say though you were very brave asking a question such as that."

Everyone laughs, especially the children.

Jay asks Mr. Wilson why he calls the longhorn 'Bob.'

"Ah yes! I named him after Robert DeNiro, the actor. He played a boxer named Jake La Motta, in a movie called Raging Bull."

"Never heard of Jake La Motta, probably before my time," says Sean with a shrug.

"He was a famous boxer in the United States, unbelievably aggressive in the ring. He boxed during, and after the Second World War." As Mr. Wilson describes La Motta, he dances around, much to everyone's amusement, throwing jabs here and there at Jay. He makes for a strange scarecrow-like figure in his old work clothes. He and his wife have long since given up worrying about their personal appearance.

He goes on, "He used to have his opponents thinking he was losing steam before launching an attack. No matter how many times you hit him, he kept standing. He lost to another champion, Sugar Ray Robinson, the first time they met, and then beat him in '43." He punctuates his words with a few right jabs to Jay's stomach, stopping just short of hitting him. "He fought for the middleweight championship and won, and then defended it in 1951 I think. He fought

Sugar Ray again in a title fight. Robinson hit him hard, but La Motta refused to go down. Gee, I remember it like it was yesterday. The commentator made me feel like I was in the ring with them. The referee stepped in to end the fight during the thirteenth round. I saw pictures later on that week." Mr. Wilson has an excited look in his eyes.

"La Motta looked like a puffer fish and he couldn't see out of his eyes. Wow, he was a mess alright, and he only fought a few more times after that, before he retired in the late '50s. He was knocked out only once in over a hundred fights."

"You seem to know an awful lot about this bloke, Mr. Wilson, how come?" Jay asks with an amused smile.

"After the Second World War, a lot of things changed, Jay, but a lot of things stayed the same. Boxing was well supported here in Australia, especially in a large stadium called Festival Hall in Melbourne, as well as in the States. It was before television. We didn't have it 'til the Melbourne Olympics in '56. The missus and I would spend time in the evenings with the family, sitting around the wireless. We would hear stuff from overseas via our short-wave wireless. Out here, if you needed help for anything, you could get it by using the radio for help. Get it, radio for help."

Mr Wilson laughs and shrugs at their vacant expressions. "Well, it *was* funny when we said it to those older than you young'uns anyway. Anyways, that's how I got to hear about La Motta and how he fought. DeNiro showed me what he was like, and my son has shown me a couple of La Motta's fights on YouTube."

Mrs. Wilson interrupts, "Plus he did a bit of boxing in the Army, and he doesn't like to talk about it much these days though."

Mr. Wilson looks embarrassed. "Come on let's get back

to Bob before the bloody thing wakes up! I've got to get the tractor."

As he walks away, Mr. Wilson turns and says, "R.E.S.P.E.C.T, that's what it's all about. When you get in the ring, or play any sport you have to have respect for your opponent. Otherwise you're not for real. Get it? Okay, good."

He turns again to Jay with a wink, "I call him B.O.B, its short for beast of burden. La Motta was a dangerous fighter, just like our unpredictable friend here."

Everyone stands around Bob discussing everything from the size of his horns, to his enormous testicles. Country people generally feel easier than their city counterparts when discussing such matters, but Dianne and the girls feel embarrassed by some of the ruder comments.

Ron teases Dianne and she starts to jokingly hit out at him for stirring the pot, so to speak, and continues to enjoy the moment.

Minutes later, Mr. Wilson returns with the tractor, cutting short the rude comments about Bob's balls. The tractor moves into position and slings are placed under the limp longhorn. He is raised slowly off the ground, and Mr. Wilson straightens him up and moves him carefully towards the rear of the trailer. He raises Bob up above the level of the floor of the trailer and expertly turns him to face into the right side of the cage, continuing forward until he is inside.

John and Sean have recovered from their recent near miss, and climb into the back section of the trailer to release the slings, as Mr. Wilson reverses the tractor out of the way.

A sudden nervous twitch from Bob catches the brothers off guard, and they both jump clear of the trailer in panic again, much to the amusement of everyone watching. Red-faced, they climb back up and release the slings, and then climb out again whilst acknowledging the applause of their audience, grumbling, "yeah ha-ha very funny... not."

John and Sean dust their clothes off and walk to their side of the trailer, locking the pins into place on the doors. They stand back, breathing a sigh of relief that the worst is over.

Mr. Wilson is saying his farewells to Ron when they hear a loud female voice from afar. It's Mrs. Wilson waving and calling out "good riddance," to the prized bull and with good reason, Bob had nearly killed her a couple of times in recent weeks.

The first occasion she had been leaning on a fence, talking with a neighbour, and not really aware that the lightly coloured red dress, which was flowing in the light breeze might somehow attract the bull. Bob the bull had charged her from the other side of the fence.

She could have been badly hurt or even killed if it wasn't for the fast thinking young son of the neighbour, who was there in the nick of time. James had grabbed Mrs. Wilson around her waist and swept her to safety, much to the dismay of his mother, and Mrs. Wilson, who yelled profusely, "what the... put me down!" at the sudden scare of being lifted away from danger.

Bob had suddenly stopped in his tracks just short of the fence as the neighbour's son, being over 6ft 5" tall and quite big and broad-shouldered, stood before him.

Mrs. Wilson attempted to compose her-self at the untimely event. Bob snorted at the tall young man standing in front of him, just behind the tree. Mrs. Wilson was somewhat taken aback by what had just happened and could not thank the striking young man enough, turning slowly to give her rescuer a big hug. James took a nervous step backwards embarrassed by what had just occurred, and politely apologised to Mrs. Wilson.

"Forgive me, Ma'am, but I just acted on impulse and was unsure as to the consequences that could have befallen you."

She spoke back to him, wishing she were fifty years younger, saying, "if only I was fifty years younger..." and then, for a brief moment, having thoughts of being in a loving embrace with the young man before her, when a passing car's horn snapped her out of her brief interlude. Realising what she had just said, she retreated flustered, to continue chatting with her neighbour. She cursed herself inwardly for saying it aloud, but in the back of her mind, not regretting a word of it.

The second time had been only yesterday when Mr. Wilson was putting Bob into the holding area. Mrs Wilson had been watching when Bob had heard the creaking sound of a shed door she was peering out of. Bob had turned his head and, upon seeing Mrs. Wilson who was wearing the same red dress, he suddenly took off, heading for the door.

Mrs. Wilson swore under her breath, "oh shit," and without hesitating, she quickly shut the large wooden door. Mrs. Wilson put the crossbar in place just as Bob reached it but still, a tilt of his head was enough to knock her sideways off her feet. She landed on a stack of hay bales, narrowly missing the tines of a large pitchfork which was lying close by on the ground.

Unaware of all this with his back turned away from Bob, Mr. Wilson closed a gate that was keeping Bob in the holding area.

He rode his quad bike around to the front of the shed, oblivious to what had befallen his wife. Mr. Wilson continued on only to find his wife sobbing on the hay bale.

He went to console her but she dismissed him with a wave of her hand. Her crying was partly caused by yet another near miss, and also because she wanted her husband to know she'd had enough of life on the land and wanted to be off the farm.

He tried hard not to laugh at her woeful expression, but she didn't miss much and caught him with a backhander to his stomach.

They had been diverted by the sound of the phone ringing nearby.

It was Ron Williams calling to confirm he was coming to collect the bulls the following day.

Subsequently Mrs Wilson lifted her-self off the hay and had difficulty walking past her husband undeterred, with her nose fully up in the air. Ignoring her husband on the phone, she went straight to the house for a cup of tea, which she'd planned to only make for her and not for that smirk of a husband.

She'd also decided that she and she alone deserved the last bit of cake, which she had also been planning to share with her husband.

BACK AT THE loading area everybody laughs, but that's short-lived as Mrs. Wilson gives them one of those stares.

Everyone drops their heads in embarrassment before she remarks, "I should think so."

Ron is asking the three brothers where they're heading to next.

John tells him, "We're off to Margaret River in Western Australia. There's a property we're working on over the next few months, before winter. The owners were in a car accident. Oh yeah and get this. Sean met this girl, Sarina, back in Melbourne, and the randy bastard has persuaded her to meet him there."

Robbie was still hanging around and overheard what happened in Melbourne, and decided to quickly take her leave without any embarrassment.

"Sarina says she can nurse the owners back to health, as well as helping us on the station. She's a registered nurse, and, would you believe, she can handle large machinery, like bulldozers, excavators and such like."

Ron turns to Sean and asks how he'd met Sarina and talked her into meeting him on the far side of the country. Sean explains it's a long, complicated story involving a chance encounter in a cafe in Melbourne, a few days earlier.

JOHN AND SEAN had noticed Sarina as soon as she came into the cafe as the front door was forcefully shoved open, causing a metal stop on the floor to break. The door crashed into a bench next to a row of chairs, smashing glass over the bench and across the floor. Luckily no-one was sitting there at the time.

Everyone in the cafe had stopped doing whatever they were doing and looked towards the loud noise. Sarina had cursed a few words under her breath, hoping no-one had heard or saw what she did, but they did. Sarina didn't flinch at the attention and offered to pay to fix it. The owner dismissed the offer and said she can sit over in the corner at her usual table, while she waited for the rest of her workmates.

She was a stunning, young Italian-looking woman with dark, dishevelled hair, hazel eyes, and pearly white teeth, with a big loving smile that could light up a dark room. Sean was convinced she was used to turning heads. Her eyes somehow met

Sean's, and when he asked if he could join her for lunch, she readily accepted.

John realised immediately that Sean and not him had succumbed to Sarina's irresistible charms with the opposite sex, and retreated back to where Jay had also watched and felt just as annoyed, as it all unfolded in front of him.

A few minutes later, a group of men from her work arrived at the cafe and voiced their disapproval of the attention Sarina was receiving from Sean.

She responded to their taunts by kissing Sean squarely on the mouth. All the workmates dropped their heads in mournful defeat as a couple of them felt sure they were in the hunt... but now that's the end of their quest.

Not surprisingly, this cemented the instant attraction they were both feeling, and not long after Sean popped the question about her meeting him in W.A. Amazingly she agreed immediately.

Sean proceeded to leave her, saying I'll see you in W.A, and they kissed again to the Bronx cheers from the patrons, and the manager, who shed a tear while crying.

WAITING for a pause in this romantic monologue, Mr. Wilson turns to farewell Ron and his family. They are about to enjoy time away together after the final trip on Ron's schedule, staying at a secret beach location somewhere along the East Coast of Australia.

Ron isn't saying where that is, much to the annoyance of the family, especially Dianne who doesn't like surprises.

Ron climbs into the cab of the semi as Dianne and Stephanie clamber into the large sleeping compartment behind him.

It's fully air-conditioned or heated throughout, and able to sleep four people in comfort and it has pretty much most of the mod cons you would get in a medium sized caravan.

It's Bridgette's turn to ride in the front passenger seat and she fastens her seatbelt as Ron starts the engine, pulling out of the loading area while waving goodbye to the Wilsons.

It's about a five-minute drive from the loading area to the main road along a dirt track cluttered with numerous potholes and ripples, that haven't been smoothed out for a while.

Every time the family tries to discuss their impressions of Bob, their voices vibrate with the continued swaying and jolting as the prime mover lurches from side to side between the potholes.

The children start laughing over their vibrating voices, causing Stephanie to get a bad attack of hiccups. They all give up trying to talk until they finally reach the main road.

After a few minutes, all is quiet in the prime mover as it disappears into the distance. Then Stephanie hiccups again and they all laugh as the truck heads towards Steering for an overnight stay, before taking Bob and the other bulls to the abattoir in the morning.

Meanwhile, in Melbourne, other events have occurred that will bring different types of people into the conflict... including a few nasty ones as well.

8

(COP THAT)

S omewhere in the city centre of Melbourne, Senior Constable Scott Taylor approaches a wide and convenient flight of steps, that lead up to the front of an aging government building.

He is wondering why the architects back in the day didn't realise how the population would not only grow, but grow old as well.

So, why so many bloody steps... really. Already balding at thirty-eight, Taylor is a likeable knockabout bloke, popular with his fellow officers and to members of the public, who he has had more than the average regular dealings with.

Handsomely single and standing six foot four inches tall, he'd entered the force later in life than most of his fellow officers. This makes his judgement a little more tempered than that of some of his younger fellow officers.

He is dressed in his neatly-pressed-for-the-occasion uniform as he climbs the thirty-five steps at the front of the building, grimacing from the pain in his right knee – a result of too many hard knocks during his sporting career.

He struggles to open a door that takes him into an open hallway. Large oak doors, with carved features in them, line either side.

Inside a room three floors above, a meeting about his future is about to get underway. Scotty looks at the letter in his hand and then locates the room where the inquiry is being held. Going up more stairs, he mumbles to himself, "That'd be right, punished even before I get to the bloody room. More bloody stairs, bloody architects."

Upon arriving at room 153 that is noted in the letter, more large oak doors again confront him, but this time they are formed with square etchings, and a long vertical handle that just has to be pushed by a well-dressed attendant outside the room.

Entering the room, he is less than surprised to see five people sitting behind a large mahogany desk, impatiently waiting for his arrival.

The hearing concerns a high-profile journalist Jo-Anne McGrath, sitting to one side with her lawyer.

She had been investigating various underworld figures when she crossed paths with Scotty. Strangely for her, she fell deeply and inconveniently in love with him. Scotty, because he could, went along for the ride.

Everything went pear-shaped one evening when Jo-Anne and Scotty were in bed together in her flat and the bedroom door had suddenly flown open to reveal a stocky, bald figure dressed in long black pants.

HE STOOD at the end of the bed wearing expensive shoes, a tight fitting shirt and sporting a spectacularly broken nose.

This was Con, a stand-over man employed by his uncle known as 'The Boss.'

Jo-Anne had been steadily compiling a dossier of highly incriminating details about 'The Boss's' operation. Con had not expected to find a burly cop in bed with his intended victim... let alone a naked one. Introductions were less than formally polite and ended in Con lunging at Scotty, who wasn't exactly dressed for the occasion. He'd blocked the first few wild haymakers thrown by Con, but eventually copped one on the nose. He recoiled backwards onto the bed, a small amount of blood coming from his nose.

He then knocked into Jo-Anne who was cowering behind the sheets to protect herself, and her dignity.

The two lovers had fallen onto the floor beside the bed, Jo-Anne with a slightly cut lip, as the fight continued.

Scotty had looked angrily at Con standing before him and clenched his fists, intent on defeating this person for interrupting his pleasure.

Scotty was up instantly and jumped onto the bed, using it as a trampoline to project himself feet first into Con's substantial stomach.

The force of the attack had sent Con spinning backwards, causing his head to crash into a coffee table near the corner of the room.

He lay motionless and seemingly unconscious while slumped on the floor, with a small amount of blood trickling from the back of his head.

Scotty leant forward awkwardly, grimacing with the pain in his right knee and going down on the good knee, just to get a better look at the damage he'd done. His body aching and stiff from the sudden hard workout, compared to what he had been doing moments before in bed.

Suddenly the crim's right leg shot out, connecting with

Scotty's bad knee and excruciating pain shot up through his leg. Scotty lost his balance and fell backwards onto the hard wooden floor. Con followed up with a crunching uppercut to the jaw, flinging Scotty backwards onto the bed.

Con flung himself towards Scotty, with his weight breaking the bed in its middle. However Scotty had expected this, and when he saw what Con was about to do, he rolled to his left before Con landed on him, and consequently he fell off the bed.

Landing on Jo-Anne again, Scotty inadvertently squashed her against the wall, with her screaming again in pain.

Con scrambled up from the wreckage of the bed and sat on its edge, recovering from the ordeal. A wry smile crossed his dishevelled looks as he relaxed his demeanour, and looked down upon Scotty and Jo-Anne. He made the mistake of thinking that if he grabbed onto Jo-Anne, he would have the upper hand – bad choice.

Jo-Anne groggily stood up to shield Scotty and grabbed a hairbrush from the bedside table, just as Con was about to grab onto her, thinking to himself, *why would you want to brush your bloody hair? That's typical of a beautiful woman.*

Then, with one quick movement, Jo-Anne had spun it around and thrust it into Con's eye, blood squirted out and over her. She was so enraged by this time that she rammed the handle of the brush deep into the eye socket. She hadn't known it then but found out later, she had penetrated the hairbrush through to his brain, killing him instantly.

Collapsing backwards into Scotty, she sobbed, emotionally relieved, but at the same time, began to react hysterically.

She screamed, "What have I done? What have I done?"

as Scotty embraced her even more, still all the while in their naked state.

She lay in his arms, and to their mutual shame, a flicker of lust passed between them. "No, it wouldn't be right," Jo-Anne murmured.

They both laughed nervously, expelling the tension. Scotty wiped blood from her face, asking if she was okay, and went over to where Con was laying spreadeagled across the bed. Something had told him even before he checked for a pulse, that there wasn't going to be one.

Scotty slumped down next to the limp body – hairbrush still intact in Con's eye – put his hands to his face and roared his frustration. He knew instantly they were in too deep. Even to contemplate the situation rationally.

As they were both standing there stark naked, Jo-Anne went over to embrace him. He pushed her away, saying, "Just let me be for a second. I've got to think how I'm going to deal with this."

Then she added, "It wasn't your fault so don't blame yourself, it was just one of those wrong place wrong time moments. Don't concern yourself with the blame game as it was purely self-defence, besides..." her tone and demeanour suddenly changed saying confidently, "the CCTV will show that it was *me* that did the killing, and it wasn't for any other reason." Jo-Anne pointed to the big lump of a man, dead on the bed before them.

SCOTTY KNEW his big challenge was to convince Force Command that self-defence was the *only* motive behind Con's death. He didn't reckon with the media furore that was about to erupt, and how this had forced Force Command into a corner.

Unfortunately, some of the more inexperienced senior police have had a weakened resolve over the last few years, due to the lack of direction from the top. Scathing reports from the tabloids, and questions in Parliament, all made it difficult for any attempt to brush the whole sordid affair under the carpet.

The Police Minister had made it abundantly clear in behind the scenes meetings with Scotty's superiors that he had to go.

It was the only way to defuse the ongoing media criticism. Scotty argued that sacking him would turn him into a martyr, and he would play this role to the hilt. But, he would be prepared to accept a transfer to a country town, as suggested by the Minister. And that's how he ended up being sent to Steering.

A FEW HOURS LATER, Scotty leaves the disciplinary hearing by a side door and walks to where he had parked his car down a side street.

He is surprised to see Jo-Anne as she walks alongside the Minister towards the waiting media who are intent on grilling them both.

As he opens the car door, a hand is placed on his shoulder. He spins around to find a young woman clutching what looked ominously like a reporter's notebook. He tells her he has nothing to say. "Is it true there was a CCTV camera in the room, and you were in the middle of making a pornographic film... and were both naked?" the girl blurts.

Scotty is about to voice his anger when he notices a

photographer over the girl's shoulder. This was not the time for further embarrassing publicity. Scotty jumps in the car, fires the ignition, rams it into gear, and speeds away.

On the way home he receives a call on his mobile from Force Command. The officer on the end of the line is clearly enjoying himself. "I'm letting you know your future. You start at your new posting next Monday. Understand?" This gave him just a couple of days to get his stuff together.

He sighs. "Okay, where am I going?"

"Look on your computer when you get home."

The phone goes dead and an engaged signal is heard as Scotty has the word 'prick' come to mind. He presses the off button.

Almost instantly it starts ringing again. This time it's Billy, a mildly slow on the uptake youth Scotty has been looking after for longer than he cares to remember.

"What's happened to you? Heard you went in with your balls intact, but came out with 'em a bit bruised," says Billy.

Scotty has to laugh at his colourful expression and then explains the morning's events, and says he's on his way home to discover his immediate future.

"How far away are you? I'll meet you there in thirty minutes and we'll have a few beers to cheer you up." "Sorry Billy, I finished them off last night to help me sleep. I've got to call someone else on the way home." "Okay, I'll see you then."

Scotty thinks long and hard before he redials. A voice answers, "Hello, this is Emma, that you, Scotty?"

"You know damn well it is, Sis, how are you?"

"Was that you I saw on the news before, you naughty boy? What were you playing at with a floozy like that?"

"You know what it's like, Em. Before I knew it we were... you know, we were up to our armpits in each other, and then well, before I knew it... bang, there's all this mess. Well, I guess I had it sort of coming."

Scotty breaks the bad news that he's being transferred to a station in the bush, probably somewhere remote.

"I'll ring you as soon as I know where, okay? I'll call soon."

As she hangs up her phone, a frustrated Emma decides to stay clear of the news for the next few days.

SCOTTY PULLS UP into the driveway of the room he's renting from an elderly lady he's known for years.

Billy pulls up at the same time on his pushbike, which has a motor attached to it.

He wears his helmet over a peaked cap, daggy fluorescent shorts, a yellow t-shirt, and slippers, because he can.

Billy greets him, "Hey Knackers, how's ya testicles going, you poor old bugger?"

"Get stuffed, Billy or I'll send you home, you peanut."

"Does the old girl have any pancakes or chocolate cake?"

"I don't know if the 'old girl,' as you called her is home, but make sure you don't eat it all, you pig, or I'll..."

"You'll what? *You're* the one who's been a bad boy. I'll have what I like."

"You're just jealous because my legs are better looking than yours, all tanned and hairless." The latter description is based on Scotty's cycling days when shaved legs were essential. He had also acquired scars on both legs from a car accident, which tragically killed everyone in his family, except him and his sister.

"Oh you will, will you, Billy?" says Scotty's landlady, Mrs

Emerson, who had been standing unnoticed by the two mates in the driveway of the house.

She is wearing a floral summer dress, a wide brimmed hat and sneakers, her normal attire while pottering in her well-kept garden.

Scotty says, "Hello Mrs Em, didn't know if you were home or not."

She turns to Billy, telling him he can help himself to cake or other goodies, knowing full well the hardships Billy has endured over the years.

Mrs. Emerson is proud of Scotty for taking Billy under his wing, mentoring him over recent years. She addresses Scotty, "What's this I hear about you, you sly fox, having an affair with that floozy?"

"That's the second time I've heard the term 'floozy' today, Mrs. Em," Scotty frowns disapprovingly.

Billy drops his bike and heads straight for the kitchen at the rear of the palatial 45-square timber home Mrs Emerson has owned since 1985, after both her parents passed away the same year.

A small and diminutive figure at eighty-three, she never married as her husband-to-be didn't return from the Second World War, dying of pneumonia in his final days in Germany, in a nursing station.

While Billy helps himself to food, Scotty makes his way to his room and opens his computer. He reads endless paragraphs about the results of the hearing, and finally discovers where he's going. Wondering where Steering is, he retrieves a map from a desk drawer and quickly locates the town.

Billy barges into the room and asks with a loud voice that sounds as if everyone in the neighbourhood could hear him, "Where you off to, Knackers?" Then the penny drops, his face changes and Billy suddenly flops dejected onto the floor. "Shit, Scotty, what am I going to do without you around?"

Scotty feels suddenly bereft also. He takes a deep breath, swallows hard and wonders how he can break the news. His throat feels dry from the lack of fluids. "Listen, I'm sorry, Billy," he says gently with a note of disappointment in his gravelly voice. "I hadn't even given it a thought until you mentioned it, so here's what we'll do. When I get settled, you can come up on the weekends, just to see how things work, okay? Depending on my workload we'll have a look at it then. But first I'll have to figure out the logistics. I've looked it up and it's about a five or six hours' drive from here, up near Mildura."

Billy nods, but Scotty can tell by the look on his face that he isn't going to enjoy the next few months.

"Besides, Billy, you'll like coming up there every weekend on the train. I know how much you love trains. Now stop being a sook, and go and get me a slice of that chocolate cake, you pig."

Billy's gloomy demeanour changes instantly.

"You're the best-est. friend ever." As he leaves the room, he nearly bowls over Mrs. Emerson. "Whoops sorry, Mrs. Em, got to feed the womaniser."

Mrs Em chimes in, "I hope for the both of you that things work out. If it doesn't, Scotty, you can send me a regular payment for all the chocolate cake he'll be eating." Mrs Emerson muses aloud about selling the house now Scotty is leaving, and the place is too big for her to be alone now.

"There's a new retirement village opened up around the corner. They haven't been able to get a cook, and I've told them I would be happy to do it for a couple of years."

"When does the village open up?"

"They're hoping before Easter so if you're going, I will put this house on the market now. Then I'll let them know I'll be there when the residents have moved in, including me. I hope it works out for the both of you. I can't imagine what Billy would be like if his two favourite people move out. And he doesn't understand the ramifications like we do.
"

She makes a scathing reference to Billy's parents, particularly his alcoholic, wife-beating father.

"She should leave that mongrel and take Billy with her. Maybe after you've settled in you could put them both up at your new digs, depending on how big they are."

"I'd have to look into that to see if it would work. I'm concerned for him too. But it's a big ask. You know what a handful he can be."

"Yes, I know he is, but I'm sure you'll make the right decision. You might even settle down there in... what's the town is called again, Steering?"

"I'm sure we'll work it out, but first I want to enjoy some of your cake with my mate." He smiles as he takes his first bite into the moist, rich triple chocolate mud cake.

Scotty wonders how long it will be before he samples Mrs Emerson's cooking again. Then he says, "Maybe someone drove through the town and then settled there, and named it after the way they came steering through?"

"Don't laugh, Mrs Em, Dad joke, it's not that funny," says Billy.

They share a laugh anyway, possibly for the last time together.

9

(YOU'RE ON THE RADIO

Dianne leans forward, taps Ron on the shoulder and asks him to turn up the radio. She's anxious to hear the program on near-death experiences.

Announcer Michael Scanlon has asked listeners to call in and describe incidents in their lives when the Grim Reaper had come too close for comfort.

"Sounds like something you should ring up about," Ron says. "After that bloody longhorn got pulled up only a few feet away from turning you into hamburger meat, you might have something to tell."

The song on the radio ends and Scanlon's unmistakeable voice fills the cab of the prime mover.

"That was Fanfare for the Common Man *by Emerson Lake and Palmer, one of the more ostentatious bands in the history of rock music, playing one of their more exaggerated works. Looks like we're in for a bit of a storm overnight and looking at the radar there's plenty to be worried about, what with the lightning and all.*

Michael Scanlon here, on Crazy FM, with you until dawn. Our usual night-time host, Maurice Conway, has come down with the dreaded lurgy. It's ten past the hour of seven on this Friday evening, so there's a looooooooonnnnnnng way to go. Now we're asking if anyone would like to call in and talk to us about any near-death experiences you may have faced recently. What determines the outcome of these situations? Who knows... sometimes its pure luck, sometimes quick thinking? Okay, the lines are open... Seems we've got our first caller. Hello, this is Michael; go ahead please, you're on the air."

"My name's Patrick and I'm from Inglewood."

"Hello Patrick! How are you feeling today?"

"I'm a bit under the weather, Michael, and I'm just coming to terms with what could have happened today."

"Rather ironic you should mention the weather, Patrick, sorry, please continue."

Patrick gives a big sigh. "I was riding my motorbike along the main drag on my way home, when this bloody car went through a stop sign and nearly took me out. I thought I'd had it. Didn't stop at the sign or even look my way."

"Do you feel you should've died? Or was this a cat's got nine lives moment in your life, Patrick?"

"I've recently broken up with my girlfriend of eight years, I found out she's being playing up behind my back. When I confronted her, she was moaning about me not being up to it in the cot over the last few months. So I went to the quack, and he told me I'd got cancer..."

There was a long pause. "To answer your question, that bloke today in the car might as well have finished me off."

"That's not good to hear, Patrick, can we go on or would you rather leave it there?"

BACK AT THE radio station Michael and Robbie his producer

are crossing everything, hoping for Patrick to continue. Their fears are unfounded as he says through the phone with a heavy sigh, "Yep, sure, okay, whatever. It's not as if I've anything else to do tonight."

"Can I ask how long you have to live, Patrick?" Michael makes his voice gentle and comforting to Patrick's plight.

"The doc told me it looks like we caught it early. He said to think positive and not dwell on the negative. So I'm hoping for a good outcome. Then there's the chemo ..."

"Well we can only hope for a positive outcome. Did you have any visions of dying in the moment before the near miss, Patrick?"

"I definitely wasn't thinking about me dying. I'd just come from a mate's funeral and I guess his death was playing on my mind. But not mine. Maybe I wasn't paying as much attention to the road as I should have been."

As Michael looks out through one of the large windows at the radio station, he expresses some empathy for Patrick in his voice, before moving on at being excited at the dramatic story, while unsure as to how the listeners will view this interview.

Robbie motions to Michael to look at his monitor, she has sent a message for Michael to his computer. The message says there has been a quick response to the way he is handling this interview, and to keep up the good work.

Michael now feels a little more confident that this interview will go its course, and takes on a more serious tone with his questions.

"Did you expect to die when you saw the car go through the stop sign? Did you have any flashbacks of your life, or of someone, or something, special?"

A short pause ensued but Patrick's heavy breathing, came through on the phone. The dramatic effect this created pleased Robbie and Michael as Patrick then began to speak again.

"My ex-girlfriend, but that only lasted for a split second before the car ..." This time there was a lengthy pause.

"Are you still there, Patrick?"

"Yeah, it's weird and puts things into perspective... kind of hits the spot."

"How old are you, Patrick, and what happened after the car nearly hit you?"

"I'm thirty-five, Michael, and yeah, it shook me up pretty badly, until I got home about ten minutes later. Then I had a beer to calm myself down. Next thing I'm throwing the bottle through the window, only I didn't realise it was closed, Mum cleans them so good. So, yeah, I guess I was a bit pissed about what nearly happened. I reckon talking it over with you has helped. I am, as you say, a cat with eight lives left."

"That's good to hear. Has this ever happened before, something so confronting that you have to question your existence, perhaps with your ex-girlfriend, or something else?"

"I dunno. Anyway, thanks for the help, man. I still feel a bit numb but I guess I'm coping. Good luck with the program."

"Thanks Patrick, time will tell. We'll take a...hang on, you still there, Patrick?"

Robbie is urgently and frantically waving her arms and hands around, and she finally succeeds in getting Michael's attention to take this next caller.

"Yeah, ya just caught me."

"We've got the woman who nearly killed you on the other line, Patrick, and she wants to apologise, if that's ok?"

"A woman, shit ... I thought it was a bloke. Sure, let's hear her." Patrick's tone changes as he continues his uncomplimentary thoughts of what he thinks of women in general. "That's typical, can't wait to give this bitch some grief."

Michael frowned, not happy with Patrick's rude comments. *"I suggest we hear what she has to say before you abuse her, Patrick, You there, Michelle, you're on the air. Hello Michelle, you there?"*

"Hello Michael, I'm a bit nervous at the moment. I heard... is it Patrick? Talking with you, and I sort of felt a bit guilty about what happened. Don't know if I should have called in or not."

"We're glad you did, Michelle, and just to let you know, Patrick is on the other line listening. First of all, if at any time you wish to stop, we'll take a break okay? Is that okay with you, Michelle?"

"Yes, I'm fine with that, Michael."

"How about you, Patrick, let's see what Michelle has to say."

"What on earth were you thinking, woman? You nearly killed me today!" There is anger and strain in his voice, as he is clearly still affected by what happened today.

"Let Michelle have her say, and explain why she didn't stop." Michael interrupts Patrick, trying to get him to calm down and not scare Michelle off the line.

"Okay, okay, sorry, Michael, I lost it there for a minute. Tell her to go ahead."

Michelle began again. *"Yes, thank you. I'd just received a phone call from a friend. Her daughter had fallen off some gym equipment in their backyard, monkey bars, I think. Sorry, I'm a bit flustered at the moment. Um, where was I? Oh that's right, um, she broke both her arms, and my friend needed me to look after her other kids while she took her distressed daughter to the hospital."*

"That's terrible, Michelle, I'm a bit taken aback, um... I hope

no-one looks at her twice. These days the mother might have a bit of explaining to do." Michal inquires.

"So is that why you went through the stop sign? I can tell you were in a bit of a panic?"

"I didn't see him and I know it was wrong, but I was thinking more about my friend. I had to get to her as quickly as possible. I realise now I should have been a bit more responsible, and I kind of over-reacted and nearly killed Patrick, but it wasn't entirely my fault." Michelle's voice is shaky and full of emotion.

Patrick's angry voice cut through. "Oh yeah it was, you stupid fucking bitch."

"Patrick, cut that out. We don't need that. Let Michelle finish or I'll cut you off. Is that clear?" Michael set out a warning. As much as this made for compelling radio, he also had to show a duty of care to sensitive matters.

There is a sniffle as Michelle interrupts, *"I'm not going to do this if he's going to... oh well... there was a huge semi-trailer on my right blocking my view. It had a load of cattle on board. I couldn't see the sign properly, and I thought I could get through okay but that's no excuse really. Anyway, you see, my dad was a racing driver and stuntman. When I was growing up he would take me out on our property and show me driving stuff he had to do in stunts, and I always tried to remember some of the things he showed me."*

Michelle took a shaky breath, *"He was killed after he returned from an overseas tour. He missed a sign and crashed on a corner. Anyway, I wasn't expecting this motorbike as the truck had just passed me, and I couldn't see anything else behind it. So I continued on through the stop sign and suddenly here's this motorbike sort of tailgating the semi. I wasn't travelling very fast. I just didn't expect to see anything behind the trailer, let alone a motorbike. Oh yeah, and one other thing, Michael, that*

I now remember. It was nearly dark and he... Patrick, was wearing dark leathers. I didn't see him until it was too late and I swerved the car away from him to stop my car from hitting him. But that's not all Michael..."

"What else could there be, Michelle?"

"He didn't have his headlights on, and he wasn't wearing a helmet."

Patrick screams through the phone, "Fucking bitch!"

Suddenly a click comes from the radio. Patrick hung up.

RON, Dianne and the children had been locked into the drama unfolding before their ears. Unfortunately, Dianne could only cover Stephanie's ears, just in case Patrick swore some more.

Bridgette is sitting there with her mouth wide open, looking at her father, who had a grin from ear to ear. Bridgette screws her face up and folds her arms in disgust at the swear word, and smirks at her father.

After a pause, Michael's tempered voice returns. *"Seems to me, you were both at fault to an extent, and you both should learn from this. It's everyone's responsibility to pay attention on the road, whatever else may be going on in your head. It's no good thinking you're more important than the next person, to get where you're going, and stuff the rest of the traffic, because it's all about me. We still have Michelle on the line. Thanks for staying with us, Michelle. Unfortunately Patrick's hung up, and we've tried to get him back, but he's not answering his phone. So I'll just ask you a couple more questions before I take more calls. How did the little girl go at the hospital? Is she back home now?"*

"Yeah, she's fine and asleep."

"Have you thought anymore about what happened today?"

"I'm getting a bit tired but thinking about it now, I realise I shouldn't have driven like that. I was tired and distracted by emotion. I didn't want to let my friend down so I just acted on instinct. Just shows what a dill I was. I was so worried and I guess it was the adrenalin that made me careless."

"Thanks Michelle; hope you've learnt something about yourself today."

"Thanks, Michael."

Ron begins nodding his head in agreement with Michael, as Michael knows about this sort of stuff now, having spent time with Ron on a couple of long trips to get a feel of what really goes on out on the roads.

Michelle's phone goes click as heavy rain continues to fall outside and is making it hard for Ron to see the road in front of him, until lightning flashes violently across the sky.

He sees Dianne and Stephanie looking kind of tired in the sleeping compartment of the prime mover. Stephanie has finally recovered from her hiccups and is sitting quietly.

Bridgette however, is wide awake and showing no signs of wanting to sleep anytime soon.

10

(LIFE ON THE ROAD)

I t's a long journey along a straight and narrow road, which is making the longhorns restless as they struggle to stay upright in the trailer.

Ron eyes the blackening skies ahead and tells Dianne and the children he needs to focus on the wet and dangerous roads to ensure he can deliver the longhorns safely to the abattoir tomorrow morning.

This is Bridgette and Stephanie's first time in the truck with their parents, and Ron tells them he needs to concentrate on the white lines and cat's eyes on the road.

"What if there are no white lines or cat's eyes on the road, what do you do then, Dad?" Stephanie asks.

"If there are no lines or cat's eyes, Steph, there are little white posts on both sides of the road with red and white reflectors on them. And you've *always* got white lines in the middle of the road. The red reflectors give you the understanding that the road goes around a sweeping bend to the right, while the white reflectors give you the understanding that the road takes you along another different sweeping bend in the road to the left. So when you're driving at night, the reflectors show you the way the road is going or if there are corners ahead. The one we're on now is like that. It's a more winding one so you can see ahead which way the road turns. A long time ago some roads never had white lines, cat's eyes, or even the little posts."

"What did the driver do then, Dad?"

"Well, kiddos, most of us truckies travelled these roads regularly, and we remember where all the hills, intersections and other hazards are. When driving in the day, we memorised the roads for the night time. It was like this a few years ago, kiddos, when we had to drive blind without any white lines or cat's eyes. It was especially hard as well when we had to face driving rain."

Bridgette pops up with, "How can the rain drive, Dad?"

"Asked for that one didn't I?"

Dianne laughs, "Can't wait to hear you get out of that!"

"Me too," Ron says under his breath. "Well let's see, driving rain is something we say when the rain is carried fast by the wind and pushed into a building, or our truck. Driving rain is so hard that when it hits you, it's like having little pins going into you."

Dianne nods her approval. "I think the jury's convinced."

Bridgette and Stephanie look terrified at the prospect of being hurt by the driving rain.

"Now on the other question you asked. When it rains, my view of what's outside the cab is affected, just as if I close my eyes like this..."

"DAD, DON'T DO THAT, YOU CAN'T SEE!" Steph and Bridgette scream at the same time.

His eyes snap open. "Sorry, I didn't mean to scare you. Why don't you both close your eyes, and see how long you can last without being scared."

Steph and Bridge look at one other and then their mother, shaking their heads with a definite, "No."

"Now, see how you are already scared?" says Ron, deciding that now was a good time to teach his daughters about a few road dangers.

"That's a good thing. You shouldn't close your eyes. And another thing that is happening a lot now is with drivers that look down and text, or especially talking on the phone. Just because you are driving, doesn't mean you can turn your head away from looking at the road, and then look at the person you are talking with. There is a simple way to figure out how far you travel, while you're driving along any road. But nowadays a lot of drivers are practically doing exactly that, using mobile phones when they should be watching the road. They don't understand the distance their vehicle travels while their attention is diverted. Every second their eyes are off the road, they're moving closer to disaster like running off the road or hitting and killing someone."

Steph and Bridgette look at each other in shock.

"Distances travelled at any speed are easily calculated at twenty five percent of the speed you are travelling. For example, at one hundred kilometres per hour, you can travel as much as twenty-five meters in one second, that's the length of a b-double semi-trailer. And it takes over one hundred meters to stop safely at that speed. A slower speed of sixty kilometres per hour, you will travel fifteen meters, that's the length of a normal semi-trailer. So you think that it's okay to look away for what you think is only a second, but in reality, someone could be dead by the time you listen to me finishing this sentence now."

He doesn't like scaring his children, but Ron knows the more they understand, the more careful they'll be. He only hopes they don't become like some of the dangerous drivers he sees every day.

"Most of the larger connecting roads these days have more than one lane in each direction, and are separated by a concrete wall, or what they call a median strip. Some have a grassed area or wire rope barriers down the middle. If any type of vehicle runs off the road, or if someone loses control to avoid an unexpected object, or has fallen asleep, then they won't crash into any oncoming vehicle going the other way. You can see which way the road is going on clear nights, especially more so during the day."

Ron sits there watching the conditions in front of him become worse, but has the time to bring a cheeky smirk on his face. This causes Bridgette to hastily fold her arms and scrunch up her face in a joking way again, to show her father she is not impressed by his smirk.

He continues with his mini-lecture, "When your mum and I teach you to drive, you'll have better skills than most other people on the road. You'll be learning about what to look out for, and what other drivers are doing. And it's only going to get harder in the future."

Dianne adds, "What Dad means, girls, is it's better to learn as much as you can, as early as you can, even at your age. Never think, like most teenagers do, that you know it all. Your father will tell you even he still experiences and sees new things every day while he's driving. Today, with a lot of migrants and young people on our roads, this is something very new to them. Even though they have the added advantage of technology, sometimes they can still take something like that for granted. G.P.S. maps showing you the way to your destination don't have the height of bridges, so if the driver is not paying attention, they will get stuck under a low bridge, or even worse, get killed. It can bring them undone by having a serious accident, and it's nobody's fault but theirs."

As they continue on, the driving rain is smashing heavier on the windscreen, making it harder for Ron to see the road ahead. The wipers are working overtime just to keep up.

Most of the continent of Australia has not seen any good annual rainfall over the last decade, and the land has just simply dried out. Rivers, dams and creek beds are empty, and animals in the wild, like kangaroos and koalas and worst of all the venomous snakes and spiders, are out hunting for water.

Along the dried-out rivers and creeks, there are many old wooden bridges that are badly in need of repair. Many of them no longer have the stability in their foundations to withstand unusually heavy traffic.

Suddenly a large kangaroo hops in front of their truck, and is instantly bowled over, much to the dismay of Dianne, Bridgette and Stephanie. It makes a loud thumping noise, as it hits the bull bar on the front of the prime mover.

Some people think that bull bars are unnecessary, but on roads where animals and vehicles meet, it's more of a safety issue with the amount of damage a large animal can do to any vehicle.

In more serious instances, it can cause the vehicle to leave the road and kill the occupants. Or it could come through the windscreen, continuing to fall and thrash about inside the vehicle, which would also injure, distract or kill those in the front seat.

Ron has often spoken of the priorities in these situations. "*First and foremost, it's better to hit the animal rather than swerving or braking hard to avoid it. Most people have no wish to kill a live animal, but a human life is always more valuable. Missing a human and killing an animal is socially acceptable, but killing a human just to miss killing an animal, is not."*

As they continue on their journey, Dianne calms her upset daughters down. The skies are even blacker now, and it's obvious the storm has been heavy ahead of them for some considerable time.

They have already crossed a number of rivers and creeks which have filled up with swirling brown water flowing at a dangerous rate. And visibility has become terrifyingly dark, like a snow whiteout.

Dianne re-assures the girls by telling them this is something their father is used to.

"His industry, road haulage, has for decades prided itself that whatever the conditions are the load must be delivered, just like the mail. Most drivers become familiar with the roads they travel on regularly, and continue on at a normal speed while ignoring the changing conditions outside. It's terrifying not seeing clearly in front of you."

"A bit like jumping out of a perfectly good aeroplane without a parachute," Ron explains. "I've got to drop these bulls off at the abattoir in steering tomorrow or I won't get paid, and there'll be no birthday presents on the twenty-fifth for you two," confirms Ron, trying again not to laugh.

Hearing that makes the girls get a better picture for what their dad does for them. Steph and Bridgette say thanks to their dad.

They are now heading down the side of a mountain, as lightning lights up the sky and the road ahead again. Up ahead, the land levels out more and becomes a bit less hairy. Ron is already looking forward to getting to where they are spending the night, before dropping off the bulls in the morning.

11

(EVERYONE HAS DIFFICULTIES)

The Lockwood family are on the short trip home from Jack's house, a journey that would normally take twenty to twenty-five minutes.

In the middle of the back seat is the latest arrival, Stephen, who is just over six months old, the latest bundle of joy for Grandad Jack.

Unfortunately, there are no grandparents on David's side of the family, as both his parents died from cancer a few years ago.

Although outwardly Pearl gives the impression of a carefree wife and mother, on the inside she wishes her own mother could have seen this newborn.

Like many women, Pearl experienced a bout of post-natal depression after Stephen's birth.

Sometimes the difficulty of a quick birth can have its own ramifications, brought on by one's own life experiences. She couldn't help thinking her mum's compassion would have nullified much of this.

Pearl had shed a few tears earlier tonight, probably due to her being overwhelmed and tired from the long journey, and not from cutting onions. While cooking their dinner of roast lamb, potatoes and vegetables, topped off with a dessert of mouth-watering chocolate mousse and ice cream.

She enjoys going to her father's place as it helps her cope with the loss of her mother, but being there reminds her she should be helping Jack more than she does.

The constant bickering between Rhys and Tiffany doesn't help much either. Like ships passing in the night, while they were out of sight of their parents' gaze and ears, they were at it again and again at Jack's place.

At fifteen, Rhys is showing promise with the local football team, and is expected to graduate into the under seventeens next year. He is well liked at school, especially by the girls.

Except his seventeen-year-old sister, Tiffany, who's too busy to waste time on her brother, glorying instead in the attention she receives from many of the more eligible boys at the school.

Pearl has read some of the more unpleasant references to Tiffany on Facebook, where the word 'slutty' crops up far too often, yet another source of unhappiness for Pearl.

In most country towns everyone pretty much knows everyone else, but it's not known around town that Tiffany was raped a couple of years earlier by a local hoon. She is still acutely ashamed and traumatised by the ordeal and frequently becomes emotionally overwhelmed by the memory.

She retreated into herself for a time of self-discovery only to find solace in being the opposite of what she was, and without the slightest thought for how she was being viewed by anyone, let alone her mother.

Pearl struggles with her daughter's mood changes. She has become something of a confused teenager, particularly when compared with her sunny-natured outlook before the rape. In those days, Tiffany was universally loved, both in and out of school.

Tiffany puts aside those demonic influences when she is with those that don't judge her by her looks, or her anger.

The Lockwoods have barely left Jack's house when the two siblings are at one another's throats, despite Stephen being fast asleep in his capsule between the two of them.

They begin to throw taunts at each other over some meaningless comment Rhys had made to Tiffany in their grandfather's hallway earlier today. Tiffany had been visited by one of the older teenagers, regularly seen playing in most of the sporting codes one could imagine. The nineteen-year-old had arrived at their house on horseback one day looking all rugged and tanned, much to Tiffany's pleasure, just as they were leaving for their holidays.

As the bickering continues, spoiling the somewhat sombre evening after dinner, David's patience has finally worn thin, and he decided he will send the pair of them to their rooms as soon as they get home.

Inevitably, the ongoing verbal battle in the back seat finally wakes Stephen, who screams his outrage.

There's barely a night that goes by without having to get up again and again, either feeding or trying to put Stephen back to sleep, and both David and Pearl are aware that Rhys and Tiffany feel life would be sweeter, without child number three.

His parents are unimpressed with their elder children's lack of consideration, and suddenly everyone is yelling at once.

The power trip takes over as to who can be the loudest and persist at who's right, each trying to get their individual point across.

They have travelled just one kilometre down the road when David realises the storm is closing in on them. He glances across at Pearl but she is pre-occupied with the ongoing warfare in the back seat.

David tries to block out the noise and battle on at the wheel, but one of his eyes is giving him trouble. He's been told by the optometrist he has astigmatism, a problem with how the eye focuses when light enters from different angles.

The optometrist had told him, *"It's causing you blurred and distorted vision, and in your case, it's hyperopic astigmatism. Being one of three types of symptoms, this gives the front surface of the eye a football shape. Something your mother had surgery on a few years before she passed away."*

He went on to explain that the hereditary condition can be corrected with glasses or in most cases, contact lenses. David was prescribed new prescription glasses, which are performing less than successfully tonight.

The road ahead doesn't help as it's becoming progressively more difficult to navigate and although David knows it well, he becomes uncharacteristically anxious.

He passes a sign warning of the snaking road ahead, which means he's about to reach the larger of the two old wooden bridges on their route.

As he enters the 40-metre long bridge David turns around to reinforce Pearl's attempts to quieten the disturbance coming from the back seat.

Rhys and Tiffany's bickering has escalated to physical jostling and without realising it, Tiffany falls against the seatbelt restraining Stephen's capsule, releasing the latch.

They are on a remote stretch of road in the Australian bush. Night time has arrived, bringing with it dishevelled emotions for both animals and humans alike. They are crossing McKenzie's bridge that spans about forty meters across the river.

It was constructed during the town's boom period during the late sixties, due to the need to handle the volume of trucks and cars heading to the Industrial area, about a kilometre down river. There are loud sounds coming from the driving rain hitting the many objects in the river, and the hard ground.

Everything is shrouded in thick rain and the subsequent spray from the wind is pushing it sideways.

Pearl suddenly screams as lightning flashes across the sky, illuminating through the driving rain. She can see a jumble of trees and rocks being carried along by the fast-flowing torrent below them. But that's not what makes her scream.

Suddenly David makes out the blur of oncoming headlights through the rain. With no time to react, he swerves hard left to avoid a head-on collision. He has almost never found another vehicle on this bridge at the same time before, and is even more confused about what is going on tonight.

They are on a bridge that has only inches between him and the edge of the easily collapsible structure, which is mixed with the torrential downpour around the very old sleepers that create a fence-like structure along McKenzie's bridge.

He struggles to hear the escalating disharmony of chaotic noise... and what sounds like the deep blast of a loud horn and the screech and hiss of air brakes, and finally the explosion of metal impacting on metal.

The two vehicles collide and crash through the weakened railings at the eastern end of Mackenzie's Bridge. David's car plummets down the ten meters into the murky depths of the torrent below, as does the other vehicle, which plummets much slower due to its size and weight. David's continued blurred vision and the constant rain, which has become even heavier over the last few minutes, is not helping David cope. Neither is the continued screaming coming from the rear of the car.

The various noises become intermingled with the gurgle of water, and voices screaming out in pain. But there is something else, something inexplicable and terrifying.

It is the panic-stricken bellowing and thrashing of what sounds like several large beasts.

Luckily both vehicles fall on the more eastern side of the river and land on the sloping embankment away, but still affected, from the rushing river torrent just a couple of meters beside them.

Finally blackness cloaks David as he descends into the realms of a nightmare. His mind takes him back to where he is suddenly sitting in the optometrist's waiting room, flicking through a magazine article about how the mind slows down when disaster approaches, taking note of every tiny detail of what is happening.

He reads on, about when a person is falling. They don't actually observe the fall in slow motion. It's not equivalent to the way a slow-motion camera would work. It's something more interesting than that.

It's all about memory, not a fast paced perception.

Normally our memories act like a filter, by not writing down most of what's passing through our system. The brain is still recording until the individual recovers from whatever extreme crisis they're in.

To enhance what they are seeing is delayed, and then, when they recall that experience, it feels like it must have taken a very long time. But really in a crisis situation, they are only getting a peek into all the pictures, smells and thoughts that usually just pass through the brain and float away, never to be seen or heard of again, forgotten forever.

Mixed with the sound of human moans, the bellowing of the animals is gradually superseded by the encroaching darkness.

David slips into unconsciousness.

12

('AVE A GO, YA MUG!)

It's payday for the drinking classes of Steering, and many of them are gathered in the local pub as they are most Thursday nights.

Storms are bringing much needed rain and a steady downpour has soaked the area over the last few hours. The conditions outside are humid and wet, and it's quite a change from the continued overwhelming heat over the last few months.

Sitting around their usual tables, in a corner next to the main bar, are most of the older residents who are quite content in listening to Michael Scanlon on the radio.

In the opposite corner are the five brothers, known throughout the town as troublemakers. Other young males are chatting up the local girls. With only one thing in mind as the drink takes effect, the more suggestive their chat lines become.

One young man called Jack, although he doesn't know it yet, has succeeded in pulling the girl Nick had his eye on. Rick turns to his older brother, realising what's in store and warns, "Watch yourself Nick you know Jack's a bit testy."

Nick ignores his well-meant advice and heads straight over to his intended victim.

Aware of what's about to develop, the publican, Ian Milton, decides, with the help of a few others, to evict all five brothers.

As usual they're becoming troublesome and rowdy. Luke is the most placid though, so Milton tells his helpers to go easy on him.

Ian's foreboding 135kg masks his gentle nature, but tonight he's determined to show off his menacing side. He approaches the brothers and tells them politely it's time to go.

Nick immediately sneers his contempt and tells Ian to go and have carnal knowledge with his mother. He follows this up with a wild haymaker of a right hook, missing Ian by half a metre, but connecting flush on the shoulder of one of a group of ladies unlucky enough to be passing the action, on their way back from powdering their noses.

It's Katrina who cops the punch and worse still, it bounces off and smashes into the right side of her jaw. Katrina is the daughter of a local councillor so when she hits the floor, a tense silence descends over the crowded bar.

Instantly one of Milton's mates, who is known for his first aid skills, pushes through the crowd and kneels down beside Katrina's prone form.

For some reason this is the signal for most of the patrons to erupt into a melee of flying fists. And more than one of the antagonists is female, giving as good as she gets. It's almost as if the falling rain outside, which is ending the long drought, has sparked a similar venting of relieved tension in the pub. Only it's not raining drops, it's raining blows.

Someone behind the pump calls the cops as one patron is seen flying over the bar and lands on him, knocking him to the ground. Rick motions urgently at his four brothers, especially Nick, that it's time to leave for Luke's initiation. They head for the back door, leaving Rex wondering what had just happened.

Smoke from the pub's fire wafts up and out of the top of the chimney, hovering above the car park below, where five figures are seen running for Nick's SUV. Nick and Ryan climb in the front and the other three scramble into the back, Luke is sandwiched once more in the middle. He's used to being the target for his brothers' taunts and beatings, and just because today is his eighteenth birthday, doesn't mean anything is about to change.

One of his earliest memories was the time his brothers had surrounded his cot. Their mother had caught the boys in the act, spraining her ankle climbing a ladder outside Luke's window in the process. Without warning, she had noticed something being taken out of Nick's pocket, but at the time she had been unsure as to what it was. As the sunlight had come through Luke's bedroom window, it glistened.

She did not have to wait long for a scream from Luke, who had obviously been suddenly awakened from his deep sleep. She'd thought it was a knife that was in Nick's hand, but to her relief, it was a metal water pistol.

A scream of pain was all the boys needed to hear to let them know that their silent cruelty was up.

This made their punishments worse than usual, inspiring the boys to further malicious reprisals on the defenceless Luke.

In retrospect, he'd eventually worked out that all they were doing was repeating the same torment meted out to them, one by one, by their brute of a father.

Heading away from the pub Luke wonders what's in

store for him. The twins, Ryan and Brian, had managed to put themselves into the local hospital on the night of their twenty-first birthday. So Luke knew he wasn't going to get off lightly. Nick took after his father, Tom, whose heavy drinking and random brutality may well have stemmed from seeing action in Vietnam, from where he returned suffering Post Traumatic Stress Disorder.

The boys' mother had learned of Tom's condition and the couple underwent counselling in a vain attempt to save their marriage. In the end it was their mother, Edith, who raised the children, but the damage had already been done to all of them, except Luke. The price he paid for his comparatively pain free childhood, was the jealous hostility of his brothers.

When Edith finally fled the marital home, Tom was given free rein to raise the brothers as violently as he pleased. On one occasion, they stole lollies from the local store and were brought home by the police to face their drunken father. As soon as the custodians of the law had left the house, Tom set about the four older brothers with his belt, inflicting a savage flogging on each of them. Luke only copped a slap on the backside, something his siblings deeply resented, *and something that would most likely not be allowed to happen in today's society, even though it still does*, Luke thinks to himself.

As the brothers climb into the SUV, they discuss the planned surprise for Luke. Nick gives Ryan a reassuring slap on the thigh, as he turns the engine over and the vehicle growls to life.

The SUV takes off flat out across the packed car park, weaving in and out of the other vehicles and narrowly missing a dog. Nick lets the animal know how lucky it was, "Maybe next time, dog."

He turns sharply onto the main road heading west, and as police cars race with their sirens wailing up to the pub, he swerves into a side street leading to an industrial area, a few kilometres west of town.

Ryan realises his vision is blurred. *Maybe it's the alcohol* he thinks, but when he asks Nick, his brother tells him the same thing is happening to him. Through the heavy rain a vivid flash of lightning sears across the sky, and Nick is momentarily blinded. Just long enough to obscure the bridge straight ahead, and the unfamiliar dark shape looming out of the gloom.

This is all the warning Nick gets before the SVU slews into a semi-trailer, part of which is in the river with its trailer at an angle wedged into the wooden bridge. The SUV bounces off the intruding trailer and careers over the edge of the bridge. It's as if someone had turned on a slow-motion switch.

Inside the SUV Luke is nursing an open carton of beer cans on his knees, and one flies off, striking Nick on the back of the head, and smashing into the front windscreen. Nick turns to see where the can came from, just as another can flies towards him from the inside of the SUV, causing a nasty gash on his forehead.

The sudden impact forces Nick's head back into the seat rest as blood begins to flow from his forehead.

The large SUV comes to an abrupt stop after spinning more than three hundred and sixty degrees, as debris had cascaded around the brothers inside the spinning, plummeting and tumbling SUV.

The vehicle has ended up with its rear end on top of the sleeper of the prime mover, and its bonnet is pointing skywards, almost vertically. Only the wedged trailer section of the semi-trailer stops the SUV from toppling over backwards, and into the raging river below.

Inside the SUV, the boys groggily realise the sky is directly above them. Amongst all of the loose items in the SUV, one of the pens has found an opportunity to be released from the floor, consequently stabbing Brian's left eye, and he cries out loudly in pain, receiving a poke he wasn't expecting.

Begrudgingly he turns to Luke to see if there is any damage done to his eye, as it continues to rain heavily outside.

Because of the noisy rain thumping on the outside of the SUV, Luke has to speak loudly so Ryan can hear him. "Keep it closed for a just few minutes until it settles down. It isn't a good idea to try and open it. No, you'll have to wait for the initial stinging pain to subside." Luke advises.

"Where the hell did you learn that crap from?" Brian says, as if he cared less.

Luke answers as if this was just an ordinary situation, "On one of the first aid courses during Venturers, I think... no, it might have been when I was in scouts. I can't remember."

Luke shrugs his shoulders and is about to say something else when Brian says, "don't care when, how, blah-blah-blah, Just make the bloody stinging pain go away."

Luke acts how he acts when his brothers are not around. To him it's a simple but caring gesture, regardless of whether the person is a total stranger, or a prick of a brother.

"I'll have to wash it out with some water, but as we don't have any, you'll just have to wait a bit longer."

"What about some beer, would that help?" Brian asks.

Luke shrugs again. "It *could* make it better, but it might also sting a bit."

Brian growls in frustration, when Nick laughingly says to Luke, "Yeah, put some beer on it to see what happens." Rick and Ryan join in the laughter, unaware of the terror about to befall them.

Luke grabs one of the beer cans off the floor and having not realised what is about to happen, opens the can and accidentally sprays Nick all over his face with foam, as the cans having been shaken due to the forces of the accident.

This brings about a stinging sensation upon Luke from Nick.

Nick screams at Luke for what he did to him and says loudly, "luckily I can't see you to strike out at you... you shit."

Brian remarks, "That would make two of us," bringing more laughter with the exception of Nick, but Luke has an accomplished grin on his face. Although he couldn't hurt a fly, Luke has a sense of finally having outsmarted them all, especially Nick, and wonders if there will be another opportunity tonight.

Luke did not speak, not wanting to further his punishment any more than it needs to be, given the circumstances. And thankfully the darkness shrouds his triumphant demeanour.

Only their seatbelts are stopping Nick and Ryan in the front seats from falling back down onto the other three.

The air bags have deployed, and as their general panic subsides, the brothers have come to the stunned conclusion that they have all survived... for now.

13

(SQUARE PEG ROUND HOLE)

Slowly and carefully, Ron turns the semi left onto a dirt road and then travels another two hundred meters, before easing onto the larger of two wooden bridges, which will finally take his family on their way to the hotel they are staying at overnight, in Steering.

Ron leans over to speed dial the radio station's number into his phone. The truck is nearly at the far end of the forty-metre-long wooden bridge when Ron thinks he hears an ominous creaking noise amongst the heavy rain. Maybe he should have stopped and opened the driver's side window or gotten out of the semi-trailer, and checked the bridge before crossing. But playing with the phone distracted his thoughts.

Then he hears a voice on the phone saying, "Hello."

It's Robbie, Michael Scanlon's producer, and when he doesn't reply, she hangs up.

In the cabin of the prime mover, Ron is suddenly tossed about like a rag doll, his body smashing into a series of hard-edged sections of the vehicle, bruising his ribs. Flying debris resembling sunglasses, a couple of the kids' books and a few pens, and various other bits and pieces are scattered and flung around him. Then a violent collision between his head and the gear stick renders him unconscious, with a deep cut over his left eye.

Flying through the cabin is Ron's heavy log book that has fallen straight onto the seat belt latch, releasing him to the unknown gravity inside the cab, as the prime mover slowly plummets down to the waiting torrent below.

The absence of his seatbelt means Ron is finally hurled through the already smashed front windscreen of the truck, into the raging river below. His limp body is picked up instantly by the fierce current and washed downstream by the force of the storm-driven water. He is carried along with limbs of broken trees, stumps, boulders and other debris. Thrashing about him are animal bones scoured from the depths of the once dry riverbed. His body becomes tangled in the branches of a tree, careering along with the current.

DIANNE AND STEPHANIE are trapped inside the sleeping compartment, which is resting against the splintered timbers and broken roadway timber beams, on the eastern most side at the bottom of the collapsed bridge.

Bridgette lies unconscious in the front seat with a slight cut on her forehead, blood trickling down her face while it is slumped against the side window.

Then, through the shrouds of rain, come another set of headlights and the sound of loud rock music that is instantly overcome by another noise.

It's the screeching of brakes and the awful sound of metal scraping against metal.

And still being heard above the thundering rain is the

bellowing of large beasts as the moaning of trapped and hurt human voices goes on.

The undercurrent to this jangled disharmony is the thunderous roar of the water below.

The river has overflowed along parts of its banks before and after, as it slightly narrows at Mackenzie's bridge and has spread out across the countryside, covering everything in its wake. Daylight, when it comes, will reveal the tops of only the tallest trees left visible.

A CAR CARRYING a family of five has collided with a semi-trailer, transporting a cargo of pedigree Texas longhorn bulls. Moments later, a second car containing five drunken males has ploughed head-on into the wreckage.

The trailer carrying the bulls is leaning precariously on the bridge, wedged against a light pole that is somehow still flickering in its attempt to stay alive.

The trailer's cab is half immersed on the eastern side of the torrent that the river has become.

All five occupants trapped inside are unconscious or concussed, and the first car is slightly pinned beneath the semi, half submerged in the river. Their new car also has a large wide sunroof made of Perspex, and a sliding wooden section underneath, shielding them when it becomes too bright or sunny.

The raging torrent of water is rising around them, chunks of shattered bodywork is floating around them.

As the prime mover came down on top of the Lockwood's family car, stopped only by its connection to the trailer, it shattered the Perspex, showering most of the broken pieces on the family inside. The force allows various objects to be tossed around in the rear of the vehicle, blending in with the various pieces of camping gear and packages packed tightly for the journey home. Other items found their way out through the open sunroof, and into the catastrophe outside.

The vehicle is positioned facing forward, and the front rests slightly upwards against a timber beam of the bridge, to the oncoming river as it flows over the part of the bonnet not covered by the prime mover.

The edge of the fast-flowing river goes up the front window and down the back window, then finally away further down the river. With the speed of the river forcing the water along, it's not allowing some of the river to penetrate most areas of the doors or roof that might be vulnerable.

The second car carrying the five brothers comes to rest on top of the prime mover with its bonnet pointing skywards. This slightly squashes the prime mover cabin down onto Dianne and Stephanie, who are precariously trapped inside the sleeping compartment.

One of the panic-stricken bulls tries to extricate itself from the tangled wreckage of the trailer, but succeeds only in knocking itself out, blocking any hope of escape for the remainder of the terrified animals, except for Bob, the pride of the herd. A slight toss of his massive head is enough for him to break free from his enclosure. The remainder of the trapped bulls are becoming progressively more enraged and frightened, bucking against the confines of their stalls inside the now vertical trailer.

Five bulls have, since the accident, succeeded in extricating themselves from the wreckage, and plunged down into the river. Even their huge bulk is insufficient to save them from being washed along in the current. They finish up in an area where three are able to scramble up the banks, and onto solid ground.

They will remain there for a few hours before heading aimlessly back towards the crash site. The other two have drowned, and have been washed away downstream.

The trailer sits precariously on a slight angle, shaking with the force of the bulls' desperate struggle to break free. Bob is at the top of the trailer, thrashing in agony from a piece of thick wire that has been forced into his left eye during the crash. He finally frees himself from the trailer and tumbles out, catching his left hind leg on its railing.

The leg snaps, partly tearing it from his body, causing him to fall and smash his head against the side of the trailer. Blood pours from his broken leg down onto the car below. He bellows his fury and pain as he hangs helplessly from the tangled wreckage of the trailer.

Stephanie and Dianne are trapped inside the sleeping compartment of the prime mover, and gaze in horror as an animal's eye, wide with fear is seen dangling outside their side window. A leg is carried downstream below them. Something or somebody is hanging by its clothing on a nail on the bridge, suspended over the raging river.

Even though the temperature of the water is quite warm, there are signs the swollen river is beginning to subside.

Ron has vanished somewhere down the swollen river, having landed on a partly submerged tree as remnants of a long-ago simple creek, before it became a river.

Part of the tree has jammed his left arm, breaking the skin but not his arm, causing him to lose a little blood. However, the water has made the skin around the wound slightly close, preventing more blood loss as he loses his fight to stay awake.

～

ON A REMOTE STRETCH OF ROAD, somewhere inland along the East Coast of Australia, night has arrived, and a storm has passed. The wind has died, and the land is quite still, and slowly the valley begins to be enveloped in thick fog.

Inside the darkened bedroom of a nearby farmhouse, John Meadows sits up and nudges his sleeping wife, asking her if she heard a strange noise... a loud bang.

"Shut up, John. Just go back to sleep, it's bloody raining, you idiot," she murmurs.

He does so reluctantly, mumbling that he's sure he heard something.

The next ten hours see a horrifying fight for survival by fourteen human beings, a herd of longhorn bulls, and something else.

Surviving the accident is one thing, surviving the night is another, and with a little torment from Mother Nature's Fury... anything is terrifying.

14

AUTHOR'S EXPERIENCE

While on their way home from holidays Dennis and his family were caught in the aftermath of Cyclone Yasi, which had reached as far south as Victoria. Minutes away from going through Charlton, they were redirected to the township of Donald, where they endured floods in the town around them. On the second morning Dennis spoke to a fellow truckie asking, "how can I get out of here." The truckie directed them to a dirt road and they were soon on their way home. They were however able to capture photos of their experience.

Not having any experience with the damage caused by cyclones, Dennis was not able to comprehend what anyone has to go through when experiencing a cyclone on a regular basis.

15

(WRONG PLACE, WRONG TIME)

F ive young brothers aged between eighteen and twenty-two, united this night by a cocktail of terror, anger and alcohol, are about to confront something so terrible, it could end the lives of any number of them, and destroy forever the minds of the remainder. That something is more powerful, more destructive and more vindictive than anything their worst imaginings could ever have conjured. It is also hanging upside down by a partially severed leg, separated from them only by the thickness of a...

ALL OF NICK'S anger stems from the drink-riddled impression that someone deliberately lured them into crashing their vehicle. In the front seat, Nick and Ryan are the first to articulate and attempt to come to terms with the awful circumstances they must face, in the immediate aftermath of the collision. The airbags have saved them for now from anything worse than painful cuts and bruises. They are slowly coming to the realisation that they are trapped and sitting in the now vertical SUV. They are able to see over the top of the deployed air bags, in the murky blackness outside the spotted windscreen.

There is something improbably large, something jerking and changing shape, coming in and out of their limited vision.

Its movements are punctuated by deafening roars and bellows of rage, pain and fear.

Nick says to Ryan, his voice blurred with blood, "is it me, or is there a big black balloon that seems to be getting bigger in front of us?"

Ryan wants to ask Nick to repeat himself, but fears the inevitable snarled response, so he says nothing. Nick, realising that the airbags are still inflated, and due to his intoxicated state, calls out to everyone that all will be okay. Then their world explodes in their faces.

Their horrible screams stir the three brothers in the back, waking them out of their semi-concussed state, in time for them to witness something unfathomable coming their way. But, thank Christ it's getting to Nick and Ryan first.

The image in front of the pair bursts through the windscreen as if it were paper. Little nuggets of fractured glass cascade over them both. And then come two thin, curved, yellowy white arms that somehow end in sharp points. These two apparitions come to an abrupt stop, one buried deep where Ryan's nose used to be, and the other penetrating almost the whole way through Nick's chest.

The three brothers in the back watch helplessly as Nick and Ryan are gored and torn again and again. They now realise there are horns mounted on each side of a massive, slavering, one-eyed monster's woolly head. Several times, the horns slash through the upholstery of the front seat and wave perilously close to the three cowering young men in the back. The minds of all three have snapped in different ways.

None can comprehend what they are seeing. Brian and Rick have become delirious and are convulsing and vomiting.

Luke is rigid, almost comatose with terror.

Bob's entire form keeps coming into view through the shattered windscreen and then disappearing as he thrashes violently in his attempts to extricate his back end from the wreckage. He is swinging, almost like a pendulum, and every time his head smashes back into the interior of the SUV, more flesh is torn and gouged from the by now ragdoll forms that are motionless, and slumped on what remains of the front seat.

As the two bodies are repeatedly tossed and thrown into one another, more blood and intestines splash and squirt over the three surviving brothers in the back.

Brian, Rick, and Luke gradually become unrecognisable from the blood and gore coating their faces and upper torsos.

Brian and Rick have finally slipped more into blessed unconsciousness. Only Luke remains witness to the evolving horror. He wonders whether this is the end of everything. The torment he's endured at the hands of his brothers. This awful vision... is it going to cut short any attempt he may make in the future to end his siblings' tyranny?

Bob's repeated assaults have finally severed the steering wheel. One of his front legs is protruding through it as he convulses, as if to rid himself of it. He strikes Ryan in the middle of what is left of his face.

It's that one powerful lunge that snaps Ryan's neck, like a

DENNIS LUKE

crack from a whip, his head dangles, perilously flopping at a hideous angle.

Nick, prior to the point of death from the bloody goring he has suffered, while Ryan's head is lolling backwards on his shoulders. There is also, mixed up with this realisation, a flashback vision of himself, in the act of raping a girl in a drunken stupor a few years ago.

In a solitary moment before Nick dies, he has feelings of elation. Then his final thought is an all-encompassing fear, and behind it the knowledge that his lifetime of pretending to be fearless has left him with all the more to fear. He is overcome by fear. It is his last conscious thought before he slips away forever into darkness.

Fear is in us all. The most fearless have far more to fear. It's how we deal or overcome it that separates us from the rest, but in this case, Nick died experiencing fear.

The last breath of life in both of them had arrived simultaneously. Bob's thrashing has, by now, reached such a crescendo of convulsing violence that he snaps his own neck, mere moments after he has done the same for Ryan. The huge bull's form shudders to a gradual, swaying stillness.

In the back, Luke has descended into a state of almost euphoric oblivion. He dreams of the time in his cot when his brothers sprayed him with the water pistol.

As he comes round, he imagines seeing their faces peering down on him. Then he realises in a brief interlude of cold reality that it's not water he's covered in, but blood, slime and something that feels squishy and lumpy. He looks to either side of him and a sudden vivid flash of lightning reveals Brian and Rick marred with the same revolting mess. The sudden flash illuminates much more, far too much for Luke to take in.

There are two tangled masses of broken limbs, faceless skulls and more blood and slime where Nick and Ryan were sitting seconds ago. There is also something glimpsed through the shattered windscreen, something immense, its gentle swaying at odds with its sheer bulk. The lightning and the tumbling crescendo of the thunder that follows it are strong enough to wake Brian and Rick.

As they lurch back into consciousness, both once again begin vomiting uncontrollably. Luke points speechlessly at the front seat, but the flash has died away and all that's visible in the gloom is that great bulk swaying gently through the front windscreen. Realising what they had just gone through, Rick and Brian begin to laugh together and, feeling slightly better, ask each other if the other is okay, and if the other is able to get out of the car safely.

Luke says he's fine, except for the blood, but Rick and Brian couldn't care less about him.

Rick says nastily, "you're lucky that's all that's wrong with you, you should be thankful you weren't in the front instead of Ryan. That's where you were going to be but luckily for the commotion back at the pub, we had to keep an eye on you, just in case you decided to skip out and hide on us."

Rick and Brian want retribution, and don't care how they get it. The single factor tempering their rage and their response is their youngest brother, Luke, and wanting to make him suffer. The sudden realisation surrounding them makes Brian, Rick and Luke want to get out of the vehicle, sooner than later.

All three young men are in deep shock, and covered in the gore of their dead siblings, but they are somehow responsive enough to know they must free themselves from the confined and horror-filled tomb, the SUV has now become.

16

(STOMACH'S HUNGRY)

Scotty Taylor is reaching the end of the long drive to Steering, but pangs of hunger force him to stop at the last town before his destination. It had looked like a pleasant enough little place before he called in at the local store, and found out first impressions can be deceiving.

He climbs out of his fifteen-year-old station wagon, loaded to the hilt with his gear, and stretches extravagantly to ward off the stiffness from a five-hour drive.

He finds himself stumbling face forward, and ends up on his backside on the pavement outside the store. He climbs laboriously to his feet and slumps and stumbles towards the wire door. "Oh crap," he says to himself, wincing in pain as his stomach growls. Something hot and nutritious would put him back on his feet.

An elderly woman who flings open the door into his path brings him up in an abrupt halt. He hopes this old woman would get out of the way quickly so he could at least sit down somewhere inside. She gives Scotty the once over, grunts disparagingly, and walks off.

Finally, he makes it inside the store to find an elderly

bain-marie containing tired looking meat pies, dim-sims and chips. Over in the corner, next to the drinks machine, is a large fridge containing a variety of ice-creams, and other stands are scattered around the general store, for children and overweight adults looking for any rubbish they could get their hands on.

After looking around for whatever reason, as one felt compelled to do so to perhaps give the impression it is all too familiar, his eyes land on the lady behind the counter.

If he thought for one second he was going to be treated like a local, or at least with a bit of respect, then he can forget it.

She mutters something in his general direction, not one word of which he understands, but before he can ask her to repeat herself, she blurts again very quickly, "Haven't got all day, sonny."

Despite her rudeness, Scotty opts to use his charm, hopefully to get something out of her a bit more appetising than the contents of the bain-marie. But before he can speak, she's at him again, speaking as though her words were in a race against each other. "Can't make up your mind, sonny?"

He'd hoped he could use his charm to try and get her to slow down, after all, isn't that what happens in a country town? He's had enough of these bush manners and barks impatiently and slowly, "two pies, three dimmies..." and not thinking much of it as it's normal city lingo, adds, "Some dead horse."

No please or thank you. The woman's face becomes even more hostile.

"I keep horses out in the backyard, you ignorant bastard, so less of your crap!" Then she adds, "Gimme twelve dollars twenty!"

Noting that her name badge reads '*Mavis*' he sheepishly tries not to catch her vile stare, which would kill anything if it were a laser, Scotty places a cold drink on the counter and says, "This, and one of those donuts with the coloured sprinkles on top."

"Seventeen-eighty, suppose ya want a bag with that?" she blurts out like a drag racing car.

Scotty hands over a twenty with a contemptuous, "Keep the bloody change for your wonderful service." But then his mood and facial expression changes abruptly as he sees something move behind the curtain in the back part of the shop.

Mavis notices the same thing and goes behind the curtain to re-emerge with a gorgeous looking young woman in her early twenties. She has long locks of curly brown hair and a stunning figure. For the first time in his testosterone-fuelled life, Scotty's response is one of sympathy rather than lust.

Just as Mavis is ranting about the lack of real men in the town, Scotty remarks, "That's a lovely beauty spot you have there." He's referring to the small, disfiguring birthmark, just beside her beautiful, full, mouth-watering lips, and below those piercing big blue eyes, temporarily marring the girl's beauty. He means nothing malicious by his remark. It is merely a clumsy attempt at a compliment, as she seems embarrassed but quietly flattered by his forwardness.

Awkwardly he leaves in a hurry through the wire door, climbs in the station wagon and parks across the road under a tree. The thought of eating inside the store while the woman watches him... is unthinkable.

Back inside the store, the owner and her daughter giggle to themselves about the handsome stranger with the abrupt manner. *And if only he knew what a big fool he was.* They began fantasising about the handsome young man that recently stood before them.

WITH THE GREASY tucker still sitting uneasily in his stomach, Scotty drives on to Steering to find a note on the door of the police station, located in the centre of town. The note instructs him to phone a nearby neighbour who has the key to the station.

Once inside the building, he is glad to locate the toilet, then he decides to settle down for a quiet night. He wonders how Billy is faring, and how he will cope with the long journey up here. Then the phone rings. It's Bert Logan, the local senior sergeant from the headquarters in the last big town he drove through, telling Scotty to meet him outside the Steering pub, apparently there's a bit of a blue getting out of hand.

He climbs into his uniform and does as he's told, driving the police car a short distance to the pub where he finds Logan and a number of other officers standing in the packed car park, outside the bar door.

Bert shakes his hand and then points at the door and says, "Well... get in there son, and don't hold back."

Scotty opens the door and is instantly hit in the face by the stench of stale beer and tobacco, and the noise of the knockdown drag-em-out stoush that is going on inside. And it's not just the blokes who are going at it. He can spot a few women at the centre of the melee as well.

Suddenly a woman is flung into his arms. She looks up at him and as her face lights up and she squeals, "Hello, gorgeous."

Scotty reels back, repelled by the stench of her breath,

and grabs her by an arm and frogmarches her back outside to the divvy van. "Any men you bring out, put them in here, okay?" The senior sergeant instructs him to put the woman with the other females already over under a tree outside the pub. He does so and passes back through the pub door to be confronted by the huge frame of a bloke blocking his way. It's Ian, the publican. He thrusts out a meaty paw and begins to introduce himself.

At that moment, someone behind Ian aims a vicious blow at the publican, but Scotty is quick enough to pull him sideways by the hand as he's shaking it. The blow intended for Ian lands squarely on Scotty's shoulder, making him recoil backwards.

He rights himself and grabs the assailant by his left arm, twists it up and behind his back, then grabs a handful of his hair and drags him outside to a second van. The door is thrown open by Logan, and Scotty flings the now subdued patron into the rear of the van and he collides with a couple of blokes already squatting there. Both men complain about their rough treatment and hurl abuse at their captors, who pay no attention to them as Scotty turns back again.

Ian comes over to thank Scotty, who was about to return to the fray, but instead accepts the publican's second offer of a handshake and introduces himself.

"The name's Ian, I'm the publican, and the owner of this salubrious establishment. When you've had time to settle in, and things are a bit less hectic, drop in for a meal and a drink."

Scotty glances across at Logan for approval or otherwise, and is told, "Don't worry about it. You're not in Melbourne now so take a deep breath and relax. You'll be fine." He stops and half grins, looking Scotty hard in the eyes. "I know about how you ended up here. I'd probably have done the same myself.

Anyway, come and see me in the morning and I'll give you the lay of the land. Sorry I wasn't there at the station to welcome you, but I've only just got back from leave myself.

Nothing changes much, regardless of whether you're in the bush or in the city. Steering's no different from anywhere else these days. People have good days and bad ones and that's just life. It's not always this entertaining."

As the various officers are about to leave the now subdued pub, a call comes in from the Emergency Services, asking for assistance in diverting traffic because of rising floodwaters. Scotty is despatched to a part of town near the river to check that none of the houses dotted along there are under water.

He climbs into his police car and types the address of the riverside street into his G.P.S, glances behind to make sure he's clear to pull out onto the main road, and heads off into the darkness, unsure of what he has got himself into on this eventful night.

Due to the storm, all the roads around the crash site have been blocked off by the emergency services, who are none the wiser about the crash. It has become quite noticeable to all concerned that visibility isn't as good as what it was, compared to when they'd arrived at the pub.

17

(THAT'S JUST CRIMINAL)

"JOHNNO," screams the Boss, as footsteps can be heard coming from the two floors below and getting closer. Johnno doesn't use the lift. He likes to show the Boss and others in the group that he's fit and healthy. If he needs to make a fast getaway, he can. As for the rest, they can look after themselves.

Nearly all of them are larger than life Italians who always have difficulty cramming into the lift with the Boss, who is no lightweight either. Brawn is prized more highly than brains amongst this mob. If a shootout with the police is required, deciding who would survive would be a bit like winning the lottery for one so lucky, but alas, probably not with this lot of dense minders.

In a building above a barber's salon on Lygon Street, in the northern part of Melbourne's city centre, a door opens to the expansive loft on the third floor. Johnno enters with a swift spin of his body, allowing the door to close quietly behind him. An almost gentle and silent click of the door lock could just be heard within this dark and spacious old timber room.

He ruins his graceful entrance by snivelling across the loft. "Yes Boss, you called for me?" He asks in an assertive but subdued tone.

"Will you knock that off? For fuck's sake, Johnno, one of these days someone's gunna pop you full of holes, and I won't give a sweet goddamn if they do."

Johnno scours the room with his wide young eyes, looking up at the angry faces. He gets the impression that any one of them would take pleasure in doing him bodily harm. His antics are a bit over the top at times. He turns to face the Boss and asks nervously, "What you want, Boss?"

"Go and get me the 'Book of Fools' in the basement. It's next to the fridge. And while you're at it, get me two bottles of '85 directly opposite the fridge. You got all that..." hesitating... "Johnno?"

Sounding like a snake hissing, he replies, "Yesssss, Boss." He moves quickly to the door, turning to catch the room full of big, hardened men laughing at him. So he slams the door hard, much to the Boss's annoyance as his large frame jumps up at the sudden sound.

Mario Sculini arrived with other immigrants during the seventies once he'd decided to go it alone. Too many of his Sicilian cronies were being rounded up too quickly for his liking. He distanced himself from their more conventional activities like drugs and money laundering. He concentrated instead on his dealings in the booming construction industry, using his restaurant as a cover for his extracurricular activities.

Jo-Anne had been investigating those activities when Con had paid her his ill-fated visit. She has since gone into hiding as a result.

Johnno flies down the stairs three at a time while nearly knocking over the Boss's niece, Lara, at one of the corners of the stairwell. She gives him a big smile, thus causing him to miss a step and stumble downwards, falling in a crumpled heap at the bottom of the flight of stairs.

Embarrassed by his awkwardness, he springs to his feet and continues on to the basement.

As he is about to open the door, he realises he doesn't have the keys. He curses loudly before turning round and flying back up the stairs. He is about to burst through the closed door to the loft when he remembers the protocol, he takes a breath, and knocks lightly before entering. He pokes his head around the edge of the door.

"You forget something, Johnno?" The Boss is dangling a bunch of keys in his hand, much to the hilarity of the other men in the room. Seething in humiliation, Johnno tiptoes over to the Boss and retrieves the keys whilst again noticing Lara, who is sitting quietly on the sofa.

She has an amused but warm smile on her face and it's clearly aimed in his direction, much to the displeasure of the Boss. "Don't come to me if you ever get involved with that one. He's a klutz and his age of eighteen should be his I.Q and he is more trouble than you need," the Boss tells her.

"Oh, he's okay, Uncle, he just needs some TLC," she responds.

"Okay, now that you're over twenty one, you're old enough to know your own mind. Me? I'm just looking out for you, like I promised your dead mother I would."

Flying back down the stairs, Johnno is a little more prepared this time for any more unexpected oncoming humans, as he finally reaches the basement cellar and unlocks the door.

He enters a room filled with numerous smells, one of which he instantly recognises. He's prepared to risk the wrath of the Boss, only for the supreme joy of sampling the pleasures of his personal stash of imported chocolates.

The Boss marks them off every time he has one, two, three, or the whole box in one of his stuff his face moments, which he did yesterday without even sharing with anyone, except his niece.

"Greedy bugger he is without sharing them with me except his niece," Johnno grumbles, then he goes over to the wine cellar and removes two bottles of 1985 chardonnay, before going to the fridge and searching through various documents, eventually coming up with the Book of Fools. It's bound inside a hard cover and has a lock on it that only the Boss has a key to open.

Johnno examines the book, like he has many times before, curious about the title – the Book of Fools.

He shrugs his shoulders and walks out the door, closing and locking it behind him. He stands there motionless for a moment, wondering if he has forgotten anything. Then he bounds back up the stairs once more while taking care not to drop the bottles.

He knocks on the loft door and hears Lara's voice telling him he can come in, and that nobody's going to shoot him. Trusting her gentle voice, he enters slowly around the door.

He anticipates wide grins on all their faces, and that included the Boss's niece, much to his displeasure, and to which he remarks with a scowl on his face, "ha ha very funny." Johnno takes the wine and the book over to a large mahogany table, at one end of which sits the Boss. "Here you go, Boss," he says in that quiet tone the Boss is not familiar with.

The big man leans backwards, enabling him to get a key out of his vest pocket, and unlocks the Book of Fools.

"What's in the Book of Fools, Boss?" Johnno asks misguidedly.

"None of your fucking business," snarls the Boss, dialling a number listed in the book.

"Hey, Boss, no swearing, there's sensitive blokes around." Johnno dares to say this with the intention of protecting Lara.

To his surprise, the Boss glances briefly at both of them and apologises. But, then he beckons Johnno over and whispers in his ear, "Get stuffed."

THE BOSS IS RINGING a phone in a small single-room apartment just round the corner. There is a kitchen/dining room and a bedroom. A king size bed inside the bedroom has to be entered at the bottom end of the bed, as the sides of the bed just touch the walls. But with his large frame, Milo is quite content to be able to have such luxuries, considering what he didn't have before now.

A large man, dressed in a soiled tracksuit and long curly hair is sprawled across the bed. Milo is watching a Tom and Jerry cartoon with rapt attention. He's concentrating hard that he's slightly dribbling.

The ringing phone is an annoyance. Milo enjoys cartoons partly because people get shot, blown up, pushed over cliffs and run over by semi-trailers, but they always get up and dust themselves off as though nothing had happened to them.

Sometimes he wishes a few of the people he has been paid to kill would react the same way. But that's what you get from a simple mind. He doesn't realise cartoons are only make believe.

Now that he has to wait to watch another episode. Milo picks up the phone and says, "Hello, Boss." One thing you can always rely on Milo for is loyalty. "On way, Boss," he says after listening on the phone for a minute, speaking with a guttural, central European rasp.

He has been under the Boss's group for the last few years, since being dishonourably discharged from the army in the Ukraine. He grew up there with his large family and over time, gained enrolment because of his follower, not leader, nature.

Milo has been attributed with a number of kills, the last of which was one of his immediate superiors. He'd fled to Australia aboard an illegal boat through pre-arranged links, and began working for the Boss.

BACK IN THE LOFT, loud and elephant-like footsteps can be heard leading from the lift to the door. There is a loud knock. One of the minders opens the door, as a man built like the proverbial brick shithouse ducks and sways his huge frame into the room. His sheer bulk seems almost to shrink the loft and its occupants. The floor creaks under his weight as he walks toward the Boss.

It made those already in the loft a little uneasy, fearing the floor could open up and they would all be taken down with him to their deaths. The door is closed behind him by one of the minders, but then opened again immediately when the Boss orders everyone except Milo, to get out.

The big men troop through the door one at a time, turning sideways to squeeze through the narrow entrance. Lara takes Johnno out into Lygon Street into the restaurant for dinner, while they wait for the Boss to join them.

"What's up, Boss?" asks Milo when the last footsteps fall away.

"You remember that fucking woman journalist that killed Con, my nephew?" The Boss says, realising he can swear as much as he likes now, as there is no one around to offend.

"Yes, that was bad thing, Boss, what can I do to make better?"

"I need you to follow her to find out what she's up to, and then let me know. Later, I'll tell you when and where you can see her off, and that fucking copper she's been seeing. I heard he's gone bush somewhere, but he's got a mate still living here. The journalist might get in touch with him to find out where the pig's gone. Now you got your orders, you know what you need to do. Let me know when you're on to something, okay."

"Yes, Boss, I'm thinking this is terminating. What's my take?"

"It's twice the normal fee and a bonus as long as there is no comeback on me."

Spoken in his unique broken English, he replies, "Understand. Talk soon, Boss."

18

(WARNING-WARNING-WARNING)

"It's a quarter to eight here tonight on CRAZY F.M., and this is Michael Scanlon. We have Wayne from the S.E.S on the line. Got some bad news for us, I hear, Wayne?"

"Yes Michael, the tropical storm has hit with a vengeance, as we expected, with some of the district already under water. So we're asking residents in the areas not already affected to pack up and leave unless you're on high ground, even then you should consider leaving for town, before this gets out of hand."

"What areas are most at risk, Wayne?"

"Mainly the western and northern regions at the moment, as that's the direction the front's coming from. It's travelling slowly at the moment, but it's important to understand what's happening here. As you know, we've had over ten years of drought, and the ground's been rock hard for so long. This will cause the flooding to move around the district quicker, making it flow faster than if the soil was soft."

"What are the chances of the entire district being under water, come morning?"

"The weather service says the system is slow moving, and some of the district could miss out on the storm's worst effects. It goes without saying that it's better to be safe than sorry, to evacuate sooner rather than later, but it's all very possible, and for some people it might already be too late. It's hard to know who is still out there."

Michael is getting anxious about his next question and doesn't know when to stop at just one. His voice peaks. *"Is the tropical storm building or weakening as it enters our district, and do you know where it's heading once it leaves us? How much more rainfall should we expect tonight?"* He is nervous about the answer and thinks, *phew, did I say all that?*

Wayne has a chuckle, and then replies, "According to the weather service, it'll diminish in its size as it moves further south, but it will intensify. Before it leaves this district, they are expecting between three to five hundred millimetres more over the next twenty-four hours. After that, it will head towards the Mildura-Renmark region. And by all accounts, it will continue on through some of the western towns in Victoria. Then it will move on to some of the Melbourne suburbs around the southeast, then towards Phillip Island. It's unlucky it will arrive just in time for the penguin parade, which they have mostly every night of the year."

Wayne takes a breath before he reveals the major news. "Figures from the weather services say they are expecting the tropical storm to dump between one hundred to one hundred and fifty millimetres down there over the next forty-eight hours. This will cause major flooding in most areas around Melbourne's southeast."

"Thanks Wayne, we'll talk again in about an hour. Back with more of your calls soon, as I take another break! Phew. All this rain coming, I'm just overwhelmed by it all as I know you all are too, and all this humidity doesn't help either. Everything feels

clammy and sticky and dry and it's still early, and I'm stuffed already, oh poor me." Michael gives out a big sigh as he looks at Robbie and says, "I don't know if I can last doing this til morning, Robbie."

"I'll take over from you sometime during the night if you need a break."

"Thanks, it'd be great if you could manage that."

19

(WHERE AM I?)

V alley fog, which settles into the hollows and basins between hills and mountains, is a type of radiation fog. When cooler, heavier air, loaded with condensed water droplets, is trapped beneath a layer of lighter, warmer air and hemmed in by ridges and peaks, it can't escape, often lingering for days. Being one of three types of fog that is relevant to this story, radiation fog forms in the evening when the heat absorbed by the Earth's surface during the day, and is radiated into the air. As heat is transferred from the ground to the air, water droplets form. Sometimes people use the term 'ground fog' to refer to radiation fog. Ground fog does not reach as high as any of the clouds overhead. It usually forms at night.

Fog that is said to 'burn off' in the morning sun is radiation fog. Freezing fog happens when the liquid fog droplets freeze to solid surfaces. Mountaintops that are covered by clouds are often covered in freezing fog. As the freezing fog lifts, the ground, the trees, and even objects like spider webs, are blanketed by a layer of frost. The white landscapes of freezing fog are common in places with cold moist climates such as Scandinavia, Antarctica and Southern Australia.

≈

YOU COULD CUT THE AIR, or in this case, the fog, with a knife. Those unlucky enough to be conscious in the aftermath of the disaster are immersed with an overwhelming feeling of numbness, and uncertainty as to their whereabouts.

The speed at which the floodwaters are receding in the river is incomprehensible. It has emptied as fast as it filled. Everything is ominously quiet, apart from the chirping of unseen crickets, and other nocturnal insects. Occasionally the quiet is broken by creaking sounds from the trees and the wrecked timbers of the bridge.

Raindrops occasionally fall from nearby trees into the river, and you wonder where it fell, as you try to move, but you're motionless. The overall impression is of something claustrophobic, dark and foreboding as the fog envelopes you.

It has become even more numbing to the point of wanting to say something, but the brain is a blur, your mind is a blur, and your mouth is dry. Your heart is pumping so loud you can hear it banging away in your chest. Passing out is not an option, as you're already there. You have a lump in your throat that stops you from speaking, even though you think you have the words to say. Your head is spinning and you can't see or feel anything, except maybe what's next to you, or on you.

If you're lucky enough to have someone close to you to embrace, then good, as some might find it difficult to know how to reach out to anyone. As people find it hard to talk about things that are troubling their lives, so are quite happy to go it alone till it's too late... or not. Your eyes dart from one place to another, but it's all in vain as you can't see anything, and the fear is just terrifying, and it's even worse if you're a young child in a dark and claustrophobic environment, and you've never seen this much fog before.

Here is where Dianne and Stephanie are, still trapped inside the sleeping compartment of the prime mover, and their situation is rapidly deteriorating.

When the trailer fell from its upright position, slightly level with the raging river, it allowed the brothers' car to fall into the river. This allowed more water into the prime mover's sleeping compartment, and after some time, a massive log which was carried by the swollen current, smashes into the now weakened chassis of the cab which was already violently stressed by the forces of the accident, splitting it into two sections.

The other part of the prime mover with Bridgette still in it, falls into the eastern side of the river and is taken down the river, passing what looked like a body hooked onto a branch. Luckily the section containing Dianne and Stephanie remains intact as it speeds down the river, like a floating bathtub.

THE SUV HAS BROKEN free from the wreckage and floats down the river, the body of Bob the Longhorn swirling along beside it. Rick, Brian and Luke scramble out into the flowing river, and, as they are swept towards the bank, Luke is grabbed by his two brothers and held fast against a tree root.

From there they are able to scramble up the muddy bank with their clothes soaked through, before they all collapse exhausted on the wet ground, with some parts of the river still only just visible.

Luke is relieved to be out of that vehicle, which has brought about so many bad memories. Regretting a chance to escape from the torment he was going to cop, he lays still, looking back on his hardships over time, comparing it to how he feels right now, and what the situation overnight might bring.

The rain has now subsiding, and the wind has become non-existent, along with the milder cooling temperature surrounding the valley. It becomes all too apparent to them that it has become increasingly foggy. It's as if the brothers are incapable of speech, or maybe it's simply that they can't bring themselves to discuss what they had just witnessed, of the incredibly violent deaths of their brothers, Nick and Ryan.

Instead, they now lay a few metres apart, each of them heaving with exhaustion. Everything is cloaked in a thick, sickly sweet fog. Luke, typically, is the first to think of helping others involved in the accident. He, like his brothers, is dimly aware that more than one bull was involved, and they may still be dangerously close. But he has no idea of how many humans, animals or how many vehicles have come to grief.

Luke's breathing has abated as he senses an eerie night ahead.

THE SLEEPING COMPARTMENT, still containing Dianne and Stephanie, has become wedged on the river's eastern bank. Stephanie asks, her voice trembling and choking, "What's happening, Mummy, where's Daddy and Bridgette? I'm scared, Mummy, are we going to die?"

"I'm not sure what happened to your Dad, you know

him, he'll find us, and he'll have Bridgette safe and sound with him." Dianne has no idea where she and Stephanie are, nor what they should do next. All she is sure of is the need to reassure her daughter that they are going to survive this ordeal.

Just then, something bumps roughly into the sleeping cabin, dislodging it from the bank and sending it swirling down the river once more. The pair of them screams for help.

Dianne and Stephanie are startled by the sudden jolt. However, their positioning keeps the partially broken cab from turning over and stops it from falling completely into the river.

Luke sits up after he hears their screams from the other side of the river, and tries to imagine where they are coming from.

Brian grabs him and says, "Forget those screaming bitches. We need to get out of here."

Two of the surviving bulls in the vicinity are startled by the screams and run headlong and directionless into the fog. It's a sound in the dead of night of someone screaming in pain, and terror. It suddenly erupts from the area where the bulls are stampeding. Brian leaps to his feet, his hair standing on end, but he can't see anything in the gloom.

In his panic, Brian strays too close to the riverbank and suddenly the ground gives way beneath his feet. As he starts to tumble out of sight, Rick makes a grab for him and is dragged down into the river by his sibling.

Luke cautiously goes to the crumbling bank, where his brothers have just vanished from view, wondering if this is his chance to get away, as more earth breaks away, making him tumble into the water too.

When Luke stops falling, he feels something grabbing

onto his left leg. Terror fills his mind that it must be either Brian or Rick. But both have been concussed. To his surprise, it's a young girl and an older woman.

Together they all succeed in getting towards the embankment.

As the drenched muddy trio scramble to dry land, Luke asks them, "How many of you are there?" Then he adds as an afterthought, "My name's Luke by the way."

The girl replies timidly," I'm Stephanie," whilst looking at her mum for some reassurance.

The older woman says to Luke. "Not that she wasn't naturally scared by the struggle to get out of the river, and she is thankful for being saved. She probably thought she wasn't going to drown due to her regular swimming lessons which saved her from certain death, as for me... that was just pure luck." The older woman tells Luke her name is Dianne. Her soaking red dress clings uncomfortably to her body as mascara runs down either side of her face. She asks Luke if he has seen a man and another girl.

"There are four in our family, the two of us and another daughter... and my husband. They were in the front of the truck and we haven't seen them since the crash. Are you here to rescue us?"

Luke tells her no, he has escaped from the same crash as them. The trio stands motionless in the gloom.

Dianne notices a strong resolve but something uncertain in the young man before her, and then she asks about the noises she heard, just before he rescued them from the flooding river.

Luke changes the subject as to not allow her the opportunity to help Luke's brothers, while he tries to figure out what to do next, and look for a way to get away from his siblings, unaware they are, semi-conscious, at the water's edge.

By this time the fog has well and truly taken hold of the area. It makes a surreal scene, with no way of clearly seeing what's around them, or where they are along the river. So they know nothing of their whereabouts and, far worse than that, nothing of their chances of survival.

20

(HELP US)

Back at the radio station, Robbie receives a frantic call from a lady called Margaret. She's inside a farm house surrounded by flood waters. Her landline is out, so she's used her mobile to call the local S.E.S and the police, who have told her it will be a couple of hours before they can reach her, due to the number of calls they're receiving. "They've told me to keep calm. Then they hung up on me, and here we are about five minutes away from climbing onto the roof of the house."

"Just hang on for a moment," Robbie says calmly, "and I'll put Michael on to see if we can get someone who is listening, to come and rescue you."

Michael takes the call. "Hello this is Michael here, can you tell me what's happening at the moment, and what can we do to help?"

"Everything around the house is under water. Is there someone with a boat who could rescue us?"

"Can you let us know exactly where you are? I hope there's someone listening with a boat to come and get you.

Can I ask what your name is, please, instead of me saying you all the time?"

"My name's Margaret. We're on the Lake Road about a kilometre from the main road, on the northern side of town. You can just see the top of the shed to the left of the house. But you'll need to be careful, as there are trees on the property that are nearly under water at the moment. We'll be swimming or drowning in about an hour."

ANYONE LISTENING CAN TELL Margaret is trying hard to choke back the fear that she and her family won't survive this ordeal. She has had a good life. However this is not the way she thought her final hours would be spent, thinking instead that it would be in her bed, with her family around her. She tells herself to be positive as her family will be looking to her for guidance in this hour of adversity.

She goes on with her directions, "As the property drops away after you enter from the Lake Road, you head towards the house and shed. Coming up the dirt road that you probably won't see anymore, you have to keep to the right of the gate. You should be able to see as there are two large trees on either side, just behind the gate. You'll need strong spotlights otherwise you won't be able to see the house. Then go in a straight line between the shed and the house as the highest point of the house is on the shed side."

Michael interrupts, "I've just had a call from a guy called Frank at the pub, and he wants to know how many of you are there stranded on the property?"

"There are five adults and three children, and I'm running low on battery, so I've given my number to your producer if you want to pass it onto Frank. He can ring us when he's about to come through the front gate. When I see or hear him, then I'll turn the phone back on. It's about two hundred meters from the front gate to the house." Michael can sense in her trembling voice of her ominous visions from the rooftop. "It's really frightening and terrifying at the same time and I'm seeing the rising flood waters around the house, and it doesn't look like we'll survive that long. She holds back the tears and crying so as to not alarm the other brittle family members, who are also standing on the roof around a very nervous Margaret.

FRANK HEADS from the pub to his car, realising, since his house is on the other side of the river, he'll have to go the long way round to fetch his boat.

Once he arrives home, he'll have to connect the trailer and check the engine starts okay, and that he's got enough fuel.

Robbie calls Frank to find out where he is, and his estimated time of arrival to the farm. He tells her about fifteen minutes from the property.

When Frank reaches the property, he flicks the switch on the boat with six stronger spotlights and starts to search for the house. The lights show in the distance that the northern part of the town is completely under water. "Bloody hell," he says loudly, as if he wanted others to hear.

He tries to think about where the lake road is, as it's somewhere off the main road Frank is currently on. As the topography in this part of town undulates quite dramatically, he eventually sees certain landmarks he knows. He finds the front gate and turns his boat into the entrance from where he can see the shed and the house. The water level is nearly covering the house.

Looking up towards the house again, he only sees a television aerial on his right and thinks to himself, *they are all dead*.

Hearing the boat, Margaret forgets to turn on her phone, and starts screaming at the top of her voice.

Frank locates the family who have moved from the house to the top of the shed, with the roof inches away from going under. He turns the boat towards them, completely forgetting about the trees, and gets his motor caught on one of them.

He gropes below the water line to find a branch has snagged around the propeller. He calls to the family, "You'll have to swim to the boat. I'm stuck on a tree and can't move." The water level has flooded not only the property, but most of the northern region of the town as well. As it is rising and not moving like a river, the topography has locked it in to the surrounds where it cannot escape. The soil being quite hard underneath is preventing the water from receding, creating a permanent fixture like a large lake or dam. It's quite flat with no sudden movements.

One of the children, named Rebecca, dives into the water, swimming across to the boat in a remarkably short time. Two of the men, Andrew and Adrian, put the two other smaller children, Amy and Jake, on their backs, and swim towards the bright lights on the boat. Frank helps them clamber aboard while wondering how he's going to get the remaining survivors, Margaret and her daughter Norma, into the boat.

Margaret won't budge from where she's sitting next to Norma, who is also a non-swimmer. Frank tells Andrew and Adrian he has to go overboard to untangle the propeller, so he can take the boat close enough to the shed, and the women can climb in.

As the water continues to rise, they are forced to stand on the roof, which thankfully is both slightly flat, and sturdy. Standing close to the edge, fearing they could both fall into the water at any moment, they embrace, saying confused thoughts about their imminent death, and their love for each other.

Almost on death's door, the women hear the roar of an outboard engine. Water continues to rise and now covers the ladies' knees. It begins to move slightly quicker than before.

Frank steers the boat over to the shed, and watches as Andrew and Adrian help Margaret and Norma climb aboard. Then he asks, "I thought you said there were five adults?"

As blankets are draped over their shoulders, a sudden movement knocks the boat off balance.

21

(PINNED, CLAUSTROPHOBIA, WHO
WANTS IT?)

P earl Lockwood is the first to return to consciousness. Her family's car is pinned beneath the SUV and the semi-trailer.

As she gazes around, subdued and deep in shock, out of what remains of the window, she sees the broken timbers of the bridge and the flowing river. She clears her eyes of the dust and dirt that has covered her face, trying to make some sense of what she's barely able to see in this dark and gloomy environment.

Thankfully the river is not running so fast now. Even so, it has entered into the car up to her knees, and it feels strangely warm. Her clothing and upper body are quite dry. Somehow, in all this chaos, she muses about what a blessing it is that they have recently acquired a decent car She could not... no doesn't want to even consider what would have happened to them if they were still in that old wreck. She turns to look sideways at David. He is still out to it and looks slightly concussed, half covered by his airbag.

Pearl leans as best she can in her rigid state and attempts to unfasten her seatbelt and, in finally doing so, turns herself around even more, so she can see how the children are in the back. For some reason it doesn't even occur to her that they may not be safe and sound in their back seats, as where else would they be?

The first trauma comes when she realises the capsule has disappeared, along with baby Stephen. Her eerie calmness changes instantly to hysteria. She knows she fastened the capsule properly. How could it have vanished?

The remainder of the back seat is obscured by various items that have moved during the accident, and is scattered somewhat, moved by the forces during the accident, and in the general gloom she can't see where her other two children are. Without realising it, she starts screaming, rousing David from his mindless state.

He attempts to clear his head, and between the screams, he works out that Pearl is babbling something about Stephen having vanished. She is desperately trying to get out of the vehicle to find him, unaware of the extent to which they are trapped.

David screams back at her, "Alright woman, stop yelling and give me a moment. I need to see what I'm dealing with." He is totally confused, until he remembers driving onto the bridge, and the crash that came immediately afterwards.

Pearl yells at him again, "find my baby, just find my baby."

"Shut up, woman, or I'll just sit here and do nothing, because you bloody screaming isn't helping."

Pearl goes quiet, sobbing to herself. David is struggling to come to terms with the situation that he is presented with, and his mind goes into overdrive to find an answer when all of a sudden he reverts back to his problem solving methods he faces at work, and shifts gears mentally to focus on this problem.

He begins to look for his flashlight and then remembers he can use the light on his mobile phone. A big smile appears at the genius idea. He reaches into his shirt pocket and on retrieving the phone, realises there is something wrong with his vision. He takes a deep breath, wipes his eyes again and squints at the phone to find the light button. He has to turn the phone around in his hand before he locates it.

He is temporarily blinded as the light penetrates the gloom into his face and eyes. "Bloody hell," he screamed, "I didn't need to be blinded like that."

How did the capsule disappear? He searches for his glasses to enable him to examine the rear of the car, all the while distracted by Pearl's broken sobbing. He now knows that yelling at her will only fight fire with fire, so he talks much calmer than before, as he tries to calm her, telling her, "We need to get out of this wrecked car before we can do anything."

He finds his glasses on the rear vision mirror and while trying to put them on, he realises they are filthy. He cleans them on his shirtsleeve and says to Pearl in as controlled a voice as he can muster, "We'll have to swap seats otherwise you'll have to get out first. For some reason I can't see why my side's blocked."

As the water sloshes around with his contorted movements, David clambers over Pearl, consequently tearing his tightly fitted shirt and popping a couple of buttons, as he pushes open the passenger side door. This allows the water inside the vehicle to flow out, quicker than he expected, into the river, and due to his contorted position and the sloshing motion, it washes David with it. He is carried along, bobbing with the turbulent flow while he is trying to stay upright towards the bank. In desperation he grabs hold of something he thinks is a branch.

It's not. It's a leg from one of the longhorn bulls. As he jerks his hand free in disgusted horror, he screams in pain as he twists it badly. He tries to hang onto the roots on the bank, but the current pulls him back into the river. He has no idea how far he is carried.

WITNESSING ALL THIS, Pearl is thrown into renewed hysteria. She's lost her precious baby, and now David is gone too. She turns agonisingly once again to search the rear of the car for Tiffany and Rhys, praying they are there somewhere in the wreckage, and still alive. She realises instantly that Tiffany is gone. Her door is open and there is no sign of her. Turning further again, she thankfully finds Rhys is slumped forward, clearly unconscious. She moans as she struggles to stroke his face, but there is no response.

Suddenly this is all too much for her, and she passes out.

MEANWHILE DAVID HAS BEEN WASHED into a side arm of the eastern side of the river, where the water is less deep. He lies on his back, the lukewarm water gently ebbing and flowing around him. He lies still, his hand throbbing. Feeling suddenly exhausted, he's almost enjoying the sensation caused by the water washing over him. He sees a blurred object nearby and realises it is part of a truck. *What's a truck doing here in the bottom of a river?*

This lifts him out of his trance, and he has a sudden flashback to the moment before the crash when he was blinded by the truck's lights. He rolls over to the cab, only to find it empty.

If only he had his glasses. He could do something to help his family and any others fighting for survival in the wake of the accident.

While lying there in the mud, he remembers that when he was looking for his phone, there weren't any bars, so he couldn't call anyone for help, and then goes limp in a defeated form, wondering how things could get any worse tonight.

22

(OH, THAT'S WHERE THEY ARE)

When farmer John Meadows moved onto his property just after the Second World War, he completed fencing off the boundaries within a year, so he had a good grazing area for his sheep. Today the property is bounded by a dirt road (a shortcut into Steering) running along the northern side to a corner, where it turns left along the western edge which is parallel to the river. The dirt road is just wide enough for two cars to pass at the same time, something that happens rarely. John has only ever experienced this on one occasion in his life, and that was when his wife was returning from the town. He'd had to pull over to let her through, as she would have gone down the ten meters of the embankment and into the river.

At this point, the lower part of the river is fifteen metres across, and its banks around ten metres high. On its far side is vacant land stretching towards derelict buildings that were once a small industrial mine. To reach the mine involves going over the longer of the two wooden bridges, continuing along a dirt track on the western side of the river for a couple of hundred meters, and then over another but smaller wooden bridge, to finally an eastern turn onto another dirt track for a couple of kilometres.

The larger of the two wooden bridges has a span across the river of around forty meters, and the smaller around thirty meters. They were initially designed for larger vehicles to deliver animals and various other goods to the area. It was decided at the time that a width of five metres would be sufficient for both bridges, so just enough room for just one large vehicle at a time. Signs were erected, giving right of way to westbound vehicles heading to the area. Westbound vehicles would go up a slight incline just before the bridge, whereas eastbound ones would face a slight downhill run continuing on to the town of Steering.

The eastern side of the river embankment is a collection of volcanic rocks left there by the local council. The dirt road was already on the western side of the river, so the council decided to forgo clearing the rocks, in favour of building another but somewhat smaller bridge. This allowed a better entry into the industrial area that is already part of the dirt road, which heads up towards the mountains, and a few hours' drive to the Wilson farm.

The bridges were built over fifty years ago when the town was prospering, but were allowed to fall into disrepair during the '80s and '90s.

An abattoir owned by Councillor Jeff Steering maintained its presence during that time. Councillor Steering owns most of the town and land in the district. It had originally been settled by his great grandfather, who migrated from the United Kingdom over a century ago. The name 'Steering' dates back to pre-Seventh Century Anglo Saxon times, and indicates someone who tends bullocks and oxen. It originates from the old English word 'steor' meaning a steer or bullock, resulting in a medieval assumed nickname or occupation, especially suited for someone with a defiant or aggressive nature, like Bob the bull.

Jeremiah Steer married Elizabeth Emery at St. James's Church, Duke's Place, Westminster, on March 17, 1684. The family's coat of arms is emblazoned on a red shield. The first recorded spelling of the family name is that of Jeffrey Steer. This was dated 1209 in the Worcestershire Pipe Rolls during the reign of King John, known as 'Lackland'. When Councillor Jeff Steering's great grandfather migrated to Australia, he changed the name from Steer to Steering.

Most of the young people in the town are employed part time. The abattoir offers jobs when it's up and running and it opens and closes depending on the highs and lows of the industry. It survives by buying stock from farmers when prices are low and selling to buyers worldwide when they pick up. This is where the brothers had been taking Luke.

23

(A HERO IS BORN)

L uke begrudgingly leaves Dianne and Stephanie on the western side of the embankment, while he goes in search of anyone else who needs rescuing. He is unaware that Rick and Brian have come around and are angry about their brother's disappearance. The thick fog is another source of their annoyance as they don't know where they are, or how to find their brother.

Luke is feeling more relaxed in his siblings' absence, despite the trauma of watching Nick and Ryan being gored to death. He is feeling his way cautiously through the fog, when he suddenly bumps into someone.

It's Tiffany, who is startled at first and however inappropriate the time, there is an instant attraction between them. Perhaps it has something to do with the almost surreal nature of their misty surroundings.

Tiffany senses movement behind Luke and gives a startled cry.

It's Brian, who says threateningly, "Well, hello there. What have we got here?" He grabs Tiffany by her arm, squeezing tightly. He turns to Rick and says, "Grab her and help me hold her down. Let's give her one."

For a few brief seconds, Brian's memory flicks back to something held in a dark part of his mind, to be retrieved only in moments of desperate need. The time Nick violated a much younger Tiffany all those years ago. And here she is again.

Brian had watched, fascinated, as Nick had satisfied his animal lust. He had known it was his turn next. But just as Nick had grunted the end of his foul appetite and jerked up from Tiffany's struggling form, it was already too late. A person had been approaching. It was a man with a dog.

Luke is horrified and appalled that Brian, minutes after watching his two brothers die horrible deaths, is still motivated by animal lust.

Although their vision is affected by the fog, Tiffany, for a moment, had a flashback, as she looked at Brian who has a resemblance of someone, but she couldn't put her finger on whom.

The experience seems to have stripped him of the last layer of civilised behaviour, leaving a vicious animal intent only on sating his various appetites. Luke pleads with Brian not to do this, but Brian strikes out, winding him. Luke collapses to the ground, doubled over in pain, and struggling for breath. Laying there in the mud, Luke has a sign of resignation on his face, which is masked by the foggy surrounds.

Brian starts to grab at Tiffany's wet clothing as Rick holds her down. Rick's reaction seems driven more by an instinct to support his vile brother than any great need for carnal gratification.

And then, without warning, a streak of lightning flashes

across the sky, illuminating the vision of Brian removing his clothes as he readies him-self to violate Tiffany. The lightning spooks a cluster of longhorns ambling past. They break into a gallop, headed straight for Tiffany and the three brothers. One of the bulls turns at the last moment, narrowly missing the three of them on the ground, but careering into Brian, who is still on his feet, half-undressed. A single horn pierces through his chest, literally splitting his throbbing heart open. Blood spews from the wound and from Brian's mouth. His eyes are wide open, but there is nothing behind them.

He slumps onto the horn as the bull tosses its head, catapulting Brian firstly into the air and then downwards into the river. The longhorn is also off balance and follows him down the bank into the swirling water. Brian lands on a rock protruding from the bank and his spine snaps with an audible crack, which could be heard echoing throughout the night.

Tiffany vomits wildly, her fear and repulsion erupting from deep within. Luke, who is still recovering from Brian's blow, tries to comfort her, but is distracted by a sudden movement in the shifting foggy surrounds. Seemingly out from nowhere his brother, Rick, is standing somewhat in a pathetic form before him. It's one on one now, and before Rick can attempt to emulate Brian's attack on Tiffany, Luke punches him hard to the temple, knocking him hard and away from him and Tiffany, and off his feet.

It's almost as if this one blow has lifted another weight from Luke's shoulders, just like earlier tonight with the beer spray in the SUV, suddenly freeing him of some emotional pain.

Luke grabs his painful left fist and says, "Shit... that hurt."

Tiffany and Luke look at each other. A somewhat

hysterical and scared Tiffany is swearing profusely at him, convinced he is as much to blame as the other two thugs. Luke tries to explain he's not like his brothers, but Tiffany's priority right now is getting out of here, wherever here is.

Luke tries to calm her with a distraction. "I need to go and help find this young girl who's been separated from her parents. Would you like me to try and take you where the girl's mother and sister are? If I can remember where they are."

Luke realises she is in no mood, or with any idea as to what to do, so he asks her to follow him back up the embankment. At first she refuses and Luke walks away with a shrug, but then she suddenly realises she would be alone and says, "No wait." Sobbing quietly, she follows him cautiously along the bank to where the fog is less thick.

Eventually they find Dianne and Stephanie huddled together. Stephanie lunges at Luke in sheer relief, giving him a big hug, while Dianne plants a kiss on his cheek. Tiffany is further confused about exactly who Luke is, and why these women are so obviously delighted to see him. This is the second time she has felt a twinge of something approaching affection for him, but she fights it off instinctively, as it has always ended in tears for her in the past. Luke introduces Tiffany to Dianne and Stephanie, saying he found her lost and confused in the river also, and can you stay together and look after each other please.

Luke says, "I have to go and see who else is alive." He bites his tongue when he realises that loved ones of these people might well be dead. "Don't move from here and try not to make any sudden noises. Because of the fog I think there's some sort of wild animals around. I'm not sure what they are, but they seem to be easily spooked. Just stay together and keep your eyes open." Dianne says "they are bulls and yes they are probably wild as I found out earlier today." But the others are too immersed in their own thoughts as to take in what Dianne had just said.

Almost against her better judgement, Tiffany grabs his arm and says, "Be careful and come back safe."

Realising what she has said, but being happy about what she said, she goes over and stands next to Stephanie, who looks nervously at her mum and asks, "Are we going to die?"

Hoping his words will bring some reassurance, Luke responds, "Wow, I don't remember anyone telling me we were going to die tonight." With that, he turns and walks off into the murky surrounds.

After a while, he squats close to the ground. He closes his eyes, listening to his surroundings, trying to block out the sounds of the river. A frog croaks close by, but there is nothing else. He glances up at where the sky should be but sees only thick fog. Wishing he had superpowers to be able to see like Superman, then realising that's a stupid idea, he closes his eyes to try again. More as a result of his intense fatigue than anything else, he finds himself slipping into sleep and with it, a vision of a large sailing vessel.

He dreams he is first mate, gazing across the ship's bow, its sails stiffened by a strong breeze. As they head towards land, a voice rings out, telling all to be ready as the ship is about to turn to starboard. Suddenly one of the sails tears, due to the strain caused by the sudden shift of direction and unexpected gust of wind. This causes the upper section of the middle mast to break off, spiralling down towards the deck. At the same time, the ship lurches hard to port, throwing a couple of the crew overboard.

Luke is standing on the edge of the ship, watching helplessly as the two crewmen disappear into the depths below.

Suddenly the dream is over, and he wakes to find an animal standing above him, urinating on him before moving away. Luke feels sick and crawls towards the river to find water to wash away the smell. Thankfully there are little puddles not far in front of him, and he begins to wash off the smelly warm urine.

24

(CHOP-CHOP)

The main building of the Steering abattoir is on the only level ground in the industrial area, located just south of the wooden bridges. The remainder of the property, including the grazing area, slopes downwards to a varying degree. It's steepest in the area south of the main building, heading down to the creek, which flows into the main river. The rest of the grazing area undulates between ridges and valleys, wedged next to the river between the two bridges.

In the hundred or so years of the abattoir's existence, it has experienced one flood, back in 1953. Most of the buildings and some of the surrounding property had to be repaired or replaced due to storm damage. This cost roughly $350,000 with most of the work being performed by only the locals with the appropriate skills.

During the recent storm, the water level around the abattoir rose above the river, as it wound its way through the district. When the storm hit a few hours ago, animals on top of the main slope became stranded. There were hundreds of sheep and cattle mixed together. Stock had been brought in from properties around this and other districts, which were being made ready for slaughter on Monday. This would bring work for many of the townsfolk for a week.

Due to their smaller size compared to the cattle, most of the sheep were forced down from the slope onto the flooded area and were drowned as they were carried away downstream. A number of them were caught on the aging wire fences surrounding the abattoir.

After the storm had passed, the cattle followed the receding water line along the creek, and onto the dirt road. Most of them were bulls, and they led the other animals back towards the town, via the larger of the two wooden bridges.

Councillor Jeff Steering, named after his great grandfather, has fought tooth and nail to keep the abattoir operating for at least six to nine months of the year. He pays good casual wages, which help many townsfolk and the town survive financially, because he makes good annual profits. A new, long-term deal has been signed recently with two Asian countries, helping to boost production and job security. The few employees, who were around yesterday to handle the influx of new sheep and cattle, were caught by surprise when the storm broke. Weakened fences had not been inspected, and had deteriorated in the drought.

The creek that flows into the river formed decades ago from the abattoir, and is about three metres wide, but less than a metre deep, with volcanic rocks dotting its surface. The creek reaches the river where the small wooden bridge is located. The edges of the river angle sightly downward in some sections and steeper in other sections, especially near either edge of the bridges. Both bridges are badly in need of repair, largely because they carry only limited large traffic volumes. Smaller vehicles can cross without any danger but a semi-trailer driver coming to the district could find themselves in trouble if new to the area.

The animals being led by a couple of the larger bulls have found their way along the creek and into the river without incident. They find it easy to head into the nearly empty river and continue on towards the larger wooden bridge.

Among the group of animals are about fifty-three sheep, fifteen milking cows, five horses and fifty-three bulls of various shapes, sizes and age. A number of the sheep and cattle, and one horse, have moved away from the main herd, seeking new grazing areas. Most of the herd has been kept awake during the storm, and by now are hungry and tired. The remainder are following the bulls upstream and are a few hundred metres from the wooden bridge and the unknown territory beyond...

25

(WE'RE BACK ON THE AIR WITH WHOM?)

Back at the radio station, both Robbie and Michael are going about their individual tasks when Robbie asks Michael, "Are you feeling okay? We're back on the air in two minutes and there's just one more ad after the weather report. You've got three callers to choose from and they're on your screen and it's your call, Michael."

"Okay... let's see... Someone called John wanting to comment on Patrick, another Michelle wanting to comment on Patrick, and Jeff Steering, the councillor. I'll go with the councillor first, so what's he calling for?"

"About the floods, and wanting to let people know about the abattoir, I guess, if it's affected by the storm, I guess."

"You do realise you guessed twice, so I guess we'll see, won't we! Let him know he's on first, and I *guess* I'll see what we can do with whatever he wants to tell us. So if he's on first, who's on second and third?"

"What?" screams Robbie, "What are you on about?"

Michael's mention of a 90-year-old movie sketch by Abbott and Costello has gone completely over her head.

"Never mind Robbie Okay, one minute to go. I'll get the

radar up so you can see what's going on, and how much has fallen and where. Ten seconds."

Then Michael hears the station intro and looks at Robbie for the thumbs up to start talking. Even though he's on air, tiredness has set in, and he's working on autopilot.

"Sorry folks, just a moment frozen in time. Didn't even know what time it was. Gee, if I'm like this now, I'd hate to think what I'll be like after midnight. Anyway, it's ten past nine here on Crazy F.M., and we have Councillor Jeff Steering on the line. Good evening, Councillor. How you going this evening? I believe you want to alert people about the abattoir?"

"Yes good evening Michael, and thanks for taking my call. Yes, I'd like to talk about the abattoir. As you and your listeners are well aware, we've had a helluva storm going through the district."

"Yes I can see it still passing us on the radar in front of me, Councillor. It looks like nearly all parts of the district have had a lot of rain, about one hundred millimetres so far. Like one of those storms that's here one minute, gone the next."

"Yes, great news for the farmers and their water tanks but not for their pasture and crops, but it's the abattoir I'm concerned about. Now, tomorrow morning, a few of the locals and I will be going down to check on the animals and the facility itself. Then we can work out if it's viable to operate as normal on Monday. If there's only minor damage, it shouldn't be a problem. Not forgetting the most important part – the animals. I'm not sure how many would have survived the storm. We might not have any left. The buildings should be okay and I'm hoping the renovations have kept the worst of the weather out. Those people already lined up for work can have at least some idea if we're delayed. That should put minds to rest. Thanks again, Michael, and as soon as I know, I'll give you an update."

"I'm not sure when this storm will finish. I'm looking at the radar now, and it's starting to show another front building. It looks like it could be in the district in a couple of hours, bringing similar amounts of rain to what we've just copped. We need to be prepared for the worst."

"Thanks Michael. I'll be in touch. I'm sure the SES and others involved are on top of it all, anyway."

"Goodnight, Councillor, I hope the news is positive. I'm wondering what it must be like for those animals outside in the storm getting drenched. I'm just glad I'm in here. Hello, John? You called in to talk about Patrick." Michael switches to the next caller.

"Yes G'day, I'm at the Lakeside Motel on the corner of the intersection, where Patrick and Michelle nearly crashed. I reckon Patrick should think himself very lucky. Michelle must have missed him by inches. Just because she was taught by her dad, who she says was a professional driver, doesn't necessarily mean she'll be good enough to survive. As I've found in years of driving, no-one's that lucky. If you're in the wrong place at the wrong time, then it's in the hands of fate."

"Well that's your opinion, John, and I'm sure there are others who agree with you. We'll see if another Michelle does too, but I'm guessing... there's that guessing word again, see what you've done, Robbie? Michelle, what's on your mind?"

"Hi Michael, well I'm actually agreeing with what you said about both being at fault."

"That's good to hear, Michelle. Are you having a good night, whatever it is you're doing?"

"It started out okay, but it's gone a bit pear-shaped. It's gone quiet now, but there was a big brawl at the pub about an hour ago. We are only just cleaning it up now. I'm glad I'm not outside with some of the other women, nursing sore heads. It was something I've never experienced before, anyway goodnight and good luck with staying awake all night, Michael."

"Thanks, Michelle, I'll try my best, I guess."

Michelle hangs up and Michael, off air, tells Robbie, "Guess that went pretty well, I guess."

Robbie asks again what he's on about and he tells her, "Go onto YouTube and type in Abbott and Costello, *Who's on First,* it's a riot. Oh yeah, and then go to Abbott and Costello again, and type in *Seven Times Thirteen Equals Twenty-Eight.* That's also a riot. Ron, the truckie, showed it to me last year."

"Thirteen times seven equals twenty-eight?" Robbie asks curiously.

"Yeah I know, I guess, right."

"Really, Michael, sometimes you can be such a baby."

26

(THE CLEAN-UP BEGINS)

Back at the pub, most of the patrons have left, with many of them going home with sore heads or bruised pride. A number, like Michelle, have volunteered to stay and help clean up the mess.

Outside the pub, Senior Sergeant Logan is climbing into his divvy van to transport the transgressors to their overnight accommodation in the lock-up.

Ian, the publican, has returned inside the pub after helping Logan load the van, and is heartened by certain patrons' willingness to return tables and chairs to their normal positions, and help generally with the clean-up. The barman, Lou Minto, approaches with the night's takings, sporting a cut above his left eye. It looks like it'll be a shiner by the morning.

Lou ambles away to find some ice to put on his sore head, as Ian goes to the office to put the takings in the safe. He returns to the bar where he hears Michael on the radio, talking to Councillor Steering. He signals to the remaining patrons to be quiet and listen.

Following the discussion on the probable immediate fate of the abattoir, they hear the interviews with John and Michelle, and Patrick's near miss. At that moment, Michelle walks back into the bar and cops a round of applause for her part. Then everyone gets on with the business of drinking and cleaning up the place.

Senior Sergeant Logan pulls up outside the police station and walks around to open the divvy van's back door. As he swings it open, he is sent reeling by the combined stench of liquor, tobacco, vomit and sundry other bodily fluids. He places his hand theatrically over his nose and grimaces his distaste. There are five blokes of all shapes and sizes strewn across the floor, most of them either too drunk to move, sleeping... or both. Logan can't and won't put them all in the cells at the same time.

Seeking to avoid injury to his already bad back, possibly due to a lack of exercise, too many beers, and an old sporting injury, he goes next door to the hardware store, removes a bunch of keys from a chain connected to his belt, and unlocks the door. He finds a four-wheeled trolley and slowly returns with it to the van.

Senior Sergeant Logan has been in the district for over thirty years, and has taken the liberty of having a spare key to all the local businesses. It has been useful if he needs something for emergencies, just like this one. Then he can avail himself to whatever he so pleases.

He struggles dragging the first drunk from the van and places him onto the trolley, reeling once more from the smell. The trolley is big and sturdy enough for two comatose bodies. Logan holds his breath again as he leans forward and grabs the next limp body's legs, pulling him out and dropping him as gently as possible on the top of the first. Not that it would matter anyway. *Why do they do this to themselves?* He mused.

After much grunting and blowing, he finally wheels the trolley down to the cells – luckily the path is straight and level – and then enters through a back door. Once inside the cell, he grunts again due to their size, weight and flopped presence. And then simply tips the trolley up, and stands back as the two drunks flop onto the cold floor. Both make moaning sounds as they reacquaint themselves with their relaxed state.

The next three are big country boys and he takes them one at a time. Two of them are half-awake and abuse Logan as he takes them to a separate cell. Local knowledge tells him it would be unwise to house all five together – there are hostilities here.

Now that they're all secure, Logan lies down on a bed he has set up just for these occasions and is asleep before his head hits the pillow. Nobody's going to drown in his own vomit on this cop's watch.

IN ANOTHER PART OF TOWN, Scotty is ankle deep in water while patrolling a major road that is partially flooded, but not sufficiently so to make it unsafe for cautious drivers.

But nobody's out and about on this foul night and Scotty's starting to wonder what he's doing here.

It's stopped raining and the fog has seeped back quicker than expected, making visibility nigh impossible for more than a few yards. He thinks about Billy arriving tomorrow morning. Knowing Billy, he'll regard the train journey as an adventure.

His thoughts are interrupted by a call from the SES, telling him he will be required for another hour, even though the water level is receding quicker than first thought. Scotty tells them, "Nobody's driven along this road since you got me to come here. I'm going home. I'll leave the warning signs up." He hangs up, tired and frustrated for being in this situation but that's just part of being a human being.

Scotty drives home and hits the sack relatively early for him. He has to be up in the morning to meet Billy on his train. He's decided to shower and freshen up before going to bed, as he is too wound up.

BACK AT THE PUB, Michelle is not sure about the attention coming her way from Gazza, one of the late drinkers. Michelle has heard his chat line a hundred times before, but surprisingly enough, warms to him. Tonight seems different. Maybe for the first time everyone is relaxed and jovial, something Michelle hasn't seen for a while. So maybe she should enjoy herself and take a chance. She has spoken to Gazza a number of times before, but for some reason tonight he's gone up a notch in the attraction stakes. Maybe it's the amount of drink she's had.

Gazza is wondering if he's onto a good thing when another patron bangs into him from behind. He turns around and as he's about to fly into a rage, Michelle grabs him by the neck and plants one squarely on his mouth. Loud, raunchy cheers echo around the bar, as they hold the kiss for what seems an eternity.

When they finally break away and get their breath back, Michelle grabs him by the top of his shirt and leads him outside to somewhere more private. With all this fog around, there's nobody to see them as they tear the clothes off one another.

27

(THAT WAS CLOSE)

What I've noticed about dogs over the years is if they are in unfamiliar surroundings, being watched or just uncomfortable, then they have an uncanny embarrassed look on their face. That stops them from doing their business until the feeling passes. They are almost shy when they use their litter box to poop. Reasons your dog might not be keen to have people around, seeing them do their business. It could be because they don't want to be attacked. Fear of punishment, as dogs are creatures of habit. So if you are walking your dog outside and they seem reluctant to have a poo, step away, give them space, but keep hold of the leash.

Frank's boat is big enough to hold ten passengers, but even so, the bump from the water is enough to send alarm signals through everyone on board.

Paddling along the side of the boat is Bert, the family's ageing dog. They are all, quite naturally, overjoyed to see him.

After pulling the frightened but game old dog into the boat, Frank realises that Bert is the fifth adult, from comments made by the other adults. And he continues to navigate his way along the river, being ever careful to watch out for partially submerged trees.

The receding water level means that although having gone as far as he could, Frank is still fifty metres short of the trailer. Frustrated, he moors the boat against the bank and helps the family clamber out from the rear.

As they climb the slippery bank, someone remarks on how foggy it has become. Someone else says, "I think I heard noises coming from the river down near that old wooden bridge."

No-one responds, so the comment is promptly forgotten in the scramble to reach the top of the embankment. Then as they are guided by Frank, they start walking in the direction of the town.

Their path along the embankment is hampered by volcanic rocks, adding to their sense of being disoriented by the fog. Some are perplexed as to what to do, but they are all talking amongst themselves as to how to get out of this unstable situation.

As for the three girls, they are scared of the surrounding fog and cling as close to the adults as they can.

Bert the dog, on the other hand, is happy that he going for his evening walk, even if it is at a different location. But he has to stop as nature calls and is glad no-one can see him poop.

The dilemma has made them realise the only safe way through is to keep abreast of each other in twos or three's, with the children holding hands, except Frank, who is not only guiding them through the maze of volcanic rocks, but he has tasked himself with looking after Bert. He is enjoying his newfound companion. It is taking the misjudged boat landing off his mind too. He can watch Bert lead the way through the maze of volcanic rocks ahead, and hopefully back to the pub for a well-earned beer.

Trying as hard as they can not to lose anyone, they finally reach the entrance to the larger of the two wooden bridges, known only to a few of them. They pause, wondering what to do as they look down along this damp, dark and even more foreboding place that they dare not venture into. It looks worse than where they have come from, as the creepy and shifting foggy surrounds is more claustrophobic than expected. So they move on towards Steering, showing no interest in seeking any refuge on the wooden bridge. It is too damp and dark. They are more interested in somewhere less threatening.

They continue on towards the town and the pub, for some warmth and rest from their ordeal.

Being above the valley, Frank finally realises he has one bar on his phone and in relief, phones the radio station and tells Robbie, "I thought I'd ring to let you know the family are all safe and well. We're two kilometres from the pub at Mackenzie's Bridge, you know, the larger of the two wooden bridges. Should be at the pub in about an hour, unless you can call someone at the pub to come and get us, as I don't know the number."

Robbie puts Frank on to Michael on air, and Frank says, "Yeah, um if anyone is listening? A few people I have rescued here might struggle with the journey. Could someone come and get us? We're going to need a couple of cars, if that's okay."

Michael offers to call the pub in case they didn't hear the message. When he does, he's told two cars, including one being driven by Michelle, have already set off to look for them, probably about halfway between Mackenzie's Bridge and the pub by now.

Michael thinks to himself, *'hope they get back to the pub before the next storm comes.'*

28

(COOOOOOOEEEEEEEEEEEEE)

David has decided to move away from the empty cab, which is now sticking half out of the water, as the river has receded. First, he has to work out which way to go. He is disorientated by a combination of the ordeal that he has just gone through, his painful and badly twisted hand, and the thick fog.

He cautiously stands upright in the water, using his good right arm to help, and suddenly winces in stunned pain. He puts his aching left arm inside his shirt in between the only two buttons he has left intact, thus making a sling out of the sopping garment. He is wary of taking a another step forward in case he trips on something and then falling and damaging his hand further, and of running into whatever animals are around.

'*Now what do I do?*' He thinks to himself, trying to figure out which way is which. There is no movement of any sort with this bloody fog so unbearably thick.

Nearby, and unknown to David, Luke is also trying to work out exactly where he is in relation to the town. Luke, on the other hand, has recovered and stands upright at the same time, unaware of anyone else within cooee of him. Suddenly he hears someone sneeze, as if they're only a short distance away.

"Who's that," Luke calls, speaking quietly but loud enough for his voice to travel that same short distance. Standing there motionless, Luke is half in fear, half in hope as he waits for a reply.

David responds immediately, cursing at the unforeseen sneeze and consequent pain shooting through his hand. "My name's David and I've just been in a terrible road accident. I've no idea where I am. Please, can you help me? I think I may have broken my hand, and I can't see much without my glasses, as I lost them some time ago."

"Sure David, the name's Luke and I'll try and come to you. Just stay where you are. Keep talking so I can work out which direction I should head. But keep your voice down, there are some dangerous animals close by."

"Are you alone?" David asks, hoping whoever it is there are others around the crash site with similar intentions.

"No, I'm not but I've found three other people, a woman, her daughter and a teenage girl."

Focused on the thought of getting as much information and as quickly as possible, David blurts out "What's their names? My entire family's missing. I've lost all four of them. I think they're still in my car."

Luke, sensing impatience from David, calmly replies "I don't know, we got to exchange names, but in all this confusion, I've forgotten, but they're all female if that helps." He stops talking as he reaches David.

"It doesn't sound like my family, but I guess I'll find out soon enough if this bloody fog clears."

"Which hand do you think is broken, David?"

"It's the left one."

"Okay, I'll walk on your right side. Let's just take it slowly. There are bits of debris strewn around the empty river. I'll try and get us back to where the others are."

"How far are we from the accident?"

"Why?"

David responds. His voice is slurred and his body aches from the ordeal. He is leaning forward as though he thinks he is going to fall headfirst again into the slow running river that's above their ankles. "I think my wife and three kids might still be in the car. I'm terrified of what's happened to them."

"Let's get you to somewhere safe first, and then I'll think of what we'll be able to..." Luke suddenly stops mid-sentence. David realises that Luke had stopped talking and is about to respond when Luke replies, "Best not to concern ourselves with 'what if's' at this stage, and I'll go and check on your car. If I can find it, okay? We don't have much further to go. Save your strength for the climb up the slope at the edge of the river. Depending on where we are, it could be quite steep."

David continues to be anxious about this environment and for his family, and begins to wobble around, not knowing what to do. He feels helpless for the first time for as long as he can remember.

They arrive at the riverbank and both work their way up to the top of the slope. David slips and curses quietly in his frustration and worries over the whereabouts of his family.

Strange to think a short while ago he would have been glad to see the back of them, at least temporarily.

When they finally stepped onto the top of the embankment, the look on David's face is of triumph. He attempts to throw his arms up then suddenly realises his error when his left arm bloody hurts. He tries to ignore the pain as he is just happy to get to the top of the steep embankment, giving the impression he'd just climbed Mount Everest.

They walk along the edge of the embankment and find all three women where Luke had left them. Luke calls out quietly that he has found someone in the river. Without hesitation Dianne and Stephanie rush to him, hoping it is Ron.

They try hard to hide their disappointment, but Tiffany is ecstatic and goes to hug her father as Luke stops her. She begins to yell at him for doing so, when her father explains about his broken left arm.

Tiffany soon realises she has jumped the gun on remonstrating at Luke again, and walks away, not realising she can no longer see where she is going. She awkwardly apologises to the young man, as she is as overwhelmed as to why she is in two minds about him, and it is only making her all the more irritated.

Luke asks Dianne and Tiffany, "Can you all look after David? There are obviously more people out there who need help. Luke turns to ask Dianne, "so I'm looking for your husband, Ron, and your daughter, Bridgette, is that right?" Dianne and Stephanie nod simultaneously, too choked for words. Luke continues, "David, who am I looking for with your family?"

"That would be my wife, Pearl, our son, Rhys, and our six-month-old baby, Stephen. Rhys and Stephen were in the back seat. Stephen was in his capsule between Rhys and Tiffany. We don't know where the capsule's gone."

Tiffany starts crying and puts her hands over her face, fearing she could have been responsible for Stephens's disappearance. She wonders if she and Rhys could have done more to save Stephen.

Dianne and David look upon a crying Tiffany and go over to her to console her. But she is in two minds about Stephen and backs away from them, but for only a couple of steps, as she doesn't also wish to be alone in this thick fog. Then Luke says quietly, "Okay, I'll see you all later. Just stay here and stay together."

As he ventures off into the fog once more, and having worked his way back to where he thinks he found David, he turns to his left ninety degrees and believes, or hopes, he's facing the large wooden bridge.

He's not sure how far away it is, nor is he aware of the animals from the abattoir behind him. Stumbling through the fog, he is often even unable to see the ground he is walking on. But this seems to strengthen his resolve, even though voices in his head are telling him *'you are going to die.'*

He thinks about the girl he has just met and tries to dismiss it, when he bumps into what looks like a vehicle looming out of the fog. He runs his hand over the cold metal, giving him the impression that this is the rear of the vehicle. He goes back towards the other direction passing the door he previously found, but there's no more panel, nothing. He moves his hand forward and it encounters some form of material, and what feels like a body.

Unsure how, or as to where to put his hand, he inadvertently touches what feels like...

Suddenly whatever he's touching moves abruptly and moans slurred words. "Who's that? Who's there? Get your bloody hands off my tits, you filthy bastard."

Luke jumps back in shock, and then contains himself. He says, "My name's Luke, who are you? I'm looking for survivors from the accident. I have found four other people that were also in the accident. I have put them somewhere on top of the river for now, while I go and look for others... like you."

Having accepted his explanation of what's happened, Pearl composes herself and introduces herself to this unexpected young man before her. "My name's Pearl," she says, speaking with a perplexed tone and doesn't quite know in what order she has to say things, and just blurts out anything relevant to her situation. "What's your name again and do you know what's happened to my husband, and please..." she hesitates again, "please, can you look at my son in the back seat as I'm not sure how long I've been unconscious... asleep... I don't know..."

Luke moves to the back door, and when he opens it, water spills out at his feet. He feels around and realises he is running his hands over someone's face. He senses dried blood and feels for a pulse which seems to be okay. He thinks the boy is unconscious or has been concussed, but he's definitely alive.

Luke tells Pearl, "he's okay, but we need to decide whether we should move him or leave him here. I can't tell if he has any injuries, or how serious they could be. Maybe you should stay here with him until we can get help. I'll see if I can find anyone else."

"My other son's a baby and he's only six months old. He's disappeared from the car in the capsule. I'm not sure what I would do if I lost my precious Stephen. Can you help me please, as I'm not, as you can see, able to."

Luke is startled by this news, completely forgetting what David mentioned earlier in the night due to being slightly overwhelmed by the occasion, and is uncertain as to how to respond. "Okay," he says uncertainly, "I'll have a look around, but this fog is making everything hard to see, even right just in front of me."

"Thank you. My name's Pearl Lockwood. I'm missing my husband, David..."

Luke interrupts, relieved to have some good news, "Oh, I found him before, and do you have a daughter, Tiffany?"

"Yes, I do!"

"They're safe on the riverbank, looking after one another and some other people I've found."

"Thank God. Do you know where they are?"

"Yeah, sort of, I've been counting my steps while groping around and trying to remember directions I've been going in. Anyway, if it starts to rain again, just close the doors and you should be safe inside here. I'll see you soon."

"Do you know what time it is, so at least I know when the sun's coming up?"

"Sorry, I don't know."

"Ah well, goodbye Luke. And thank you again. Bye."

As Luke is leaving, he turns back around and in a calming voice and asks, "When did you see the capsule last?"

"Just before the accident, why?"

"That means it should be around here, somewhere. I'll feel around here, then work my way up to the top of the bridge."

Luke is starting to think all this would be easier if he had another person helping him. So he heads back to the others and lets David know he's found his wife and one son and tells him about how they both are, especially with Rhys being out to it, and that Pearl is quite happy to stay and look after Rhys, not that she has much choice in the matter.

An emotional David has realised Luke hasn't spoken about Stephen, and is horrified when Luke tells him that Stephen is missing. Without getting too emotionally involved about David's response, Luke is more interested in leaving them and finding Stephen. He does not want to spend any more time than he has to talking about it.

Then he turns around and asks Tiffany if she can help him find Stephen, because he could do with another set of eyes in this bloody fog. Expressing his annoyance, Luke doesn't feel quite comfortable with all these things going on at once, and feels he needs time to take all this in, and try to do one thing at a time.

Dianne stands up and says, "I'd rather come and help. It would be better to leave Tiffany here with her father and Stephanie." None of them can see the other faces and are unsure as to how to respond. Tiffany agrees, "Would it be okay for me to stay here? I can look after Stephanie and my father, without being on my own... with you... not that I..."

Luke suddenly cuts her off mid-sentence with a quick, "Okay, that's settled then. Let's go, Dianne."

As they walk away, David blurts, "thank you." Realising he is no help, he begins tearfully to express his gratitude by slowly holding up his right arm as a gesture.

As they venture into the fog, Dianne takes hold of Luke's hand, saying, "This is just so we don't get separated while we try to get to the bridge. God, I hope we find them safe."

Holding hands with Dianne reminds Luke of walking along the dirt road to school with his mother. They always held hands when he was little.

Luke tells Dianne they should look for baby Stephen first, and then Bridgette, and her husband. Dianne wishes she could search for Bridgette first, but she realises the vulnerability of a baby in these awful circumstances.

Luke explains how his step counting is something he taught himself on scout camps. "Occasionally someone would get lost, so I'd ask questions of those who saw them last, and the rest takes care of itself. It seems to come naturally to me." He continues, "David's wife, Pearl, said the last time she saw the capsule was moments before the accident, so it can't be that far away, Or..."

Luke stops himself suddenly and Dianne says, "Or what?" And then she glances downriver, realising the awful possibility of the capsule being washed away downstream, with Stephen inside... or not.

29

(HAVEN'T THE FOGGIEST)

Bridgette still lies concussed in the front seat of the semi-trailer, where it rests on the eastern side of the embankment. Most of the bulls have freed themselves and are long gone.

Luke and Dianne have separated to widen the area of their search. As they are only a few yards apart, they are nervously feeling their way around the crash site for anyone who might still be alive. This can be achieved only with very slow movements.

Dianne finds it quite difficult, given the thickness of the fog, as she inadvertently stumbles into a branch. It pierces her face just below her left eye, causing blood to flow down her face.

In pain and shock, Dianne calls out to Luke, quietly remembering what Luke had said about dangerous animals around. He spends a couple of minutes trying to locate her. As there is no-one within earshot, they cannot be heard as everyone else is either asleep, or too far away for their voices to carry that far.

Once he gets close enough to her to see the damage, he

DENNIS LUKE

finds there is a deep cut on the cheekbone. Luke decides they should return to the others, where the fog is less dense. The journey takes a few minutes with Luke guiding Dianne over the rough terrain.

When they return, they find that the girls have put together a makeshift bed of branches and leaves for David to lie on.

Tiffany was glad to see Luke, as too was Stephanie. Luke needs to clean the cut on Dianne's face, and David offers his relatively clean handkerchief. Tiffany passes it to Luke, and their hands touch briefly. Luke looks up at Tiffany and gives a slight grin.

He holds the handkerchief aloft for a few moments in the foggy atmosphere, long enough to dampen it. On cleaning Dianne's wound, he finds the blood flow has stopped. He wipes away the crusted blood and the mascara running down her face. If Dianne had seen her messed up face, she would have been annoyed, but she would only have put on a brave face. She would be thankful that she has survived this terror, for now.

He announces he's going back to the SUV to get the first aid kit. Tiffany asks if she can come with him.

Luke is unsure about Tiffany's resolve and has reservations as to whether she can cope in this varying climate. He is about to refuse when Dianne agrees. "Let her help. I'll stay here and look after David and Stephanie, so off you go Tiffany, but be careful you don't do something stupid, like I just did."

Luke reluctantly agrees and, as they head off into the foggy unknown, he turns to Tiffany and says, "Hold onto my hand." Tiffany happily agrees, and Luke misses the smile of satisfaction on her face.

She asks, "How exactly do you know where to go?"

"I'll tell you in the morning, if we survive 'til then," says Luke as they plunge into the fog riddled darkness.

It's then that Tiffany realises how quickly the fog has worsened as they enter into the murky depths of the fog riddled riverbank below. She begins to imagine shadowy figures that change their shape in the gloom. It was like stepping out of the shower and the bathroom mirror is all foggy, but nothing in the mirror is quite distinct. She can't make out what they are, and tells Luke, "Please make sure you don't leave me on my own. I'm terrified, this is... wow... this is scary... this fog out here."

Luke is instantly annoyed with himself for not realising earlier that Tiffany would not be able to cope in this environment. He stops in his tracks, and turns abruptly to Tiffany. "I'll take you back to the others."

Tiffany agrees as she drops her head in disappointment, regretting not being able to hold Luke's hand, but understands his frustration.

He heads back up the embankment to the top, dragging a downhearted Tiffany along. They reach the others, and Tiffany mumbles tearfully, "I didn't realise it was that bad."

Luke is gone in an instant before anyone can speak, and sooner, rather than later, she will come to the sudden realisation that being with Luke and just holding hands, is not bad at all.

Even though he too has feelings for her, he knows that dragging along someone who is nice, but not up to the challenge in this environment is not sensible. Putting his own feelings aside, he chose to leave her, for Tiffany's own safety.

This is not the time or place for romance.

The adrenaline is flowing fast through his system as he continues his search for survivors around Mackenzie's

Bridge. First he checks on Mrs. Lockwood, only to find Rhys still out cold in the back seat. Pearl is half-dozing, half-snoring in the front seat, reclined as much as she can in the wreckage to make herself more comfortable.

Looking to his left and walking slowly, Luke finds his way to the edge of the river. He walks blindly along the eerie river until he finds a more accessible section, where he climbs up the bank.

Crawling on his hands and knees, he reflects on how many hundreds of times he and his family had driven over this bridge, without ever giving a thought to how unstable it was. It was named after his grandfather Sirus McKenzie, who built them when he settled here in Steering. There has never been any water like this in the river for as long as he can remember, except for maybe the occasional trickle.

It takes him a couple minutes to get to the top of the embankment, where he collapses on the level ground, exhausted from the ordeal. He regains his feet, pulls a branch from a tree and swings it from side to side in front of him as he stumbles on, virtually sightless in the thick fog.

As he moves along, he reflects on how lucky they are it's not the middle of winter, and freezing cold. But then again, being unable to see anything is almost as bad as freezing half to death.

He finally reaches the bridge, sweeping the branch along its rickety boards in the hopes of snagging the capsule, perhaps with Stephen still inside. He is well aware the capsule may have been swept a considerable distance from the bridge. But he has to start somewhere. Knowing the dimensions of the bridge he reckons it will take between twenty and thirty minutes to search it thoroughly.

Unknown to him he has passed the bottom part of the capsule twice, when he decides to go over the bridge one last time. This time he bumps into something on the bridge, stumbling forward and knocking whatever it is over the edge. He snatches at it, realising it is the capsule or at least part of it, but it tumbles into the riverbed below. It has become stuck as the water level is quite low now, compared to about a couple of hours ago.

"Shit," he mumbles to himself and turns to head down to the riverbed. He starts down the deep embankment on his hands and knees, and then goes head first in his panicked haste to rediscover the capsule.

As he crawls on, trying to work out where the capsule could have fallen, he bumps his head into one of the bridge's timber uprights in his haste. Despite the pain across his forehead, he valiantly moves on, only too aware of what's at stake.

Hoping like hell to find the capsule, he then heads across the river to the other side. Feeling enthusiastic he soldiers on but in the back of his mind, he knows that there are at least another eight hours before the sun comes up.

Mindful of what's at stake, he moves on regardless, and continues to feel around for the capsule, opening his arms as wide as he can to cover as much ground as possible. *I once caught a fish this big,* he thinks to himself before refocusing on the job, wondering where that bloody thought came from. He wiped the smirk off his face as this is not the time or place for comedy. The capsule shouldn't be that far from the edge of the bridge.

He stumbles slowly around without finding anything resembling a capsule, and starts to wonder if it was the capsule at all.

Eventually he reaches the other side of the river, and having done that, he returns back to where he started from, and is at a loss as to where the bloody capsule went to.

He bumps into what feels like two separate vehicles and piles of debris, before to his intense relief, finally re-encountering the capsule, but no Stephen.

He wonders briefly if the baby could have fallen out when he knocked the capsule off the bridge. Or had he been swept down river when he fell out of the capsule? But there's hardly any water now.

It occurs to him that if Stephen had fallen out anywhere close by, he should be able to hear him crying, unless he was dead.

"Bloody hell, this is too much to think about. What to do, what to do? Which direction next? Whichever way is bound to be the wrong way." He continues to talk as though someone is listening to him continually ramble on and on, then realises he is talking to himself. "Uh-oh first sign silly me."

He remains sitting on his wet bottom in the river, frustrated as to what to do next. Now he is thinking to himself, *'do I go this way or that way, as whatever I do, it will be the wrong bloody decision. Go with your gut. What's your gut telling you?'*

Luke finally stands up and moves to the embankment then climbs it to look over the wooden bridge area again.

Arriving at the top, his stomach grumbles, but he dismisses it and continues over the wooden bridge, hoping to find the baby. He decides that the absence of a baby's crying means Stephen is either dead, or some distance from here.

He begins to feel uncomfortable as he searches, the amount of fluids he had consumed at the pub have finally made him realise that he is in need of relieving himself. Believing that there's no-one around, he takes the opportunity and lets it all hang out as he wonders what the others might have to experience some time tonight.

While enjoying his relief, he idly wonders what people do when they are stuck in a lift for longer than expected. Then he snaps out of it, only to think that he could spend too much time looking for a dead body only to find one, when he could be looking for Bridgette, who might be in the same predicament, but alive.

Luke has the options continually going over and over in his mind. He stands upright stretching his back, and puts his arms out and up, as if to signal 'I give up.'

Wouldn't he be better employed looking for Bridgette? *'One more sweep for Stephen, and then that's what I'll do, look for Bridgette,'* he decides.

Having crossed the bridge and the river without any luck at finding Stephen or Bridgette, he is even more frustrated at what he finds himself dealing with. Luke remembers what his brother had said and thinks of how lucky he was not being put in the front seat, where he could have been dead well and truly by now. Then he remembers the first aid kit in the SUV.

He wonders where the vehicle could be. It also crosses his mind that he doesn't particularly want to find it, nor the gruesome remains of his two brothers, splattered and smeared across the front seat.

Instead, he returns to the Lockwood car, where Pearl is still semi-conscious, and opens her door. The creaking sound given off by the door opening wakes her, and he tells her, "I haven't found the capsule or the baby yet." He tells her the white lie. That he needs to get a first aid kit from one of the cars, as David and Dianne need its contents to help them through the night.

Pearl tells him to look in the back of the car next to a big blue bag filled with baby stuff. This starts her sobbing softly to herself.

Luke opens the rear door and retrieves the kit while watching it close slowly behind him, and then he says goodbye again to Pearl.

Arriving back with the others, Luke checks Dianne's head wound first, before realising David's hand is probably a higher priority. He tries to remove the shirt sleeve and it is making David wince in pain.

With Tiffany and Stephanie looking on, he removes David's shirt sleeve to reveal bruising and more significantly, a bone poking through the skin of his wrist. The girls recoil in shock, and Luke asks Tiffany to hold her father's arm, while he applies cream from the first aid kit on to the break to stop infection.

He asks the girls to find a piece of wood suitable to act as a splint, and Stephanie trundles off and returns a moment later with something the right size.

He places it along the other side of David's arm from the break, and winds a bandage around both arm and splint, using a clip to hold it in place. Nodding approval at his own handiwork, he walks over and puts iodine on Dianne's cut face, causing her to wince at the stinging pain. He puts a couple of band-aids over the cut and as he moves away, both Stephanie and Tiffany give him a big hug.

Luke takes a deep breath and says regretfully, "I'm not having much luck in finding anyone." He asks Dianne in a continued calm manner, "What happened with the prime mover and how did the sleeper compartment split? Any ideas what might have happened to Bridgette?"

Dianne describes the accident in as much detail as she can. "The last thing I remember is Stephanie and I in the back. Bridgette was wide-awake in the front. My best guess is she and her father is still in the prime mover, wherever that is."

Luke nods, wondering if he is ever going to get any information that will help him deal with this and any other situation tonight.

He knows he can give up searching and wait here with the others till the sun comes up, or go on looking for survivors.

"Oh bugger it," he says and stands up and heads off into the fog, without saying another word.

30

(GOOD ON YA, FRANK)

Back at the radio station, Michael Scanlon is on the station phone to Frank. "Well that's good news to hear, Frank. I hope they're doing okay."

"Yes, they are, except for being a bit wet and tired, especially the old dog, Bert. It helps having Malcolm at the pub."

Michael asks, "Isn't he with St. John's Ambulance?"

"Yes, and they'll get a proper examination when we arrive in a couple of minutes."

"When you got to the property, Frank, was the family on the roof where they said they'd be?"

"No, not on the roof of the house, they'd swum a few meters to the shed, and climbed up the ladder. It's higher than the house. That was all Margaret and her daughter, Norma, could manage, and they were bloody grateful they didn't have to do it again. When I got to them, they had made their way to the top of the shed. That kept them just above the water level, as both the house and shed were just below and surrounded by the rest of the property. And we just managed to get them out safely."

～

WHEN MARGARET and her family arrive at the pub, Malcolm makes Margaret his priority and gets her to lie on a couch while he examines her. Frank didn't mention the problem with the propeller. Seeing all is well, Frank enlists the help of locals Brenden and his son Eric, to go and retrieve his wedged boat.

They use Frank's G.P.S. to navigate their way through the still thick fog, but can't locate the boat.

Walking back into the pub, Brenden, Eric and Frank go to the room to see how the family is recovering, and seeing if anyone is paying attention, Ian asks, "Would you three like a beer?" They all nod yes gratefully and meander over to another corner in the pub, with a wry smile from Eric, who is excited with the thought he was getting a beer. Then his expression quickly changes to disappointment when only a glass of lemonade is placed by a joking Ian. Brenden's eight-year-old son Eric is grateful to be on this adventure, instead of being stuck at home being bored.

Michael Scanlon's unmistakable voice is still blaring from the pub radio. *"It's 10.28 pm here on Crazy F.M., and as you heard, all's well with Margaret and her family, who are now safe and sound at the pub. I have Wayne from the S.E.S. on the phone. Good evening, Wayne, what can I do for you this evening?"*

"Hello Michael, I'm calling about the rescue and what some of your patrons from the pub did this evening. I'd like to pass on my thanks to them. I hope we don't have to call on them again tonight."

"I'm sure they appreciate your thanks. I'm sure they're listening to us as they settle in for the night."

"As most people are probably aware, most of the roads

around the town are now blocked due to the last storm. And thanks again, Michael, if I need their help again, I will surely call you again, goodnight."

"Looking at the radar, we still have a couple of hours to go before the next storm arrives, so if you're in this area, be aware as we've got more rain to come. Back soon!"

31

(WHAT'S A TELEGRAM?)

S cotty's looking forward to a good night's sleep when the phone rings, and it's Wayne from the SES. Having stood in ankle deep water for the past hour, Scotty is glad to be home in his new digs. He has showered, put on a t-shirt and shorts, and he's had a glass of warm milk to settle his stomach.

"Hello Scotty, how's it going? Don't worry I don't need you out there again, I just want to know what you left on the electronic noticeboard back there."

"Three phrases, first SLOW DOWN, then ROAD CLOSED, and then finally, TURN LEFT HERE."

"Would you mind leaving your phone on, in case it floods again? I'm letting you know this, Scotty, 'cos we're expecting another big storm sometime in the morning."

"Thanks Wayne, for the heads up. I'll be ready if it comes to that. Oh, and thanks for letting me come home."

Scotty hangs up his phone. He's looking forward to seeing Billy in the morning. He misses his little mate.

~

Back on the embankment, David is resting comfortably, and is being watched over by Dianne. She interrupts Tiffany and Stephanie's conversation to ask Tiffany, "What are you planning on doing for a job when you leave school?"

Tiffany is not sure as to how to respond to this question, as she is perplexed about her surroundings. But as she looks around at Stephanie, and especially Dianne, she composes herself with a wry smile and pretends to be interested in not only the question, but her patronising response. It is in no way offensive to either of those around her, as she just wants to be out of here. But she feels she has to bite her tongue and suck it up, for hopefully not too much longer.

And then she replies with that familiar patronising tone, "I'm not sure at the moment, but nursing or child care is high on my list, teaching maybe. It has to do with helping children, maybe paediatrics, but that's a lot of study."

"Time will tell in a couple of years and before you know it, you'll be doing something you love."

David butts in, "I don't know what's been in her head for the last couple of years. She hasn't been herself. Whether that's your normal teenager or something else, I don't know, but something's been wrong. There's been a spark today I haven't seen for a while, so we can only hope."

Tiffany feels embarrassed, emotional and sad all at the same time. But this is neither the time nor place to bring all this up, so she covers her feelings with a fake smile. Dianne has seen these signs before, although she is not sure what is troubling Tiffany.

Stephanie joins in, "I like what Luke's doing to keep us alive and safe."

Dianne adds, "Me too, he's doing a great job." Then she asks David, "What was your first job?"

He smiles, "my first job was a paper boy in the western suburbs of Melbourne. I think I was about ten, twelve... something like that. I had to get up every morning about four or five in the morning, I can't remember. I got paid sixpence, if my bike was in good working order, every week. I think when the currency changed in 1966 I got maybe one or five cents per paper."

Stephanie asks inquisitively, 'what do you mean the currency changed?"

"It went from pounds, shillings and pence, like they have in England, to what we have today, dollars and cents, and that would have been about $5 per week, I earn't. It was a lot in those days. I did that job for a couple of years, and then when I left school, I was fifteen. I delivered telegrams for a couple of years."

Stephanie asks with a slight tilt of her head, "What's a telegram?"

David explains that, during the Second World War, people were informed by telegram when a family member had been killed.

People complained that the government should have been more sympathetic, so eventually someone came with the telegram, and offered personal condolences, instead of it being delivered by a taxi.

"Telegrams marked important moments in our lives, and I know some people that have still got them in albums or from their wedding or other treasured moments," he continues.

"Wow, I wish I could get a telegram, what did they look like?" says an excited and curious Stephanie.

"It came in an envelope with a clear plastic window at the front. When the telegram was typed up on a machine at the post office and then folded properly, it would show the name and address of the person it was addressed to in the clear window. Telegrams had typed capital letters, and as you know this is taboo today." David laughs. "We know it as yelling, except when you want to get your point across. Lowercase wasn't even spoken about at all back then. Oh and there was always the word 'STOP' in capital letters, for the full stop instead of the dot as we know it today. They were usually sent to congratulate or to express sympathy, as well as to deliver money or urgent news. Many people would rush to telegraph offices when someone got married somewhere around the world, if they couldn't go for any reason. Then for a bit of fun you could send a souvenir telegram to families and friends, or even to yourself. During celebration speeches, those telegrams would be read out to everyone, especially the funny or naughty ones."

This makes Stephanie giggle a little, much to everyone's amusement, releasing some much needed laughter. David explains, "I went to Beechworth in Victoria not far from here recently and sent a message first by Morse code, which went to someone else, who then sent a telegram to my sister's for her birthday." David explains to Stephanie as to what Morse code is and how it works.

"But I do believe there are companies around that still have them today, with e-mails, Twitter, Instagram and other social media sites, that's probably why it's not around. But I'm sure there could be a market for some members of the community. Especially some of the older generations that could send one to their children or grandchildren, or even their great grandchildren." David then points out they were discontinued by the Post Office sometime in the 80s or 90s, he's not sure which.

The conversation serves to take the group's mind off

their eerie surroundings. But they're all wondering in the back of their minds, what the long fog-riddled night will bring.

32

(BEWARE: ANIMALS AHEAD)

The animals from the abattoir are stretched out over one hundred metres in the shallow section of the river. All is quiet until the sound of footsteps spooks them. They move on wherever they can in the fog-riddled river, not stampeding, but very unpredictable.

Luke hears them and stops dead, trying to work out where the sounds are coming from. He's not sure what sort of animals they are, or how many there are of them, so he walks more quietly. Then a couple of sheep stroll past almost nonchalantly. Luke fervently hopes it's only sheep he has been hearing.

He works his way along the western side of the river towards Mackenzie's Bridge, still keeping a lookout for baby Stephen, Bridgette or Ron.

Arriving at the bridge, he bumps head first into a timber object, just missing a protruding nail. It feels like a large wooden fence, so he continues on a little further before suddenly walking into something sharp and hurting his left leg in the process. "Shit...," he curses under his breath, still aware enough not to disturb any of those perceived dangerous animals, which could be close by.

He places his hand on what feels like a large tyre, and then he realises this could be the trailer, that Dianne had told him was holding the longhorn bulls. He wonders how many of them are still at large.

But where has the prime mover gone?

He goes around to the other side of the trailer but it's blocked, so he returns to the rear. He walks back along the way he came, attempting to work out how many bulls the trailer could have held. Judging by the number of individual pens, the figure would be around ten.

He wonders whether the animals he's heard are from somewhere else. Dianne had said nothing about sheep in the prime mover. Then it occurred to him, *of course, the abattoir*.

He heads back to the others, over the slow flowing river, and manages to find his way back to the top of the embankment. He eventually finds them all and he was going to mention to them about the abattoir but notices they are all asleep, except Dianne. Then he prepares for a well-earned rest as he is perplexed as to what to do next.

He gives her an update on what's been happening in the river. "If the weather worsens again, we'll have to work out where to go away from the river. I've covered the bridge twice now with no sign of Stephen, although I did find the bottom part of the capsule, and it was empty. David's wife, Pearl, and his son Rhys, are still unconscious or asleep in their car. I'm not sure if it's safe to try and move him." He yawned, "I'm stuffed, so I came back here to rest for a while. Don't you go out there? I heard some animals before in the river, and I think I spooked them. And you know I'd have told you by now if I'd seen any sign of your daughter or husband."

He adds after a pause, "I never thought I'd be involved in anything like this."

The tragic consequences of his brutal upbringing have had a varying psychologically induced mental effect on Luke, for as long as he cared to remember. Being useful tonight compared to being useless, as he'd kept on hearing all his life, has strengthened his inner resolve to come through this night without any more unforeseen sibling rivalry.

As to why they'd turned out so differently... he'll never know. Perhaps it was due to his mother's calming influence, compared to his brothers. For some unknown reason, they'd mostly all followed in their father's footsteps, making Luke the black sheep of the family. Thus allowing him time to learn how to become resilient, but seemingly remaining fragile at the same time.

Dianne says, "A completely different way of thinking is there are those that watch from a distance, as others like you try and work through your difficulties. Our lives are splashed around the world by the media and especially social media, every minute of every hour of every day. It makes you realise that even though we are all different, we are fundamentally all the same, from our beginning to our end."

Luke interrupts, "I like helping people, and it shouldn't matter if I know them or not, or what colour their skin is either, we're all in this life together. We all started out as new human beings, but it's the environment and outside influences that shape our lives. In my case, I needed to wake up to the sudden reality that I was experiencing some false impression that my life was meaningless, and I had to change like I'm doing now for my future." He yawns, feeling tired.

"Don't get me wrong this is just... I'm overwhelmed by it all. It's different to finding someone who is lost on a Cub or Joey Scout camp, this is extreme stuff, make great reality TV, don't you reckon? I've had it, I don't mean to be rude, but I'm tired, I need to sleep." Luke moves away from Dianne and drops onto an area covered by leaves around a large tree. He closes his eyes and says over and over in his mind, *'I must sleep, sleep, sleep, and sleep.'*

Dianne lies down next to Stephanie, wondering where Bridgette and her husband might be. She puts her hands over her face to stop anyone from seeing her cry. Not knowing if her other family members are dead, or in a location off the beaten track so to speak, she closes her eyes and falls asleep. Apart from the occasional trickle of water and some nocturnal creatures, all is quiet as the fog deepens into a thicker blanket across the river and valley.

Is this the catalyst halting their endeavour to continue on? It's white at night in the valley of the unrelenting fog. They know they should be looking for those that have disappeared, but in his case, Luke can only do so much, given the circumstances. The temperature is still mild enough so nobody is missing a cover over themselves.

As the time slowly continues past midnight at Mackenzie's Bridge, millions around the world are going through their daily chores. But around the crash site, their minds are empty as all the bodies are drained to exhaustion. Fatigue is a killer in many aspects in life, and this environment is at the top of the list.

If you don't understand anything about fatigue, then all you have to do is ask yourself, why I am now feeling tired?

What have you been doing over the last twenty-four hours? How much sleep have you had in that time?

A heavy meal after being awake for so long will cause that sleep to arrive quicker, as the food will sit and linger in your stomach. This will cause a chemical reaction, akin to when the light changes at sunrise and sunset, as your body clock looks forward to its normal sleep patterns.

It might be okay if you're one of the many who work night shift, as the body has acclimatised to the rigors of different sleep patterns, like members of the police and security forces around the world. But some would find it hard to acclimatise.

Unusual sleeping habits tend to affect your eating habits, and if not put in check, can adversely affect your health.

This eerie world waits to bring you more of the unexpected...

GOOD NIGHT!

33

(DREAMTIME)

S leep is a natural, fatigue-induced chemical reaction, playing a vital role in Mother Nature's design for the human body. Over the years, everyone develops a pattern of sleep unique to each individual. Each of us is affected by these sleep patterns in different ways, regardless of age.

Our D.N.A, environment, and most importantly, our character form our sleep patterns. Sleep revitalises the mind and body. Even a power nap of a few minutes while parked by the roadside does bring benefits. Depending on various factors before and during sleep, there are periods of wakefulness.

In its most extreme form, this wakefulness is known as insomnia, and often requires medication to reintroduce beneficial sleep patterns.

NOW THAT THE little shits and their father have gone, Jack wonders why his beloved daughter has been so obviously devoted to him for so long. He notices his twenty-year old cat, Yolly, named after a mate who died in the war, sleeping peacefully on a chair facing a window he likes when the afternoon sun appears. It also keeps him out of the little shits' prying eyes and thoughts, as he is more comfortable with old Jack.

At an active eighty-eight years old now, Jack was fifteen when he'd enlisted in 1943, and, like many young Australians misguided enough to seek the glory of battle, concealed his age when he signed up.

He makes a point of going to bed at the same time every night at around ten p.m., more so especially since his wife died, allowing him more 'me time' than he used to get. While she was alive, she'd never mentioned that he had any sleep disorders, save for the occasional snort after one too many beers, generally drunk in the company with mates from the war.

He always wakes around seven a.m., and potters around the house or goes for long walks... because he can. Jack hates interruptions to his daily schedule. Life is peaceful and relaxed, like the dream he is having right now about his mates from the war.

He neither knows, nor suspects that Pearl is in deep trouble.

PEARL HAS ALWAYS SUFFERED from insomnia, playing its disruptive role in her tangled and sometimes jumbled existence. Unlike Jack, Pearl welcomes intrusions in her life, and is always offering a helping hand to those in need. It's as if the lessons she learnt from her days in the Girl Guides have never left her. Not only is she a dedicated mother figure for her family, she is happy to spread her good nature outside the bounds of house and home.

She only wishes that Rhys and Tiffany were involved in Scouts and Guides, but being in a small community that didn't have any involvement like that, their passions leaned more towards sports. She vows to herself that she will involve Stephen in the Scout movement, when he grows older. Even if she has to do it herself with him, as she know David is also not that way inclined, she will go on camping trips with him as he gets older, just the two of them, regardless of what others think.

If she ever finds him, that is.

She chokes down tears as this last, unwelcomed thought intrudes on her drowsiness.

SLEEP FOR DAVID HAS, for the most part, been good, except for the constant waking, brought on by sleep apnoea, a weak bladder, and Stephen's frequent bawling during the night. But at this moment sleep is far from his thoughts. His hand and wrist are giving him too much discomfort for that.

How could he be comfortable in this dank gloomy environment, surrounded by others suffering the same lack of life's necessities?

In some ways, being in the company of strangers makes him determined not to show weakness, by whinging about his hand or his missing family. David is normally intolerant at being disturbed due to his highly stressful job in transport, and welcomes sleep at any time regardless of the time or place.

He'd endeavoured to function with a reasonable work-life balance, until this deplorable family holiday, and he swears it will never happen again, for as long as he lives.

His long working hours, and a lack of a good home

cooked meal, doesn't allow him to socialise with his family and friends as much as he would like, other than some of the people he gets along really well with at work. He would like to meet other people outside his family and work environment, as this sometimes brings about a form of depression that makes him yearn more for his bad eating habits. Laziness sets in from being tired a lot too, so it's just as easy to get what he can eat now, and let the future look after itself.

Thanks to not being at home at a regular time, like most working people who have a more balanced life, he's often had to find time for meals that were not what one would call 'healthy choices.' And with an ever-increasing continued liking for takeout, his sleep patterns are just as disturbed as his lifestyle.

And he is at pains to discover how he could ever have that life-work balance, which he can only dream about. But he now has the determination to change things around, before his weight – and anything else that might eventually – kills him.

Unfortunately, there are not enough hours in the day to do what and when he wants to, and then he gets side-tracked with some meaningless task that makes him wonder how he ever gets to sleep at night at all.

DIANNE IS HOLDING UP WELL, and so are Luke and the girls, Stephanie and Tiffany. Tiffany is trying not to allow the surrounding gloom remind her of the night of her rape.

To her surprise she wasn't feeling the least bit annoyed about her current company of Dianne, Stephanie and Luke, who do not look upon her with distain, like her mother does.

Tossing and turning at home is okay. Nobody sees her restlessness brought on by that awful memory. Here she has to hold in her emotions. To lose it, and witness the disapproval of the others, is unthinkable. She knows her father, David, is keeping his fears in check. She must emulate his control.

AS AN EIGHT-YEAR-OLD, Stephanie is untroubled by such peer group pressure, and is fast asleep, dreaming as usual about her school. That's where she has learnt, over the last couple of years, that if this is the time and place for her to go to sleep, then so be it. Before she dropped off though, she had suffered pangs of anxiety, thinking about her twin, Bridgette, and where she could be.

Her life is filled with the dreams an eight-year-old should have, and it's no surprise where her influences come from. Stephanie excels in all forms of dance and her favourite instrument is the clarinet. At home she allows music to lull her to sleep, and earlier she had replayed clarinet melodies in her head, and had eventually fallen asleep, on the leg of her new-found friend, Tiffany.

BRIDGETTE IS STILL LYING semi-conscious in the front of the prime mover. Occasionally she drifts in and out of a dread of the unknown. *Why is there nobody with her to help her deal with the situation she's in?* When these thoughts intrude, she tries to think of her father and his strength and work ethic. She thinks about how he conducts his daily life with guarded optimism, always believing things will be okay... eventually.

With that thinking, it is quite easy for her, like her sister, to lay back and let the pieces fall where they may, hoping she gets through this terrible night. Eventually she also falls asleep, while thinking of playing as many sports as she can get her grubby little hands on, like her father did when he was her age. Then her thoughts settle on her mother, Dianne.

ON THE ODD OCCASION, Dianne will fall from her normal position of grace, loved and respected by those who know her. But the odd circumstance can unsettle her. Like Bridgette, she was very much the tomboy while growing up, but still retained sufficient feminine charm for when it became required. Tonight she is revelling in the environment afforded her, and shifts between demeanours when it suits. Tonight she is feeling drained by the brooding, threatening nature of the weather.

Making sure she is the last to sleep, she finds herself wondering as she looks upon someone who, through no fault of his own, has set out to be heroic in his endeavours to help them through the night.

She lies there looking at and wondering at what Luke is dreaming about right now. No-one except Luke and his family would know how he was tormented by the brutal aspects of his childhood.

LUKE IS EXPERIENCING his normal restless sleep patterns, oblivious to anyone like Dianne, who might be watching him in his disturbed slumber. He sleeps with his body contorted, as if involuntarily preparing himself for whatever malevolence Nick might have in store for him. Some nights were more tranquil than others, but more frequently he stayed half-awake until the early morning, wondering if and when his siblings were coming to torment him.

Tonight he's just dead tired and fighting against the overwhelming desire to give up his search for Stephen and Bridgette. The toll of not having found them is playing heavily on his mind right now, as is the absence of any sign of the truck driver.

Maybe all will be revealed in the morning, just as long as he survives the night. He has already witnessed the deaths of three of his brothers, and a small part of him regrets what happened, even though he knows this means the horrors of the past are gone, if not forgotten. He falls out of a light sleep into a much more settled, deeper slumber.

RICK HASN'T awoken from his unconscious state near the top of the embankment on the eastern side of the river. General anxiety, shock and the amount of alcohol in his system have caused his collapse. He's lying next to a collection of large rocks that he believes will shelter him from whatever comes his way.

Over time, he has found a decent night's sleep essential for dealing with the rigors of full-time employment. He enjoys the knowledge that he has created an effective work-life balance, and the good money this earns him. This quiet satisfaction and having his own room have combined to help him towards a stable sleeping pattern.

Luke's twin brothers have always shared a room with Nick. Born followers both of them, they generally enjoyed trouble free sleep. The amount of alcohol they consumed on a regular basis helped as well.

RON IS NOT ONLY oblivious to his environment, but is semi-conscious, drifting in and out of a troubled uncertainty. Surrounded by water in the river that is now climbing up his lower legs, it slowly passes his contorted body. Part of which is still stuck in a large part of a tree that was torn apart earlier in the night by the lightning.

His snoring and sleep apnoea have lessened since getting married and becoming a father for the first time. But with twins and his working life, he's not sure if he would like to try for a son. As Bridgette seems more like one every day, he might just not bother.

Unlike most people in the transport game, not to mention those who sit on their backsides all day in offices, Ron's waistline and fatigue levels have never been a great cause for concern. He regularly substitutes a lunchtime nap for the junk food that most long-distance truck drivers guzzle. Often Ron will now make a sandwich he prepared earlier in the day so he has plenty of healthy food to eat, during his previous long distance journeys.

34

(THIS IS HORRIBLE)

Exhausted, David wonders why he and Dianne were able to sleep for only a short time. But rolling over in your sleep and putting pressure on a broken wrist isn't helpful to untroubled slumber.

Dianne has too much on her mind to stay asleep for long, and besides, on finding David is awake too, she decided she might as well keep him company.

Since waking at about three a.m. when David last looked at his watch, they can't believe they have talked about anything and everything for so long. "Time flies when you're in good company," she jokes to David as five a.m. has come around.

Only two hours before dawn.

Luke, meanwhile, is locked in a frighteningly real nightmare. Initially it's just the sound of something tapping, softly at first, but then with increasing force and volume. And the blows are reverberating inside his head.

Or are they crashing into his skull from the outside?

Fear pumps adrenaline through his system and he senses a deep chill, although something else is telling him the temperature is quite warm. Someone is smashing a hammer on his head, but there's no pain, just terror.

He raises his hands in his sleep to protect himself.

And then he is screaming is his sleep, "please stop!"

This has the effect of waking him, and he feels something damp on his face before the next droplet falls on him from above.

So that's what it was, moisture, raindrops, or whatever.

He wonders if his screams were audible to any of the others, and is inundated with embarrassment at the thought.

He notices there is a slight breeze and that the fog has lessened. He should probably wake the others and set some plan of action into place. He sees Dianne and David smiling in his direction. *So they have heard.*

Dianne says, "I've just thought about where we were supposed to be staying last night. Do you think the hotel people might be wondering where we've got to?"

David chimes in, "My father-in-law's probably snoring his head off right now. I wouldn't expect him to be worrying about where *we* are, except maybe Pearl."

Tiffany and Stephanie are woken by the sounds of voices, and immediately notice it's starting to rain again. *Not another storm on its way... surely?*

Now the fog has lessened, the group spot animals, largely sheep and horses, wandering through the bush nearby. Someone mentions the bulls in the truck, but Luke suggests the animals they are seeing are more likely to have come from the local abattoir.

Luke asks David and Dianne, "What do you reckon we should do now? I'm clean out of ideas, but I think we might have another storm on its way, in which case we're going to need to move, and fast."

Just as he speaks, as if on cue, a flash of lightning illuminates the river and their immediate surroundings, including the animals, who seem startled by the sudden light.

Dianne says she thinks she can see a fence, but Luke tells her it's the trailer that was transporting the bulls.

"Oh! Silly me, you could have fooled me."

"I thought the same," he says, "When I banged my head on it last night." Luke points towards the bridge and the trailer in the distance, figuring it is about a hundred meters away, telling David, "That's where your wife and boy, Rhys, are."

A crack of thunder and another flash of lightning send the animals stampeding towards the bridge. They are obviously spooked and therefore unpredictable, making it all the more difficult for Luke, David and Dianne to decide where they should seek refuge from the approaching storm.

Luke suggests climbing down the embankment and finding David's car, reasoning that it's stuck fast enough to be a safe haven for all of them from both the weather and the animals.

As they stumble down the embankment, they realise they are all a bit unsteady from their nightlong experience.

David nearly falls headfirst and is stopped by Luke from aggravating his broken wrist further. They are keeping a watchful eye on the animals on the other side of the river.

As they reach the bottom of the embankment, the rain becomes heavier, accompanied by another flash of lightning and a deafening clap of thunder. This causes the animals underneath and on the other side of the bridge, to stampede along the western side of the river.

Luke and the rest of the group choose to get back up the embankment, as another loud peal of thunder spooks the animals into a renewed frenzy. Worse still they recognise a couple of longhorns in the pack. One spears a sheep through its body, lifting the animal off the ground on the end of its left horn. The bull knocks other animals to the ground, adding to the general chaos along the riverbank. Animals are now running in all directions, making it impossible for the group to either to reach David's car, or to seek safe refuge elsewhere.

As they spend all their time attempting to do just that and watching out for animals that could kill them, they will miss any opportunity presented to them in seeing where Bridgette or Ron might be. Focusing on the job at hand, they cannot see the other parts of the river, and consequently, the torrential rain has permanently blocked them from view now.

The rain is now rapidly swelling the river once more to breaking point. Their visibility is nearly as diminished as it had been by the fog. His voice is difficult to hear in the pounding rain, as Luke tries to scream out to the others. **His attempts to speak loudly... cause him to shorten his sentences... so the others don't miss out on anything... that he is trying to say. "We have to make a decision... about whether or not we head for David's car. If this rain continues... it could well be washed away by the river... with all of us inside. If we stay here... we've got to keep out of the way... of these bloody animals... particularly the bulls. I still think the car... is the best option. We can always abandon it... if the water rises too high."**

Stephanie points to a fallen tree trunk lying across the bridge that she noticed earlier. **She screams into her mothers' ear, "We could climb down that large branch... and get into the car through the sunroof," she says.**

Nobody stops to think how impressive a plan this is, coming from the mouth of a frightened eight-year-old.

As Dianne gives Stephanie a big hug, Luke screams, **"What are we waiting for??? Let's go."**

Without any consideration as to the consequences of the decision, they all go forward headlong onto the bridge without even the slightest thought. This is what happens when you are fatigued, and are unable to explain, as to the clarity of the options that might have presented themselves to them. The rain worsens as they attempt to clamber further up the embankment, and as they slip and slide in the mud, the two girls are caught between sobbing and laughing hysterically. David is trying to stay focused, but laughing isn't helping.

When they finally reach the top of the embankment near to Mackenzie's Bridge, Tiffany decides she will be the one to help her injured father into the car, via the large branch. She's hoping this might show Luke and the others she has realised the predicament they are in.

The river is rising faster than they had calculated, and by the time they reach the slender branch on the bridge, Stephanie's brilliant idea seems fraught with difficulty. Luke still thinks it's strong enough to take their weight, one at a time starting with David.

They begin arguing over whether or not the position of the large branch needs adjusting, to make access to the car easier. The rain is making it torrentially impossible to manoeuvre the branch.

Their wet clinging hair is being blown around in all directions, as they all attempt to see what's in front of and around them, and as the debate rages. Stephanie calls out, **"Stop yelling at each other,"** and starts crying.

Dianne tries to explain that tempers are becoming frayed because of the dilemma they are facing. **"With all**

this bloody rain... and the animals here... we were just blowing off steam." This brings a curious look on Stephanie's face as if to say, *'What on earth are you talking about, blowing off steam?'*

Luke finally takes control and wrestles the large branch, lifting it into what looks like the best position. He decides it's a good idea to throw something at the car first, to wake Pearl and alert her to what they are planning. Also she can hold the far end of the large branch steady.

Luke hurls a small branch down on the car, but Pearl doesn't appear to be alerted by the thumping.

They squint over the railing, but there is no movement from below, at least it appeared from what little they can see. Luke searches for a bigger piece, and another flash of lightning illuminates the area around, allowing him to find a thicker piece of branch and the car more clearly.

The water is now up to the door handles as Luke is momentarily blinded by the lightning, Luke trips, taking a heavy fall.

The same lightning flash strikes a tree at the end of the bridge, sending it crashing down to where Luke lies. He sees what's coming at the last moment, but manages to scramble out of the way, just as the tree slams onto the bridge.

He climbs over the tree, finds a suitable thicker branch, and once again hurls it down onto the car. This time there is a resounding thud, and immediately afterwards the sunroof opens, and Pearl's head pops out.

Luke's voice battles the rain and wind as he yells down at Pearl, trying to explain as briefly as he can what they are about to do. She yells back, "okay, fine, but have you found my baby yet?"

Luke and the others look around at each other's perplexed expressions. Nobody knows quite how to answer this, so they pretend instead that they haven't heard what she asked.

Luke and Dianne lift up the end of the large branch, attempting to lift it over the edge of the bridge, but it becomes stuck in the railings.

They free it with Tiffany's help and guide the bottom end of the branch into the open sunroof. Pearl peers up at them, rain pelting down on her face, and she gamely tries to grab the branch and pull it down into the car. The heavy rain is making it hard for her to see and the branch smacks into her shoulder, causing her to fall back into the vehicle as the branch slides across the roof, and off the back of the car.

Everyone holds on as tight as they can to the other end, to stop the entire branch plunging off the car into the river. Luke climbs over the edge of the bridge, and climbs down its support timbers to the car, grabbing onto the bottom of the branch. He strains to lift it, yelling at the others to pull up on their end. Eventually, and with great difficulty, he manages to manoeuvre it in through the sunroof.

Dianne tells Stephanie to climb down first, and she does so gingerly, making sure her footing is in the right place. Her early years spent climbing frames in parks and the playground comes in handy. Eventually she makes it into the car through the sunroof and finally climbs, exhausted and shaking, into the back seat, as instructed by Luke. She looks across to see a boy lying in the seat next to the other window, and wonders if he is dead, just unconscious, or asleep.

Luke then climbs back up to the bridge, stopping Tiffany from helping Dianne onto the branch. He says, "Hang on. I need you up here, Dianne, to help David get down."

Tiffany goes next, scrambling down the branch and in through the sunroof without incident. She hops into the back with Stephanie, glad to be out of the rain, while Pearl remains slumped in the driver's seat.

She turns to the two girls and asks them if Luke has found her baby. Both look at each other, hesitate and chorus, "No."

Pearl stifles a sob and turns her back on them.

MEANWHILE UP ON THE BRIDGE, Dianne is helping David climb over and onto the branch. Luke climbs onto the slender length of wood beside him, while Dianne holds onto the branch with one hand and David with the other. Between the two of them, Luke and Dianne guide him down the branch.

David winces with the pain from his wrist and the effort involved. The combined weight of the three of them sets the branch creaking and wobbling precariously.

David eventually reaches the top of the vehicle and is lowered carefully into the passenger seat by Luke and Dianne. As he drops down, he knocks his broken wrist, sending pain shooting through his arm, but this doesn't stop him from reaching out for Pearl. They embrace awkwardly, and Pearl begins to sob, gabbling words that only David can interpret.

"Where's Stephen, and when am I going to see him again?" is the general idea of what she's saying. Equally concerned at the fate of his infant son, David tries hard to comfort her, without admitting he has no idea where Stephen can be.

The raging torrent that is the river has by now reached the top of the car, and Luke tells Dianne to get in quickly and close the sunroof. Dianne screams to be heard over the rain, telling Luke to follow her.

As she places her feet inside the sunroof, she accidentally stands on David's thighs, pushing his broken wrist against his wife's body. David screams and moves out of the way to give Dianne enough room to get inside the car.

LUKE, meanwhile, has ignored Dianne's instruction to follow her into the car, and is scrambling back up the branch. He realises there is no room for all of them in the packed vehicle. He pulls the bottom of the branch free of the sunroof, but a sudden gust of wind catches the branch, sending it spinning down onto the embankment. Luke is thrown clear and lands heavily on the same embankment.

No-one in the car is sure whether or not he's been knocked unconscious, and they become distraught, unsure of what has happened to their saviour. Dianne and David eventually struggle to close the sunroof, but it has been warped in the accident, and a gap of a couple of inches is left open. Water is entering the vehicle and starts to rise above their ankles, and is working its way up their legs towards their hips. If they can't stem the flow, water will eventually fill the car.

Dianne turns in the cramped space and asks Tiffany "is there anything in the back of the car we can use as a hammer?" While Tiffany searches the rear of the car, David grabs the steering wheel lock and hands it to Dianne.

She begins hitting it against one end of the sunroof, when David stops her, saying, "Sorry, I don't think that's helping. Maybe we should try and remove the bottom part of the interior of the sunroof, and then hopefully we can see the other side of it, and force it forward enough to close it."

"David, where's Stephen?" asks Pearl, as if oblivious to all else around her.

"I don't know, darling, Luke told us about finding you alive, and how worried you were about Stephen. He looked for him for nearly two hours in the fog, but couldn't really see or feel his way around."

"There was fog? Oh yeah, that's right, sorry. I've been asleep or out to it, I forgot how thick it was."

"I'm sorry, Pearl, but right now we need to get this roof closed before we all drown. Stephen's life is in the hands of the gods right now."

Pearl responds violently and unpredictably, "You never wanted Stephen in the first place, did you? *You're* to blame if he dies, you prick." With this she begins whacking his broken wrist. David screams out in pain, and suddenly Pearl is slumping forward, passing out once more. Emotion, fear and frustrated maternal instincts have suddenly become too much for her.

Everyone else in the car goes quiet, unsure of how to react. David breaks the silence by asking Dianne to find something to rip open the material on the inside of the roof. As the water continues to pour in uninterrupted, they all miss something moving towards them.

Whatever it is, it's slithering down one of the bridge supports, but suddenly plummets down into the river, and finds its way into and through the roof of the car... and falls down onto someone's shoulder.

35

(WE CAN HELP)

S teering's population of Five-hundred and fifty-three
residents has long remained stable, but the town has
spiralled into economic decline over the last twenty
years. During a boom period after the Second World
War, Jeff Steering, his father, and ageing grandfather, fought
to maintain a healthy and motivated environment among
the community.

The family name still commands respect for its integrity,
but there is an element of arrogance as well, stemming
perhaps from the strong ties enjoyed with those in high
places, in both State and Federal Governments. Today, with
the town facing the immediate aftermath of the floods, the
family has sought information from the SES about families
that may have been overlooked, or are at the bottom of the
list that still need to be rescued and still in need of help. The
senior management team has provided a list of relevant
properties, and phone contact has been made.

As a result, Jeff Steering has suggested going to the
Miller property first, and then working their way back
towards the town. Proximity to the river could bring

problems for the Millers, particularly if the renewed rainfall persists. In fact, the entire town could be under water within a couple of hours. Current radar reports from the weather service describe the storm as slow moving, but with the possibility of more than another one hundred millimetres falling in the next two hours.

Jeff and his helpers head off through the steadily increasing rainfall towards the Millers' property, directly in the path of the oncoming front, as it moves slowly southeast.

36

(WARNING UPDATE)

At the radio station, Michael and Robbie are intent on keeping the vast area they cover provided with regular updates from the S.E.S, and the weather services. Michael is hoping to hear from any residents with specific problems requiring assistance.

"Maybe they're ringing in just to help you stay awake," Robbie jokes. She answers a call from Wayne at the command centre in town and puts him through to Michael.

"Hello Wayne, tell us what you can about this latest storm front? It came through here about fifteen minutes ago. Jeff Steering and I were talking about it just before midnight. I saw it on the radar back then, and I had some sort of idea how long it was going to take to get here. For some reason, it hasn't done what I thought. So can you explain to me what's happening with it now, and what you expect it to do over the next few hours?"

"Hello Michael, okay, what it's doing, quite simply, is slowing down. The gap between this system and the one we had late last night has part of a high-pressure system forcing its way in between them, causing the second front to stagnate." Wayne pauses.

"As you can see on the radar, the more colourful parts are around the district and the town of Steering. This is worrying the S.E.S. as it makes it uncertain how much time they have in getting people off their properties, and who they should prioritise. This is dependent on a number of variables, which the S.E.S. has under control. And because of the first storm, there are places where the water hasn't receded as quickly as it has in other areas. Anyway we'll push on through the night, saving those who are stranded, and getting them to higher ground as quickly and safely as possible. And as you can understand, people take priority over livestock, much of which is hopefully covered by insurance."

*"It's now **ten past five** on this Saturday morning here on Crazy F.M. and I'm talking with Wayne from the S.E.S. here in Steering. Can you tell us, Wayne, how long you're expecting this current low pressure system to last for, and what parts of the district are you focusing on presently?"*

"We've got most of our volunteers out on the eastern side of the town, where it's been raining the longest. We're moving residents from there onto higher ground. Most of those on the western side of town are well above the current river level. The level of water is estimated to flood sooner rather than later. But that doesn't mean the rest of the district won't receive its fair share of rain either. And then there are the valleys near the abattoir, which are prone to flooding. But the only part likely to be affected is the river between the two wooden bridges. Nobody in their right mind would be out there at the moment. It would be suicidal. Other than that, most of the roads around Steering are flooded and cut off. Most of the shops, especially the pub, petrol station and the police station, are above the flood levels."

"That's good to hear, Wayne. I know there're a few people at the pub – they're probably relieved to hear that news. Ian, Michelle and a couple of others are looking after those folk who've just been rescued. Thanks again for that, Wayne, well talk later to get another update."

"Bye, Michael, it helps having your station keeping the residents updated. And I know you had to do a double shift tonight, so hope that's going okay?"

"Yeah, it's been tough, but Robbie has helped me out, and I grabbed a couple of hours sleep when she took over. Robbie's younger than I am, and she's used to staying out late partying, as you can imagine."

"I can indeed, on that note, see ya, Michael."

The interview ends and Michael moves on to his next caller for an update. *"I have Ian from the pub on the phone. Hi Ian, what's happening at your end, mate?"*

"Yeah, it's all quiet here, most of 'em are asleep, and it's only me, Michelle, Tommy and Frank still awake. I don't think Frank's all there, he's forgotten he doesn't know where his boat is any more, and I don't want to spoil the party. He's in the other room so he can't hear what I'm saying. We'll keep listening to the goings on for the rest of the morning, till sun up about seven."

"That's still another couple of hours away, and anything could happen before then. We won't even know 'til the morning what the full extent of the damage is. Thanks Ian, we'll talk again soon."

Michael disconnects the call and winds up his session. *"Meanwhile, if anyone wants to give us a call, if there's anyone out there still awake, please do. I was going to talk about other things, but I'll cop some zeds instead and let Robbie tell you what the rest of the morning brings."* Michael yawns loudly. *"Night, oh, hang on, I mean morning."*

(AMUSEMENT RIDE...NOT)

*S*ix inches of water along the bottom of most family cars will cause the loss of control and stalling. A foot of water will float many vehicles. Two feet or more of rushing water can move most vehicles, and even heavier ones, like SUVs and Ute's, along with the current.

REMAINING unconscious for more than thirty minutes can bring on brain damage, sometimes to an irreparable extent. But it's not always possible to determine how long someone has been unconscious or whether they are asleep, or suffering a bad concussion. An individual alone in a state of unconsciousness is obviously at greater risk.

Ron and Rhys have both been in this condition off and on since the accident. Having been thrown from the prime mover, Ron now faces the threat of drowning. The flood level has reached his waist and is rising. The force of the river is beginning to loosen the large branch wedging his arm against the bank, and eventually he falls free and is washed down the river, towards the entrance to the creek.

The flow from the creek enters the river and diverts Ron over to the western bank.

Luke, meanwhile, is climbing up the embankment moments after being thrown off the bridge. The car carrying those inside has been lifted from its secure spot on the eastern embankment, and starts to hurtle down along the river to the smaller wooden bridge.

After finding his feet, he runs along the top of the bank, keeping pace with the car carrying the others as it's swept along by the fast-flowing river. He has difficulty keeping the car in view through the driving rain, but he spots the second bridge looming ahead. He wonders if the low-levelled bridge will stop the car's progress. Will it become jammed, or simply continue speeding under the bridge and on down the river?

Then he spots what looks like someone floating in the river. His first panicked thought is that someone has been washed from the car because they couldn't close the roof in time.

Luke scrambles down the bank once more and, leaning out over the water, attempts to grab hold of the body, dragging it out of the way of the car just in time. Despite the fast-flowing current, he manages to grab the body and haul it onto and above the river level, and onto the lower part of the embankment.

At this moment, the car floats past rising up and down with the undulating flow, as if in slow motion. He can see Dianne doing something inside to the car's roof. Luke realises it won't make it under the bridge, and when it hits the ancient timbers, it makes a cracking sound, like a pistol shot.

His worst fears are realised when the car stops, suddenly jammed in the limited distance of the bottom of the river, and the bridge. Facing into the raging river, it is causing water to flow over the bonnet, up the windscreen, over the top of the car, and slightly in through the still partially open sunroof.

Helpless, Luke drags the wet and heavy body along the slight slope of the embankment, away from the river until he reaches the dirt road. He turns the body on its side, then again onto its back. He tries to check for a pulse, but can't find one, so thinking this unknown person is dead, he returns to the embankment.

He went back to the edge of the river as a flash of lightning allowed him to see the fully submerged car stuck under the bridge. Regrettably, Luke could see that if the river was a foot less, the car would have gone under the smaller wooden bridge. He hurries towards the bridge, taking about half a minute then enters the rickety sounding bridge before he climbs over the lower railing and scrambles down carefully to the car.

Placing his feet onto the cross members of the bridge, he finally makes it onto the roof of the car with little regard for his safety as the flood waters rush past him at a furious rate. He thumps downwards with his boot, hoping he's not too late, and they're not all dead.

Inside the car, Dianne squints against the torrential rain through the sunroof, praying its Luke making that noise on the roof.

He yells to her, "Open the roof and I'll drag you all out onto the bridge."

But she can't because the sunroof is stuck fast. She yells, "David's been bitten by a snake. It got in through this fucking sunroof."

Luke is surprised by her changed manner, and by this development, and curses, and at the same time, he hears muffled cries for help coming from the two girls in the back seat of the car. Then he kneels on the roof and asks where the snake is now.

"It's curled up at David's feet. It's either asleep or protecting... I don't know... guarding its prey, do they do that? It hasn't moved since it bit David. I don't know what it's doing. I don't know anything about snakes."

"Just wanted to know where it is and what it's doing, but if it's still, maybe it's okay for now. Is it under water? Just hang in there, okay? I'm going to get something to cover this opening to stop you all from drowning." He's torn between thinking what he can use as a cover, and how he's going to tell Dianne that he thinks he found her dead husband. That's if the body is her husband.

He returns to the end of the bridge and continues on to where the body lies. As the rain continues to pour down, it's still quite mild. He starts to remove the heavy, soaking clothing from the body, thinking it will do to jam into the sunroof, when there is sudden movement and a voice says, "What the bloody hell's going on?"

Luke jumps backwards in shock, "I thought you were dead!"

"Well it's bloody obvious I'm not. Who the hell are you, and why you trying to undress me, you filthy pig? Ya think I'm dead, what did 'ya want me clothes for, ya mongrel?" Luke stands there dumfounded, until the man kicks him on his leg, snapping him out of his stunned state. "Well, answer me, for god's sake...shit."

Overwhelmed by the response Luke blurts out, "Are you Ron? Your wife's trapped in the car down there in the river, and I was gunna take your clothes to stop the water from getting in through the sunroof. It's stuck open."

"Shit, why didn't ya say so, son, we could have been there by now. C'mon let's go then."

As Ron stands up, he's overcome with dizziness and nearly tumbles head first down the embankment. Luke rushes to him and turns him over. "Are you all right?"

"Just get me pants off and get over to the car, quick smart." Luke does as he's told, and by the time he reaches the car, struggling to keep standing due to the very slushy and muddy road, the water has almost reached the bottom of the windscreen.

He clambers once more onto the roof and jams the pants into the open section. "Does that help?"

"Yes it does." Dianne clambers around in the front of the vehicle, looking for some reassurance from anyone else, but they all seem to be pre-occupied with what they are all feeling. Then a frown appears on Dianne's face as she stares at the pants that were shoved in the gap. "Where'd you get these pants? They look familiar."

"I got them from your husband. I thought he was dead, but he's not, he's alive. He's up there by the bridge. He'll be here as soon as he can. He's just recovering."

All of a sudden Dianne begins speaking frantically, without thinking as to how fast she is talking, to obtain as much information on Ron as possible.

"Oh my God, How is he? Where is he? Is he okay? Give him my love." And then, she added as an afterthought while becoming flustered, "The pants seem to work At least they're keeping the worst of it out. It should be okay 'til it stops raining and the water goes down. Now, all we've got to worry about is the bloody snake."

"Okay, I'm going back to where Ron is now."

But then, as he heads back to the bridge, he turns slightly as he hears the sudden sickening sound and the creaking of heavy timber.

Almost in slow motion, he turns in time to see the bridge break into two halves, its bottom timbers heaving out of the water. This frees the car and Luke watches in horror as it's carried away down the river, and out of sight.

"Go and follow the car and see where it goes," hollers Ron. "Don't worry about me."

Luke sprints off down the track, trying to catch up to the car.

Meanwhile, some of the larger animals had gotten to the northern end of the river, past the larger wooden bridge. As there hadn't been any lightning or rain for a while, they'd felt quite safe but now had become trapped in the river with this latest round of flooding.

As a consequence, some of the smaller sheep were tossed about along the now raging river. Luke hears another crash and realises a number of the animals that were trapped in the other end of the river had begun scrambling over and bouncing off some of the fast flowing branches. Sheep are being tossed about in the current, but more alarmingly, a couple of the larger bulls have smashed into the remains of the smaller bridge, breaking it into still smaller bits.

Luke suddenly notices the rain is easing off, but still, his visibility is down to around ten metres. He can't see any sign of the car, so he continues on, watching as waves of water hurtle downriver. A large but very dead horse bobs past, and then after a considerable distance, a flash of lightning illuminates the sky and he spots the car lying on its side on the far side of the river.

Thankfully the roof is clear of the flowing water.

Luke searches urgently around for something big enough to hold onto while he manoeuvres in the torrent, and sees an old car tyre on the bank. He checks the tyre and then the river, and takes a deep breath. He wades in carefully from the side, clutching the tyre, but it's only seconds before his feet are swept from under him by the current.

He goes under water, and when he comes back to the surface, he realises he has been taken past the car and is still moving away from it, so he tries desperately to grab onto something. When Luke reaches out again, he misses a branch and goes under again, pushing his legs and arms to allow him to get to the eastern side. Luke makes one last shove and grabs onto another branch as it breaks swiftly on bending too much.

Having gone nearly a few hundred meters down the river, he found that the river was widening. The tyre long gone, he makes several futile attempts to clutch at another branch. Finally, he finds the river is widening and slowing down, allowing him to swim back to the bank he started from, but some distance downstream.

Gasping, he struggles onto the muddy embankment and collapses. Rolling over to see how far from the car he has been taken. There's no sign of it. "God, I hope this is a dream," he thinks out loud. "I'm getting tired of this brave man shit." And then he gets to his feet and starts back towards the car, stumbling on the uneven ground, noticing the odd animal corpse floating by in the river and hoping that there aren't any human ones.

As he starts moving faster, hoping they haven't drowned, he realises the rain has stopped altogether. When he finally arrives at the car, he kneels down out of breath and panting loudly, not realising those noises could alert those inside that someone is outside to help them. He has to stand up again and take a few deep breaths. He then kneels down again to look at the occupants through the front window. They all seem senseless...or maybe dead. Frantically, he taps quietly on the window and to his relief, both Dianne and Tiffany stirs.

The car is sufficiently far enough out of the water for Tiffany to open the door, Luke grabs onto the open door and pushes it backwards until the hinges snap. Then he drags Tiffany out of the car and onto the embankment, and then does the same with Dianne.

Rhys, who seems to have come around at last, is checked by Luke to see if it's safe to move him.

Satisfied his injuries are not serious, at least not visibly so, Luke pulls the teenager clear and then Stephanie. Luke wrenches the front door open to find David and Pearl slumped together. More alarmingly, he can see the snake stirring in the muddy water at their feet.

He speaks as calmly as he can. "Are you okay, Pearl?"

"Yes...who's that?"

"It's me, Luke. Is David okay?"

"No, I'm not sure."

"Okay, I'll be back in a second."

"Have you found Stephen yet?"

"No, I bloody haven't," replies Luke, with more venom than he realises. Then his face changes to regret and shock, he can't believe he just said it that way. He realises all these experiences tonight must be getting to him quicker than he thought, as he has never reacted like this for as long as he can remember.

Tiffany yells at her mother as she has wanted to do for

such a long time, but Luke takes her away without realising the built-up anger that is ready to explode, as she bites her tongue in frustration.

38

(SHE LISTENS TO THE... RADIO)

Enthusiasts have a knack of improving their toys. Just like Ron when he brought this new prime mover. Adding another set of 24 volt batteries under the bonnet. So that the function of the mobile phone especially, and the radio, could function in all kinds of situations, like the one now faced by Bridgette.

Bridgette still lies semi-conscious in the front of the prime mover, that's still resting on the town side of the embankment. After the trailer fell into the river, most of the bulls had managed to struggle free.

Slowly Bridgette moves her head away from the side window, sitting upright and opening her eyes. They flicker as she tries to focus on her surroundings.

The darkness doesn't help.

She turns her head to see her father but finds only an empty seat. She twists around to her right, looking for her mother and sister. To her horror, she finds the compartment gone. It hits her like a blow to the stomach. She's all alone.

She screams out for anyone who can hear her, but after a while she collapses, exhausted. She begins to sob quietly. The heavy rain is still hitting the outside of the prime mover, and she realises nobody can hear her over the heavy backdrop of falling water.

The front of the prime mover is lying almost to the top of the eastern side of the embankment, the noisy river surging past.

Where is her family? What if the river comes into the cab? Realising the absolute helplessness of her situation, her sobs and screams merge into a desperate wail.

After a while, she stops as nothing is coming out of her mouth, and she slumps back into her seat. Looking around the inside of the cab, she sees the radio and phone on the dash. Bridgette undoes her seatbelt and turns on the radio that hasn't been affected by the crash, and there's still plenty of current from the batteries. She hears a voice, Michael Scanlon. She listens, hoping she might learn what's happened to her family.

*"Michael Scanlon here on CRAZY F.M. and it's **twenty past five** on this wet and eventful Saturday morning. We have Wayne on the line from the S.E.S."*

Bridgette stops crying, astonished at how much time has passed since, she looked at the phone with a shocked look on her face. Since...it's what time?

"How's it going out there, Wayne?"

"It's still raining in most parts of the district, Michael, but nearly all the heavy stuff has passed and it's headed towards the western part of the state before turning towards Melbourne. They won't get as much as we got here as it's breaking up now. The worst is over. I'm even expecting sunny skies for the rest of the day."

Bridgette likes the sound of that. She yells at the radio. Her muddled brain thinking someone might hear her.

"That's when the sun finally comes up in about two

hours from now. We'll get to see what and where the real damage has been done to the district."

Bridgette yells again at the radio that she could drown if someone doesn't come and rescue her soon.

"At the moment, there are a few annoying showers around, but I'm only expecting them to last for about another half an hour at the most. As for the flooding, the worst part has been in the river on the western side of town. To our knowledge most of, if not the entire, town's population has been accounted for, except for a couple of families. They could be out of town for whatever reason, and we won't know 'til about midday. Luckily no lives have been lost so far, and we hope there won't be any, but it's too early to tell. As for injuries, well that's something else we're not fully aware of either. The number of people rescued by the SES, including that family at the pub we discussed earlier, won't be known 'til later in the day. The only concern we have here at the command centre is another possible storm later in the week. Hopefully we can clean up as much as we can from this one and be ready for the next one, if and when it comes."

"Thanks, Wayne, for your time and the updated information. I'll call you again in about an hour to see if you've got anything further to report. Bye for now."

"Thanks again for your support, Michael. I hope things can calm down a bit now."

Bridgette realises from all this that nobody knows of their situation. Her eyes light on the phone. She picks it up and can hear a woman talking. She tries to get her attention by yelling into the mouthpiece, and quickly becomes frustrated when there is no response.

The phone line is somehow still connected to the radio station, from earlier in the night when Ron called Michael.

But Robbie is unaware of Bridgette, because the light above the switch is not working, and the switch is in the up position. The switch needs to be in the down position for Robbie to hear, but some of the equipment in the station hasn't been fixed for a few days. The light above the switch has failed at this time, and therefore Robbie is none the wiser about Bridgette's screams.

Although the station has had a number of callers from around the district over the last few hours, most have said that they are okay. Calls have been from either those still at their properties, or from truckies on the roads in between towns on the outskirts of the district.

39

(LET'S PARTY)

Back in the prime mover, Bridgette is listening to all this music and wishing Michael would stop discussing the weather and do something about co-ordinating her rescue. Even more frustratingly, she can still hear voices on the other end of the phone, but no one is listening to her yelling and screaming. On a brighter note, she notices the sound of the rushing water around her, thankfully seems to be lessening.

"Is THERE anyone out there in radio land wanting to call in at this god forsaken hour? Robbie, what's it like being awake at this time? I'm usually off with the fairies."

"You don't really think about the time if you're having a lot of fun dancing, or making out with someone on the dance floor. Then, before you know it, four, five or possibly six hours have passed and it's time to go home, and you get into bed and hit the pillow. The next thing you know it's Sunday afternoon and, depending on how much you've had to drink, you could have one *hell of a hangover that won't go away 'til the next day. But I know what I'll be doing tonight, if I can get out of here with all of this bloody flooding! Each and every one of us girls will be texting each other about six p.m. and decide where to go."*

"How many girls are there?"

"There are about thirty five of us, and sometimes some of the girls might bring their partners along, but it's better with just us girls. If they have partners hopefully they won't find out if we let our hair down. As they say, what they don't know won't hurt 'em."

"Thirty five, bloody hell, even I might have a chance with at least one of them. And who knows I might just be ready to settle with someone on a more permanent basis, so look out. I think we'll leave it there Robbie, just in case someone underage is listening to this."

"Bloody hell, Michael, it's five in the morning, not even the farmers are up for their morning milking. The only others listening are the folks at the command centre, a few truckies and whoever's listening at the pub."

BRIDGETTE CAN'T BELIEVE what she heard, and starts to giggle at what Michael said about underage kids listening in at five a.m. Well she's underage, and she's listening, even if she is in the middle of nowhere.

She tries again to get someone's attention on the phone, but after a few minutes, sits it on top of the casing, disappointed. The water outside has almost become a trickle, and Bridgette leans against the back of the seat and wonders where her family are. As the river continues to slow down, she watches the amount of debris being carried along with it, wondering where it's all coming from.

A song comes on the radio that she recognises and she sings along with it. There is no-one else around, so she lets her voice get carried through the night. Above her, on the top of the bank, there are a few of the bulls and animals from the abattoir. They turn their heads upon hearing Bridgette's voice, but then they go back to what they were doing, nothing much.

40

(FOLLOW THE LEADER)

Back in Melbourne, Jo-Anne, Scotty's journalist lover, has been working hard tracing his whereabouts. She is determined to rekindle their relationship. She is waiting at the railway station for Billy, who she has discovered is on his way somewhere to meet Scotty.

Billy is due to catch a train that is heading for a strange sounding country town in North Western Victoria, called Steering.

Unknown to her, Jo-Anne has been followed to the station by Milo, under instructions from the Boss to eliminate both her and Scotty.

The Boss had told Milo in their recent meeting in the loft that Jo-Anne's snooping is starting to have an increasing effect on his business interests. He has ordered Milo to contact him when he's taken care of both his targets.

A message comes over the loud speaker at the station, *"All passengers on the train to Steering, and all stops before, are advised that the train has been cancelled and replaced by two coaches. All passengers should proceed to the rear of the station, where you will find the two coaches. Please show your tickets to the stationmaster. One coach is stopping at all stations until it reaches Bendigo, the other will travel express to the end of the line, from stations between Bendigo, Steering and then Mildura."*

Neither Milo nor Billy have any idea where Steering is, and Milo decides to strike up a conversation with Billy who, in his innocent way, looks up at this big man standing to his right, and wonders if he is also confused about which coach to catch. Milo asks, "Where you go?" and Billy tells him Steering.

"Me too," says Milo.

They approach the stationmaster and are about to ask him which bus they are on, when the station master turns to a colleague. "We can get moving once these knuckleheads get on their right coach."

Unfortunately, some people can sometimes get ahead of themselves by thinking that everyone has some idea as to how things in this world work. Well even when you have come across a situation that you have experienced before, the person on the other end of your request can be annoyed with your lack of knowledge. You can hear it in their voice that they are frustrated. Maybe they should be a little more open to your indecision, rather than giving way to their impatience, but then maybe it's because they don't want to be there in the first place.

Deeply insulted, Milo grabs the back of the stationmaster's collar, lifts him off the ground, and forcefully asks him to repeat what he just said. "Now you can give apology to me and my short friend here," he growls in his Ukrainian accent. The stationmaster is terrified at the sheer size of Milo, and sheepishly apologises to them both. Milo puts him down gently, and he points nervously to the second of the two coaches.

Jo-Anne, who was patiently watching the proceedings nearby, climbs aboard the relevant coach, leans her seat back and prepares for a nap. Milo does the same, and leans his seat back, looking forward to some much needed rest. He sets the alarm on his watch, just in case he misses the stop and loses them. He squirms in his seat as the lump in his right side is making him uncomfortable.

He says to Billy, "I hope you don't mind, because of large size I'm going to sit on own, so I can spread out bit more, as one small seat not comfortable for big Milo." He realises immediately he should not have spoken his name aloud, but nobody seems to have noticed.

Billy nods and replies, "You stay here, and I'll go over there. There are many other empty seats available. I think I understand why they the cancelled train."

Jo-Anne observes all this, reflecting that where they sit is unimportant, as long as she can keep an eye on Billy. She's not sure whether or not Billy has seen, or recognised her. Milo lifted the centre armrest and found a more comfortable position to rest in the twin seats.

Billy is also comfortable and ready for the long journey ahead.

41

(PLEASE HOLD MY HAND)

Finally the rain has stopped, the wind is non-existent, but the fog has quickly returned to replace it as a barrier to good visibility. Tiffany and Stephanie are looking after Rhys, who is still a bit drowsy. Luke asks Dianne to find him a long stick so he can deal with the snake, which is still curled up at David's feet.

Luke is about to plan his attack on the snake when Pearl asks him again about baby Stephen. At this point Dianne returns with a branch, giving him an excuse to ignore Pearl's question. Instead, he asks her if she knows where the snake has bitten David.

"Somewhere on his neck, and I think it was only once, but I can't be sure. I saw it slither down to where it is now. It's been there ever since."

Luke guesses it's probably been a couple of hours since they all went down the tree into the car, and because neither he nor Pearl has been able to find a pulse, he wonders if David could be dead. He knows he will have to deal with the snake before he can get David out of the car. Guessing how difficult that's going to be, he decides to fetch Ron to help him.

Luke told Dianne and Stephanie earlier the good news about finding Ron alive, and they had both wept with relief. He says to them now that he hopes he can fetch Ron to help get David out of the car.

Then he stops abruptly and says, "Oh shit, that's right."

"What?" says Dianne anxiously?

"The bridge is broken in two so there's no way I can get to Ron, and he can't get to us unless we wait for the river to go down, and that could be another hour. And we can't forget about Bridgette and the baby, bloody hell, where the hell can they be? This is ridiculous. It's about five in the morning, there's about another two hours to go before Sunrise just before seven am, and we can't see anything, and I'm stuffed again."

Dianne asks him to sit and asks how do you know when the sun comes up? Oh I just know shit... shit... sorry didn't mean to say that, as Tiffany comes over to console him. He pushes her away, telling her he just wants to be left alone to think. Dianne tells Tiffany, "Let's go over here with Stephanie and Rhys, to see if we can think of what to do."

Tiffany feels rebuffed, but realises how shattered Luke must feel. Tiffany has feelings towards him more now than she had during the night, because of what he has done for them.

He says in a tired voice, "Do we wait for the river to subside or what?"

She doesn't reply, but turns and follows Dianne to where the children are. Stephanie and Rhys are talking about how older people are always arguing, and Tiffany asks Rhys grumpily to explain their conversation.

"Mind your own business, bi..." Before he has a chance

to finish, Dianne puts her hand over his mouth, making Rhys realise he's with people he doesn't know well enough to be his normal abusive self. Obviously he still has a hatred for Tiffany.

Tiffany taunts him sarcastically in return as if the last few hours never existed. "Rhys has got a girlfriend."

He is about to lash out when Dianne intervenes, telling them both to grow up. "This isn't helping us get out of here, so I'm asking you both please, whatever it is that you two have against each other, this is neither the time nor place, so shut up."

Neither takes any notice. "Wish you were still asleep," Tiffany yells at Rhys.

"I wish you were dead, you bitch."

Shocked at this vicious bickering, Dianne grabs Stephanie and returns to Luke. "We're heading towards the bridge. As far as I'm concerned, those two can stay where they are. I'm not having them behave like they are in front of Stephanie. It's a bloody disgrace."

Luke gets to his feet, and the three of them start walking back to the smaller bridge, while Tiffany and Rhys continue their verbal stoush at each other in the background.

Suddenly they stop, realising they don't want to be stranded in all this fog with dangerous animals around, and run to catch up with the other three. Dianne tells them not to say a word, and Luke orders Rhys up the front with him, then tells Tiffany to walk behind with Diane and Stephanie.

Tiffany is about to say something when Luke interrupts, "If you or Rhys so much as say one word, I will make sure you regret it, that clear? I don't need this shit, so shut the fuck up." He stares menacingly at both of them, reinforcing his words, mindful that it was probably the second time he has said that word in all his life. But he realises sometimes you have to, especially for those that need that sort of aggressive jolt. They drop their heads and do as they're told, but Stephanie has a shocked look of bewilderment, as this is the second time in as many hours she has heard that word.

After the way Luke has said it, she now knows the difference, compared to how it is used by some of the other students at school, who only say it to act tough.

Tiffany is hesitant to object to his demands, and feels compelled to take his advice.

Luke continues walking slowly, avoiding as best he can all of the rocks in their path, when the moon appears suddenly from behind a break in the fog, illuminating a group of longhorn bulls and other animals about ten metres ahead of them. The animals show little interest, all is still, and quiet again, as the moon disappears.

As the fog thickens, Luke tells the others to stay where they are, and climbs down the bank to the river's edge. He goes into the water to see how deep it is.

Up ahead, Ron has recovered, except for bruised ribs and an absence of pants. Thankfully he is wearing boxers.

The temperature is quite mild, so he doesn't feel cold, but he notices the fog thickening in the river. He stands up and calls out quietly, hoping someone is close enough to hear him. Luke stops, listens and looks around, thinking he heard something. He waits until he hears it again, and calls back quietly also, but not loud enough to spook the nearby bulls. "Stay where you are, Ron, if that's you, but keep it down, there are bulls around. I've got four others with me."

"Okay," answers Ron more quietly.

Luke continues to gauge the level of the river and decides it is shallow enough for a crossing. He heads back to the others, but has difficulty initially in finding them in the thick fog.

When he locates them, he says, "I've found a way to get to the other side of the river where Ron is. It's only a couple of feet deep. It'll take us a minute or two to cross as the current has slowed right down. Hold hands in pairs and take it slowly, there's a lot of shit in the bottom of the river." Stephanie giggles at the swear word from Luke. "Wave your free arms in front of you, in case there are any branches, okay?"

Stephanie whimpers in disgust and walks close to Luke after being hit by some dead animal, and the fog seems to thicken still further. Rhys says in an awed voice, "This is scary stuff, like out of a movie or something."

Stephanie responds, "Wait till you hear what you missed while you were asleep, you'll be glad you slept through it all, especially getting washed down the river, trapped in your car."

"How did you get into the car after the accident?"

"We climbed down a branch from the top of the bridge, but that's probably when the snake got into the car at the same time. We were too busy with the rain and the climb to notice it. We all got in the car except for Luke, and when we got washed down river, he found us and got us out."

Rhys shows disappointment at missing the hairy ride, but Tiffany, as usual, springs a surprise statement to further annoy Rhys, "knowing you, you would have shit yourself, you weasel."

Luke turns angrily and tells Tiffany to knock it off, or else.

Tiffany, realising she has again spoken out of turn, stands quite still without saying another word. But Luke could see on her face there could be more angst coming from Tiffany unless someone else like Dianne could help him put her in her place.

Together they might be able to bring an end to all this unknown anger that Luke somehow thinks has got something to do with her being hurt, or bullied in some way, like he's experienced.

By the expression of confusion on his face and a fondness he has for her, maybe sooner rather than later, all will be revealed.

Arriving at the embankment Luke calls out to Ron, who responds from nearby. Luke wades to the river's edge and scales the bank, followed by the rest of them.

When Dianne and Stephanie reach Ron, its hugs all around as Ron winces from the squeeze. Luke notices Tiffany and Rhys looking distraught and comforts them about their own parents.

Dianne says, "Oh my god, I forgot to get your pants from the roof." Dianne finishes by taunting Ron for his lack of trousers.

"Don't worry yourself, I'll get them when we go back to get their parents, okay."

Dianne then comes over to join Luke in consoling Tiffany and Rhys. Just then, a flicker of hope showed on Tiffany's face as she looked across at Luke, for whatever reason, she found strength in him.

Then Luke asks Ron, "I'll need your help in getting Tiffany and Rhys's parents from their car down the river." With that Luke and Ron head back through the thick fog, climbing down the bank and into the river, where Luke warns Ron about floating debris and overhead branches.

As they stumble along the riverbed, ever mindful of the steps they are taking, sloshing into the water, Luke gives Ron the lowdown on what has happened since he was thrown from the prime mover. Ron listens intently and asks, "So you haven't been able to find Bridgette or Stephen, then?"

"No, I've looked everywhere. For some reason I haven't seen hide or hair of either of them."

"Sounds like I've missed out on a fairly eventful evening then, where the bloody hell could she be for god's sake, this is very disturbing" says Ron.

"Yeah, pretty much so, I'm hearing ya, we need to find Bridgette and Stephen sooner rather than later."

After some time, they reach the smaller bridge.

"It's only about another five more minutes from here," says Luke. "But there are some dangerous looking bulls up top, so let's stay in the river. The car's on the edge of the river, so it shouldn't be too hard to find. Oh yeah, sorry, I forgot to tell you, we can't get them out 'til we get rid of the snake. It's curled up near David's feet."

"What snake? Great, that's all I need. I'm afraid of snakes. Jesus, bulls and snakes, what else haven't you told me, son? I guess we'll have to deal with the snake first."

"Not necessarily. If we can open the door and pull them out quietly, the snake might just slither away or stay asleep, like it was when we left the car about an hour ago." As he says this the car looms out of the fog. "Great, here we are."

As they move closer to the car, Ron starts to become a bit nervy by the apprehensive expression on his face. Snakes are not part of his lifestyle.

Luke gets to the car, and he leans over into the now open window, to describe to Ron what he can see on the inside of the vehicle. "Now the snake should be... oh shit."

"What *Oh shit*?"

Luke replies hesitantly... it's gone."

"Shit," panics Ron, "where's the bloody thing gone? Thank God we've just had a break in the fog and the moon's full, so we can see what we're doing." Ron looks around here and there for the snake. Luke replied "I'll go round the other side and see if I can spot it. Maybe Pearl will know what's happened to it."

Both men walk slowly round the car to the driver's side, where Luke opens the door and they peer nervously into the interior. There is a muffled mumble from Pearl, who is slumped half under David, who doesn't seem to have moved since Luke had left earlier.

Ron asks Pearl if she was awake then follows up with, "Where's the snake, Pearl?"

Pearl was still clearly in a daze but lucid enough to respond. "What snake?" She's clearly in another world.

"You know, the…"

"Oh, sorry, that's right. It started moving a while ago. It came up David's body near my shoulder then over the left side of my face, I just froze. It's probably gone now."

"Hope so," Ron interrupts.

Luke asks, "Did that all happen after I left you here?"

"Yes, I must have nodded off, is there any news, Luke? You know, Stephen?"

"No, I'm sorry, Pearl. I've looked everywhere I could think of, but no sign yet. I've got Dianne's husband, Ron, with me. We're going to get you and David out of the car, and back to the bridge with the others. Then we'll wait till the sun comes up, okay?"

"Hello Pearl."

"Hi Ron some night, hey, are all your family safe?"

"No, we're still looking for one of my daughters, Bridgette. When we get you both back to the bridge, Luke and I will go looking for your baby Stephen and Bridgette."

"Okay," says Luke, "let's get David out of here, Pearl."

Luke and Ron grab hold of David's arms, and, after a

great deal of pulling and heaving, and cursing quietly from Ron's strained and aching body, they get the top part of his limp form out of the car, and they all collapse onto the ground. More straining effort finally gets him onto the bank. Neither has genuinely confronted the possibility they are dealing with a corpse.

Despite this, they exchange wry grins as Ron winces in pain again before they both get Pearl out.

Luke asks, "are you sure you can put up with this, you don't sound that good."

Ron being Ron just grunts, makes a weakened motion with his good arm and quietly speaks without Pearl hearing, "Let's get this over with before I can't do any more."

She hides her embarrassment by joking about her weight, which is even greater than David's.

Ron says comfortingly, "Don't worry about it, Pearl. My wife, Dianne, had the same concerns. Let's just get you out of here, and we can see how David's going. Now lift up your arms."

Luke and Ron grab an arm each, but it's a struggle even to move her. Ron asks, "Can you push with either or both your feet on the steering wheel, or maybe the gearstick first, then the steering wheel? This will give us a better grip on you. Right, on three, push up on your right leg and we'll pull at the same time. Okay, one, two, three, *go*, push hard... that's it, there we go, got you now, keep pushing your feet against the seat."

While this is going on, Luke is quietly relieved that, finally, someone else is making the decisions and dictating the action.

Finally, Pearl's body emerges from the confines of the car, and the three of them collapse on the bank.

Unfortunately Pearl lands slightly on Ron's body and

again he winces in pain, but he is thankful the worst is over... he hopes.

"I'm glad that's over, boys, thanks for that. Now can we check on David?"

Luke interrupts, not wanting her to see David if he's dead, "Sure, Pearl, Ron and I'll do that. You need to rest a bit, because you haven't moved a lot since the accident, and you might struggle walking back to the bridge."

Ron says, "Well, we've got two options here. First we can leave him here or..."

"No, please, we can't do that," Pearl begs, fighting back the tears. "Can't we take him with us, somehow?"

Ron says, "Well, that's the second choice, but I'm not sure how far Luke and I could carry him with the terrain and all. Besides, I don't think I'm up to it at all, with this beaten body of mine."

Luke adds, "There are still those bulls out there, and it took us about twenty minutes to get here. So it would take us twice that at least, then we've still got to find the kids."

Ron backs him up, "Sorry, Pearl, but I think it's better to leave David here 'til the sunrises. It's not long now, according to Luke, before we could hopefully be rescued. I don't want to sound heartless, but it's not as if he's going anywhere."

Luke adds, "Besides we need to get you back to Tiffany and Rhys. They could do with some parenting right now, if you know what I mean."

She sniffs, "You're right, I know. Since Stephens's birth and what's been going on with both of them, sometimes too many things happen at the same time. We, or I should say, *I* have struggled with all of this lately, and I haven't any answers and I don't even know what questions I should be asking, to help me through whatever it is. I'm just void of anything like I'm almost numb... nothing." Then she remembers where she is and says, "Oh I'm sorry about that, for going off with the fairies... where were we? Oh that's right. It just seems hard leaving him here alone. Maybe I should stay with him."

"No, Pearl, let's go and just take it slow, okay?"

Before leaving, they make David's limp form as comfortable as possible on the bank. Nobody wants to check for a pulse and there seems to be shallow breathing coming from him.

Struggling along, Pearl soon realises how hard it would have been to carry David over the rough terrain.

As they proceed, they hear mooing from the cows on the far bank. Luke is thinking back to the trauma inside the SUV, and reflects that once he's out of this mess, he's got a life to look forward to without constant bullying and harassment. Luke has an expression of something showing the feeling of relief, as well as a more relaxed demeanour that brings a wry smile to a somewhat previous expressionless face. Luke knows everyone has problems, but until now he was more concerned about helping others.

Everything else that's happened so far brings a slight grin as he turns back to look where he is going.

Ron looks across at him, "You okay, son?"

"Yeah, I'm fine."

"You looked like you're in another world."

He nods absently, "Yeah, hopefully it's a much better one." Ron and Pearl look at each other curiously, wondering where that came from.

After what seemed like a marathon in getting Pearl back to the others on the embankment, they finally reach the spot where they left Dianne and the three children, and Luke calls out quietly to get a fix on where they are. When they emerge from the fog, Pearl hugs Rhys and Tiffany, and a still wincing Ron enjoys another gentle hug from Dianne and Stephanie.

Luke stands off to one side, glad to be free of any involvement for a moment. But he still can't help wondering what it must be like to be part of an ordinary, or a less dysfunctional, loving family.

Ron says to Dianne, "It's about time Luke and I went to look for the two children," and, turning to Pearl, he adds, "We'll do the very best we can. I promise you that." Turning to Luke, he says, c'mon, mate, let's go and do what we can. I know it'll be that much easier once the sun comes up, but as you well know, time is not on our side."

Luke asks, "Do you want to do a side each, or should we stay together? There's not much water left in the river, so it's just the fog we've got to worry about."

"What's on your mind, Luke?" I get the impression you've been in control pretty much most of the night, so go with your gut, son, and let's keep doing what you've been doing, okay?"

"Okay then, let's go this way and we'll see... *or not with this bloody fog...* what happens next."

42

(MORNING)

As the fog thickens, Bridgette leans gently against the glass window in the door. Having exhausted all efforts to raise someone with her screaming and singing, she slumps into the seat and drifts off once more into half-sleep, while remaining still vaguely aware of the low volume of music on the radio. She has given up trying to make contact with anyone at the radio station, via the phone. After hearing the sun will be up in a couple of hours, she muses that this should make her discovery easier for anybody searching for her.

As she is in the main section of the prime mover that runs on batteries of a twenty-four volt system, it enables her to have the radio on, and allows a lot more power for the bigger phone on the dash. Because the prime mover has a booster on the phone this will enable her to call anyone she likes, given the phone has a better signal than an ordinary mobile.

"Goooooood Morning," Michael's voice tries to emulate the late Robin Williams from the movie *'Good Morning Vietnam.'*

*"It's **ten past six** here on CRAZY F.M., Robbie and I have been on air since six last night. Our night jock has the dreaded lurgy, so we've been standing in for him. We've been focusing on what's been going on around the district in the wake of the terrible floods we've been experiencing. Wayne from the S.E.S joins us again from the command centre. Hello, Wayne."*

"Yes, hello and good morning, Michael."

"For those just joining us this morning, is there any news to report on what happened overnight, Wayne?"

"Most of the district is underwater, and there's still a few people left over from those rescued from properties around the area. At this stage, Michael, there's not much more to report arising out of the last hour. I'm hoping everything stays quiet until the sun comes up in about an hour."

"Well, that's good to hear, Wayne. Have there been any severe animal losses around the district that you're aware of?"

"Yes, quite a lot of the animals on various properties have perished unfortunately. There are a number of sheep and horses amongst the animals that are missing. So over the next few days, there will be a separate focus on retrieving them. Depending on the condition of the dead ones, they'll probably be taken to the abattoir, if that's a feasible option, or we may have to dispose of them in some other way. I'm sure the agricultural guys from the shire offices will deal with that as they see fit."

"Okay Wayne, that all sounds a bit grim. I'll talk with you in another hour, and let's hope it remains quiet as you say. See ya, Wayne."

"Goodbye Michael."

"Well that's the latest news, folks, we won't know what the extent of the damage is for another hour come sunup. So for now, we'll just keep moving along with music, unless someone wants to ring in to tell us how they survived last night."

. . .

BRIDGETTE IS sound asleep as the fog continues to thicken around her, and the surrounding area.

For anyone on foot, it's one step at a time.

43

(WEATHER, WILL IT OR WON'T IT)

Without warning, the weather pattern changes as a small cell rapidly develops into a full-blown storm, and it is guaranteed to wreak havoc as it deepens.

Dr. Walter Ahern, from the Weather Services, arrives at work at his office in Melbourne, and climbs the two flights of stairs to his office.

In the last forty years, he has never once taken the lift, even when he's called to the seventh floor for meetings.

Arriving at his desk, he turns on all his computers and other relevant electrical equipment, and then removes his jacket. The temperature inside head office is quite cool, compared to the humid conditions outside on Queen Street, in the middle of the city where the Weather Service offices are located.

Walter brings up the radar with rainfall figures for the past twenty-four hours, and is shocked to learn of their immensity, particularly since yesterday's forecast predicted only half that amount. He browses over material dealing with the storms that passed over the Steering district overnight, and, from the information in front of him, concludes that the worst is over.

He goes back over yesterday's forecast to see where they might have missed something which could have foretold of the flooding that has inundated the Steering district.

To his surprise, he notices a new cell developing, and, realising its potential for further havoc, calls the command centre immediately.

Wayne answers his call. "Weather room, Wayne speaking, I'm the head of the S.E.S. here in the Steering district."

"Dr. Walter Ahern here from the Weather Services head office in Melbourne. I was hoping to talk with one of the weather staff, who could let me know what's been happening in the Steering area overnight please. I'm also calling about a cell that has just developed on the Western side of Steering. Have you spotted that as well, Wayne?"

"Yes, I saw it about five minutes ago, and the weather people don't remember seeing it on the current forecasts, so they're doing the calculations to figure out why it's turned up, and what it's going to do over the rest of the day if they can, Doctor Ahern."

Wayne's voice becomes a little strained from the pressure he and the weather people are under, especially now with this new cell.

"As you can imagine, things have been pretty hectic overnight, and this new cell isn't going to help. We have been using the local radio station to broadcast weather reports throughout the night, and I was just about to call them when you rang."

"Okay then, please let them know if they need my help,

I'll be right here in my office looking into it, as well as checking on what happened last night. Can anybody help me with that, Wayne?"

Wayne can hear what sounds like Dr Ahern typing on his computer. Wayne would very much like to get off the phone, but out of respect for Dr. Ahern, he bites his tongue, goes through the motions, and hopes this call finishes sooner rather than later. "Well I guess I can, but I'm a bit pre-occupied with this latest change. Okay if I fill you in later, Doctor Ahern?"

"Sure, in the meantime I'll do my own research. Okay, bye."

As the good doctor hangs up, he is quite perplexed about what happened last night, and is disturbed about why this new cell turned up. He begins to check out what rain fell and finds that the cell is not only a big one, but another slow moving one. That is of great concern as all the rivers run north over that area, from the Great Dividing Ranges back towards Mildura, on the Victorian and New South Wales border.

Wayne's phone rings again as soon as he puts it down.

"Robbie here from CRAZY F.M., is that you, Wayne?"

"Yes, that's me. That's weird. I was just about to ring you guys. Something's developing, and we may need to put out another warning. There's another storm brewing from the west, and going by the way it's forming, it looks like it could be quite dangerous over the next hour or so. When I know what it's going to do and when, I'll ring you back with an update, if that's okay with you, Robbie?"

Robbie goes on air while Michael catches up on a few zzzzzz." Thanks Wayne, we'll talk soon. That was Wayne at the command centre on the phone. There's another storm on the way, and they'll get back to us when they know more. We'll keep playing music till he phones us back."

44

(A BLOKE CAN TAKE ONLY SO MUCH)

Luke and Ron are standing on the top edge of the western bank of the river, trying to decide how they are going to work their way through the thick fog. Unexpectedly the wind picks up, carrying away wisps of fog as it strengthens.

They exchange worried glances – as they both suspect something new is on its way. Luke says, "I don't like the feel of this. The last time the fog disappeared, it bloody poured rain again. Christ," he screams, catching Ron off guard. "What did I do to deserve this? And now this bloody rain again, just when I'm free of my bloody brothers. I was the one that suffered at the hands of my gutless brothers. Not the other way around, Shit, I wish I was dead."

Ron suddenly realises why Luke has been acting strangely, "I know this is rough, son, but maybe together we can get through it. By morning you'll look back over all this and you'll be a stronger man because of what you've been through." Luke looks at Ron, wondering why he couldn't have had someone like him to guide him through his troubled childhood. Maybe he's finally found a friend he can turn to.

"Also, at night we all have heightened emotions. We don't generally feel them as we're usually asleep. But at times like this we've got each other to get us through it. If you were on your own, it would be very different. But I'm here with you, son." Then his face breaks into a grin, "But it's only because you know your way around better than I do." Luke grins despite feeling sad, as Ron continues, "I need your help to find my daughter and the baby... what's his name again?"

Luke mumbles, "Bloody Stephen."

Ron was thinking if he could get Luke to say the baby's name again, it would change his thinking, and get him to return his focus to the job at hand. So he pretends he doesn't hear. "Bloody who?"

Luke begins shouting, "Stephen. That's the baby's bloody name, Stephen."

Ron is about to reply, when something goes plop on top of his head. It's either bird shit or something else that's wet. Then, whatever it is, hits again, and again.

"Oh, Christ, no I think it is that rain again. What are we going to do? There's nowhere for all of us to shelter if it's going to be another storm like the last one. Maybe we should head back to the car. Although Pearl doesn't look like she could manage another trip like that again. Do you know where your car finished up?"

"No I don't. It could be anywhere by now, given what happened to Pearl's car." Luke doesn't mention the bloody mess still sitting in the front seats of his car.

"And you've no idea where the prime mover is either, or the trailer. Who knows where that went...?"

"Well if it's empty and accessible, we might be able to hide in it, if it's safe from flooding."

"Let's go and have a look around the other end, where the accident happened, and I guess we'll see what we see."

They climb down the bank and begin to walk along the riverbed as the rain increases into a deafening, torrential downpour. They both cringe at the pounding on their heads, and are forced to squint to make out what's ahead of them.

Luke, who is leading the way, has his hands out in front of him to avoid walking into some unseen obstacle. Then he touches something wet and slippery. "Stop," he turns around and calls out quietly to Ron, who isn't expecting it, and nearly knocks Luke over. This makes Luke stumble into the animal in front of him, startling it. This causes other movements all around them, and Luke realises they've wandered into the middle of the herd of longhorns and other animals.

Luke yells, "Run to the bank and don't stop. Just keep going."

Once they get there, they scramble up the bank, while in the riverbed below them, the bulls and other animals have started running headlong into the rain, towards the larger of the two bridges.

The two men watch as they stampede into the remains of the bridge, then stumble and bellow in their panic as they begin falling over or knocking into each other.

The noise is undercut by bleating and neighing from other animals from the abattoir. Some attempt to clamber up the slippery banks on either side of the river, but most of them just slide back into those behind them, adding to the chaos.

Ron mutters, "Gee, I hope I don't come back as an

animal, don't know how they cope carrying on like that only to get slaughtered, and finish up on my dining room table." As he speaks, one of the larger bulls rolls back down the bank, knocking over three of the following bulls.

Luke says, "Let's go somewhere safer. Looks like all the mayhem is happening here."

They watch through slight breaks in the downpour, as a number of the bulls and other animals are dragged down the river towards the smaller bridge. There is a sudden blinding flash of lightning, followed instantly by a deafening rumble and roar of thunder.

Several other flashes follow, and their eyes adjust, but not enough to see any sign of the prime mover or trailer, let alone Bridgette or Stephen.

"Doesn't look like we're going anywhere soon," yells Ron.

Luke nods yelling his agreement, "What do you reckon we should do?

"Maybe go back to the women and ride it out."

The defeated looks on both their faces speaks volumes for their plight. What are they going to tell the others now?

THE FOUR WOMEN and Rhys find themselves some limited shelter under a large round tree with long, wide branches, hoping it will protect them from this new storm.

An enormous deafening crack of lightning is seen by all as it flashes across the sky, followed by another noisy, vibrating bang of thunder. As they again try to look skyward, another lightning bolt strikes the very tree they are under, and sends a large branch crashing down towards them, as Luke and Ron arrive just in time to get Tiffany and Stephanie out of the way.

The rest just looked on, shocked at what had just happened, as they were on the other side of the enormously wide tree, and didn't expect anyone, let alone Luke. And they were even more surprised to see Ron, especially Stephanie. Tiffany grabs Luke in a moment of her heightened adrenaline and pulls him towards her. Looking as dishevelled as can be and with her hair flying all over the place, her wet clothes struggling to cling to her soaked body, she then plants a firm kiss on Luke's mouth, while all look on in relief, happy that Luke and Ron arrived just in time.

Stephanie plants one on her Dad's cheek, but not Dianne, who is also caught up in the moment, and does the same to Ron, like Tiffany did to Luke.

Pearl just hugs Rhys and kisses his forehead, as Rhys just stands there looking like a stunned mullet.

The rain continues to fall heavily, both on and around them all, as they stand there watching the continued light show. As it is still quite warm, they all gather around each other in a group hug, thankful for the efforts of a still hurting Ron, and a sombre-feeling Luke.

Luke however is not used to this type of gratitude in his miserable life, except when his mother had praised him with her own special hugs and kisses on his cheeks or forehead. But with Tiffany around, he thinks in a moment of reflection, he could find the time and effort to maybe get used to all this kissing, hugging and love stuff.

45

(YOU'VE BEEN WHERE?)

*W*ith all the satellites and other technology around the world today, stranger things have happened to enable you to get at least one bar on a mobile phone, showing that anyone anywhere could call the emergency services, unfortunately not at this point in time in 2011.

BRIDGETTE AWAKENS FROM ANOTHER MINI-SLEEP, and wipes her eyes, trying to focus once again on the call to the radio station. A small amount of light has begun to filter through the landscape surrounding the river, and she can just make out figures of animals along the banks and in the riverbed. She wonders why the river is so low, given the rain that fell overnight, and what's happening around her now. Luckily the back end of the chassis, of the prime mover is stopping the prime mover from being swept away, as she watches this latest storm outside continue, while she sits inside the protected prime mover.

She hears an engaged signal coming from the phone.

Someone at the radio station must have noticed the line was dead. Bridgette replaces the phone in its cradle, picks it up again and presses the redial button.

It rings as she silently prays someone will answer her call. Miraculously, a female voice comes out of the top earpiece. Bridgette is speechless for a second, just gazing at the phone as a voice says, "Hi, this is Robbie from Crazy F.M., who's calling? Hello, this is Robbie from Crazy F.M."

THERE'S NO RESPONSE, and Robbie is about to hang up when the unmistakeable voice of a child says just two words, "Yes please."

"Hello? What's your name, sweetie, and how old are you?"

"M-my name's Bridgette, and I'm eight years old... and I've been trapped in my dad's prime mover all night. I'm all alone, and I don't know where I am, can you come and get me quickly, please?"

Robbie can't quite take this in.

"Just hold on, Bridgette and I'll put you on to someone else. You can explain to him what has happened and where you might be, okay? Hang on a second."

Robbie bangs violently on the studio window, hurting her hand. Michael is resting his head on the bench in front of him. He looks up, half-asleep and annoyed at being disturbed. Robbie points to Michael's monitor and talks through their connecting line, making him aware of the dramatic nature of the call.

Michael jumps up, realising immediately the importance of the situation. He fumbles to get his headphones on, presses the relevant button on his panel to receive the call, and then he says, *"Hello Bridgette, this is Michael and you're on the radio, so what is happening to you, and where are you?"*

"I've been stuck inside Dad's truck all night on my own, and I don't know where anyone else is... my Mum, Dad, or my sister. I'm frightened. I know we were heading into a town, and I think it's the town called Steering. We were all going to stay at the hotel for the night, but we didn't get that far. I'm glad the sun is starting to shine, but can you come and get me quickly, please? It's raining hard again and I don't want to drown. Please help me."

"Do you know maybe where you are at the moment," Michael asks, still in a daze after being up most of the night. After the relatively drama-free night, he can't quite process the unbelievable story she is telling him. He partly wonders if he is still asleep and having a bad dream.

"What's the last thing you remember, Bridgette? How did you get trapped in your truck?"

"The last thing I remember I was trying to see where we were going. Dad and I were finding it hard to see out the windscreen. It was raining hard... like it is now, and Dad said this is like driving blind, and I think I sort of understand now what he meant. Then we were going over a bridge and we didn't see this car. Dad hit it and it was too late, and that's when I went to sleep... I think."

Michael is more awake now, excited at the thought of what he is being told and concerned about the child. He tries to remain calm and hurriedly says to Bridgette, *"What sort of prime mover is it? What load were you carrying? Do you know that, Bridgette?"*

"It's a new one. Dad bought it last year. It has everything, just like a caravan. But we were going to a hotel 'cos it's a better place to clean up after a long journey. We've even got a shower that pops out at the side."

This brings a smile to Michael and Robbie's faces, as Michael continues, *"What's your Dad's name, Bridgette?"*

"Dad, Oh its Ron, but I remember him going through the front windscreen of the truck."

"Is that Ron Williams? He has a trailer he uses for carting animals." Feeling somewhat emotional, he feels concerned for Ron as he would for anyone in this predicament.

"Yes! That's my dad, and we were carrying bulls with large, long horns, but I don't remember what they were called..."

"Texas longhorn bulls, does that sound right?"

"Yes that's what they call them. There was this mean one in the back someone shot with a dart."

"Do you mean a tranquiliser dart fired from a rifle?"

"Yes, I think so."

"I remember going out with your dad on a couple of trips. He showed me how many drivers don't really know much about driving, and how it's easy to become lazy. Okay, I've got the police on the other line, Bridgette, and they want to know your dad's phone number, so they can call it and while they're talking to you, they can work out where you are. You okay with that, Bridgette?" Michael asks.

"Does that mean you would have to hang up on me? What if they can't make it ring? What would I do then?" Bridgette begins to cry.

"They will be able to as they are part of the emergency services, and they have the technology if there is little or no signal, so it will be okay, okay? Unfortunately, Bridgette, they have to have a connection to be able to locate you through something called a G.P.S."

"What do I do if nobody rings after you hang up on me?"

Michael isn't sure how to answer, so he looks up and his facial expression is enough for Robbie to realise this is something Michael needs help with, and so he passes the call back over to Robbie. "Hello sweetheart, this is Robbie, the lady you spoke to first. I have an idea. What if you stay on the line, and you give us the phone number, and we'll give it to the police. We'll transfer you to another line, and then we can help you work out how to answer their call. This way we can help you press the right button, so you don't get disconnected from either of us, does that sound like a good idea, Bridgette?"

"Yes, I like that idea, when will that happen?"

"When you give us the phone number, we can then pass it on to the police, and then they will call you while we stay on the line, okay, Bridgette?" Robbie's voice is calm and reassuring as she switches off the connection so no-one else can hear the number.

"Yes, the number is zero, four, zero, zero, one, two, three, six, five, four. Did you get it?"

"Zero, four, zero, zero, one, two, three, six, five, four, is that it?" Robbie writes down the number and repeats it back to Bridgette.

"Yes, that's it. I can see it on the phone, it says private."

"Now, it should say 'take call' or something like that, and then answer, okay? Press that button and say, 'Hello, this is Bridgette,' and someone from the police should answer from where they are calling their end."

"Are you sure this will work? I'm scared of losing you, and I'm not sure, and I don't know what to do, can I keep talking to you, Robbie, and I'll wait 'til someone comes to get me, can I do that, please?" Bridgette starts to cry again.

"Listen, sweetheart, we're not going to lose you, I promise you. Now, can you tell me how many others were there in the truck with you, and do you know what happened to them?"

"I don't know. I saw Dad go through the broken front window, but the part of the truck that has the beds and other things in it, where Mummy and Stephanie were...I don't know where they are either. It's gone."

"The reason why I'm asking is if they need urgent medical care, then we need to get to them as quickly as possible. Maybe there are others, like you said, in the other car, and they might need help urgently also. Because you're okay, you are okay, aren't you?"

"Yes, I don't have anything wrong with me."

"Okay then, if you're okay, then we need to get help to the others as quickly as possible, just in case they have really bad injuries, do you understand, Bridgette? It's really important that you answer the call from the police, so we can send help for everyone, and not just for you. Can you do that for your mother, father and sister, please, Bridgette?"

Michael continues to allow listeners to hear what is happening and not music.

BRIDGETTE HAS her finger millimetres away from the answer button, and for a moment hesitates, bringing her hand back to her chest. Then she takes a deep breath, hoping she won't lose Robbie and be alone again.

After what seems like an eternity for all those listening, Bridgette then moves her hand away from her chest and pushes the answer button on the truck phone. And then to her great delight, a brief moment passes before a female voice is heard.

"Hello, is this Bridgette?"

"Yes this is Bridgette, who are you?" There is excitement

and hope in Bridgette's voice, replacing the scared, upset Bridgette.

"My name is Elizabeth and I'm a Senior Constable in the police force, can you hear me okay, Bridgette?"

"Yes I can, Elizabeth."

"You can call me Liz for short, okay? Would you like to say hello to Robbie as she is still on the other line?"

Robbie has a big smile that Bridgette can hear in her voice, even this early in the morning, "Yes, I'm still here, you okay now, Bridgette?"

This has pepped up Bridgette somewhat, and as she shuffles around a bit in her temporary accommodation, she replies with some enthusiasm, "Yes, I'm okay. I'm so glad this worked and I'm feeling better now. I'm very tired though." She yawned.

"So are we," Robbie and Liz say in unison.

"What's going to happen now?" Bridgette asks curiously.

"Well, while we're talking to you on the phone, some people are working out where you are," replies Liz. "Do you know, perhaps, where you have come from today, and where you were heading, if that's at all possible, Bridgette?"

"We were at a farm in... I think, in the south-eastern part of South Australia. We were heading about a couple of hours in the other direction when it started to rain, that's when it got dark. I remember Dad telling us about white lines, cats' eyes and things on posts that I think were red and white, and going over a mountain... and can I ask a question? What's a G.P.S. and how does it work?"

Robbie begins to explain to try and distract the young child and keep her awake. *"A G.P.S. is a location device, and it will help the police find you. Now while you were at school, one of your teachers taught your class about the planets in our solar system."*

"Yes I remember about them and they go round the sun."

"That's right, well this is sort of the same way your mobile phone works, so let's pretend okay Bridgette, for a moment that you are the sun. All the planets are going around the sun... that's you... Now the way this works with your mobile phone is the same where the sun gives off rays. Your mobile phone gives off waves of a different kind. Then when the sun's rays go to Earth they don't bounce off, they create a warm feeling, right? But with the waves from your mobile phone, they are sent too many different satellites around the Earth. Just like the sun and the planets, but when they hit any three satellites around the Earth, the signal bounces off each of them and bounces back to where you are now."

Bridgette feels a little confused by the explanation, but she thinks she understands and tells Robbie so.

"What happens next is at the police centre here in town, because they have your phone number, it's continually sending out signals to these satellites, and they can track where these signals are coming from. Then they locate where the signal bounces back using all three satellites, which are positioned like a triangle around the Earth. You know what a triangle is, don't you?"

"Yes it has two bends at the bottom and one at the top."

"That's right, Bridgette, so thinking about the sun and the planets, where would you be in the triangle?"

Bridgette remains silent for a moment as those listening await her answer with anxious looks upon their faces. Then Bridgette speaks quietly just in case her answer is wrong, "in the middle."

"Well done, Bridgette, that's correct, your teacher will be very proud of you."

Bridgette could hear voices in the background. She

recognises Liz saying, "It looks like the far north-western part of Victoria."

Then another voice that sounds further away says, "We've got the co-ordinates."

Immediately contact is made with the search and rescue squad and the local police station at Steering. When they realise the town is about five to six hours from the city, they alert the air wing to send a helicopter. Elizabeth comes back on the phone, while Robbie and Bridgette are talking about what happened last night.

"Excuse me, Bridgette, this is Liz again. We've located where you are near a town called Steering."

"Yes!! That's where we are. We are in a river and we fell off a bridge called Mack... something, and there was this car coming the other way, and that's when I fell asleep. Do you think it will take long to come and get me? I'm scared I might drown," Bridgette asks urgently.

"I'm afraid it will take about an hour, sweetheart, but we've been in touch with a policeman in Steering, and he's on his way to where you are right now. He'll tell us how we can best rescue you, and your mum, dad, and your sister."

"That's good news, Liz. Can we broadcast on the radio about what's been happening with Bridgette?" asks Robbie.

"Yes, that's fine but don't mention the location. Only that a young girl has been found safe and well, but from all reports, there could be more needing help."

"Will do, thanks Liz. Are you still there, Bridgette?"

"Yes I'm still here." Bridgette is getting tired, her voice is slower than before, after all the excitement with the phone call, and finding out she is to be rescued very soon. She begins to wonder how her parents and sister spent last night, and hopes they are all alive, especially after watching her father go through the windscreen.

"I'll keep this line open for you to talk again to Michael, and you can tell him about what happened to you last night, until the police arrive to rescue you. Is that okay with you?"

"Yes," she whispers, sighing quietly to herself.

"Okay, just hang in there, Bridgette, and Michael will talk with you soon. You're being a very brave little girl."

"MICHAEL SCANLON here on Crazy F.M. and we've been in touch with the police, and they have located a young girl trapped somewhere near Steering. As you have been hearing, we had a call from Bridgette earlier, telling us about her situation, and we were able to get the police involved. They have tracked her down using that wonderful G.P.S. and have located her position. There is a possibility there could be more people trapped where she is.

"We'll keep you updated when we find out who else is in need of help. The police have mounted a rescue operation, and should be at the location in about an hour from now. Let's hope all is well with any other people they find there. Now we still have on the line, eight-year-old Bridgette, and she has asked if she could stay on the line with us until the local policeman arrives. Hi Bridgette, how are you at the moment?"

"I'm feeling frightened still, but I should be alright if you keep talking to me until the policeman arrives."

"Don't worry, sweetheart, we won't lose you. Now do you want to tell us what happened to you last night?"

46

(LOOK AT THAT)

Hearing a continued sound while you sleep allows your mind to play tricks on you. What you believe you're hearing compared to what is actually happening, is so far apart it makes you wonder for a few moments where you are. These sounds do not fully describe where you think you are. Some however are easy to distinguish like raindrops or howling winds, but constant ticking could be construed as a multitude of things.

It could be a clock for example or someone dying for a smoke, but they are not in a position to do so as they begin to click the lighter in a rhythm to that of a clock. Then there's an indicator click when a vehicle's turning or pulling into the kerbside, and then it stops, only to begin again as your mind is wondering what on earth is going on. When you begin to awaken from your slumber, it's not until the bus stops outside the railway station, which you finally realise that you're even on a bus, arriving in the town of Steering.

~

MILO WAKES FROM A DEEP SLEEP, initially disoriented by the unfamiliar surrounds of the coach. Then he realises, from spotting a shop sign the coach is passing, that this must be the town of Steering. He sees Billy and Jo-Anne, still asleep in their seats, as the coach pulls into the kerbside.

Milo and a couple of the other passengers stand up and go to the front of the coach, stepping down into the warmth of the morning. As usual Milo's sheer size attracts a few stares, accentuated when he stretches luxuriantly and exposing his midriff. Luckily the others are in front of him, and they are unable to see what he is carrying, tucked firmly in the back between his pants and his large bottom.

Realising he's being laughed at, Milo attempts to cover his protruding waistline, and then approaches the driver to ask where the men's room is. Before he sets off in the direction indicated, he turns in time to see Billy and Jo-Anne getting off the coach. He watches Billy going to the side of the bus to retrieve his luggage, while keeping another eye on Jo-Anne.

He doesn't want to lose sight of either of them. Unfortunately, the call of nature is an urgent one, and Milo is obliged to head off to the men's room.

When he returns, everyone, including the coach, has gone, except for a couple of dogs looking for scraps.

"Fuck," he says to himself, when a man driving a horse and cart comes down the road.

The area is covered in wet brown dirt, and has a few shabby looking old buildings around, and apart from a couple of the other passengers who are being picked up in more modern vehicles, the horse and cart is now in front of him, and the town, after all the rain overnight, is completely desolate.

Milo asks if he's seen a young bloke and a pretty girl. "They leave me behind. I go to toilet."

The old man looks at this strange and somewhat large form in front of him and lifts up his hat and scratches his forehead in absolute wonder, thinking what such a person would be doing in Steering. Then the old man replies, "Only a policeman, a young man, and an overdressed woman sitting in the back seat of the police car... why?"

"Was in men's room and them giving me directions before left, I want to thank, but they gone. I do same now. What direction they go in?"

"The copper asked me for directions to the old wooden bridges. Said he was new in town. So I guess that's where they're headed. Mckenzie's bridge, it's not that far. You just take that dirt track off the main road over there, and follow your nose, okay?"

"What is follow nose?"

"Don't worry about it. You'll need to get going if you want to catch them at the bridge."

The cart pulls away with Milo scratching his head, thinking maybe he'd gone back a hundred years. He turns in the direction his informant had indicated. He feels around his back again making sure his insurance is still snug in its position.

EARLIER SCOTTY HAD RECEIVED a call to go to the wooden bridge two kilometres outside of town, to investigate a distress call from an eight-year-old girl trapped in a vehicle in the river. On his way, he had passed the bus station and, to his amazement, spotted Jo-Anne and Billy standing by the side of the road, looking as if they had only just made one another's acquaintance.

He pulled up and said abruptly, "What the bloody hell are you two doing here?"

"Come to see you," grinned Billy. "You were supposed to be picking me up at the railway station? Only the train broke down and..."

"Never mind that now, I'm on an emergency, you'd better both jump in. You can give me your excuse later, Jo-Anne."

As they head west along a slightly wet dirt road, Jo-Anne tries to strike up a conversation with Scotty, and is told in no uncertain terms to be quiet. He is finding it hard not to show his dissatisfaction with her. She looks dishevelled and unattractive, nothing like he remembers her. Jo-Anne tried to explain she hasn't had time to tidy up after the five-hour coach journey, most of which she'd spent with her face squashed up against a window.

As they drive along the winding forest track, Billy remarks, "I've never seen so many trees in my life before. I reckon it'd be good to live here, Scotty."

"Let's see how things pan out over the next couple of months," replies Scotty testily, his mind on other things. "Don't get your hopes up. I've got a big responsibility in this town, Okay? Let us just enjoy our time together, and we'll see what we see."

As Scotty goes around an unexpected sharp corner, he has to skid the car to a sudden stop, causing everyone, especially Jo-Anne, to lurch forward, hitting her forehead on the seat in front of her that Billy is sitting in.

A tree has fallen across the road in front of them and he requests the help of Billy to move it.

As Jo-Anne expresses that she would like to help also, Scotty gives her another vile stare that she interprets as *'stay in the bloody car, woman,'* then says, "Billy and I will deal with this, you stay put."

As they were heading back to the car, Billy notices a family of koalas in a tree and is rendered speechless, his mouth wide open until Scotty says, whilst trying not to smile, "close your mouth, Billy, you'll let the flies in. Then he adds quietly, "there is lots of wildlife here so you better get used to it, Billy. If I let you stay, of course." A brown snake slithers across the dirt track in-between them and the car.

Meanwhile Jo-Anne is looking disconsolate in the back of the car, while she is trying to avoid his nasty glances.

Billy's hurt feelings can't wipe the excited expression from his face. Billy thinks to himself that he couldn't be in a better place on Earth than in the Australian bush, first thing in the morning, with natural bush sounds ringing in his ears.

Suddenly, and quite loudly, a number of kookaburras start laughing, and Billy is stunned at the incredible noise coming from the trees above. He says to Scotty, "Are they kookaburras? Wow... that's just an amazing sound coming from up there."

Scotty just grabs Billy and they head over to move the tree from the roadway, while Jo-Anne is also mesmerised by the real life kookaburra laugh resounding throughout the trees. She sits there with a slight attempt at a smile that appears on her face. *Then the familiar song comes into her head from her primary school days. Laugh kookaburra laugh... thinking what a wonderful place to be.*

By the time Scotty finally reaches the entrance to the bridge, the rain has begun to clear, and the sun is peeking over the horizon.

MEANWHILE, Milo is literally plodding on foot in the same direction, the ground squishing under his feet from then overnight rain as he meanders along this dirt track, in the middle of nowhere, but still a long way behind his prey.

He's fascinated by the sights and sounds of the Australian bush too, and is blissfully ignoring the warning from the man in the cart to watch out for stray animals, as well as any wild ones. Suddenly a large brown snake slithers across the track in front of him. He pulls up with a start. *Probably*, he thinks, *it's out looking for water in the hot environment.*

He hopes he doesn't have too far to go before catching up with the police car, wherever it's heading. He wishes he'd found a cab, but there didn't seem to be any around when he'd left the coach at the station.

As Milo rounds a bend, he is brought to a sudden stop when he sees his first wild kangaroo. A big old grey leaping over a hedge on one side of the dirt road and taking off ahead of Milo.

Startled, Milo reaches for his gun, but quickly realises this is neither the time nor the place for taking pot shots at the local wildlife. Then out of the bushes comes a second, even larger eastern grey.

It stops only a few feet in front of Milo, seemingly mesmerised by the large human. Moments pass as they size up each other, and then come a whole mob of roos of all different shapes and sizes, hopping onto the dirt road.

The original male makes a grunting noise before bouncing off after them. To his right is obviously the mother, with a joey in its pouch. The joey and the mother look at this strange human before them, and then the mother turns her head and follows everyone else. Meanwhile the joey is still struggling to look at Milo, as its head peers around the side of its mother's body, as the mother bounces off into the distance. Milo thinks to himself, *'Good job I live in the city, too many strange creatures here in bush.'*

As Milo rounds another bend, he spots what looks like a police car parked some distance ahead, and moves into the bushes to avoid being seen. Keeping to the side of the path hidden by the forest, he continues slowly towards the police car, noticing a familiar figure in the back seat.

He takes out his revolver while taking care he doesn't stray into the visibility through the car's side view mirror. As he opens the door, Jo-Anne is startled and is about to scream. Being confronted by a large man pointing a revolver in her face is not an everyday occurrence, even for a hardened reporter.

Milo motions to her with one finger to his lips to stay quiet and beckons her out of the car with the revolver. "Where copper gone?" he asks in his guttural voice.

She is about to speak when they hear voices coming from the river. Milo grabs Jo-Anne's arm and frogmarches her towards the voices, warning her again not to make a sound.

SCOTTY AND BILLY are oblivious to what is heading their way and continue to search along the river for an eight-year-old girl.

Slowly, through the trees, the sun comes up over the horizon, bathing everything, including a distant mountain range, in an eerie, luminous glow. This has the effect of burning off the last wisps of fog.

Scotty picks up the sound of voices from the other side

of the river and calls out, "This is the police! Can you make your way across to this side of the river, so I can establish what has happened here?"

A male voice replies, "Will do," and at that moment, the cab of the prime mover, suddenly revealed by the last of the clearing fog, looms into view.

A little girl climbs groggily out of the cab, only a few metres from Scotty and Billy. She runs towards them as the group from the other side of the river scramble up the bank.

Stephanie, Dianne and Ron are wreathed in smiles, mixed with tears of relief, as they are reunited with Bridgette. Dianne finally asks, "My little angel, where've you been all this time?"

"I've been in the front of the truck ever since Dad just disappeared through the windscreen, and everything went black. When I woke up, I could hear someone talking on the phone, but they couldn't hear me for ages and ages, and I went to sleep again. Then a nice lady talked to me and she got the police, and they talked to me as well. And then he came." She turns to point to Scotty.

They are all standing around listening to Bridgette's description of what happened to her last night, when a respectful cough is heard behind them. It is the type that is usually made when someone wants to get your attention.

They all turn simultaneously to see who it is...

47

(OH NO, NOT AGAIN)

Every morning, for as long as they could both remember, their rooster awakens the farmer and his wife from their slumber. Not for one minute do they ever seriously consider getting rid of the noisy fowl. Yet, every morning, their first conversation canvasses the option.

"I think it's about time we got rid of that rooster," mumbles Katherine.

"What?" says John, rolling seductively to her side of the bed with his early morning erection signalling his intentions?

"Was it me, or did it rain heavily last night?" He asks.

"I didn't know you could hear all that rain. With your snoring, it's a wonder I got any sleep at all last night." She starts singing. "It's raining, it's pouring, and the old man's snoring."

"At least I don't sound like a freight train."

Ziggy, their blue heeler makes a whimpering noise outside the bedroom door, as the pair of them begins to make their customary exchange of well-seasoned, early morning, affectionate abuse.

"You're a bitch."

"You're a bastard."

"Bellyache."

"Charlatan."

"Whinger."

"Shark."

"Swindler."

"Crook."

"Fussy boots."

"Double dealer."

"Gripe."

"What's a gripe?" asks Katherine.

"It's someone who complains about something in a persistent irritating way, like you do, you fake."

"Moaner."

"Imposter."

"Phony."

"Grump."

"Pretender."

"Fusspot."

"Quack."

"Mongrel... and nag."

"God, I love it when you talk dirty to me," she chuckles.

Ziggy has heard all this before, and knows only too well what it leads to, and as the noise gets louder and louder, he heads discreetly into the yard, out of hearing range.

Sometime later, when the commotion has finally died down, Ziggy sticks his head though the back door, checking to see if they've made it to the kitchen for breakfast yet.

Both of them are sitting at the table, stark naked, munching on cornflakes. John notices Ziggy's head, gives him a whimsical look and says, "What's wrong with you,

Ziggy, cat got your tongue? Looking for some tucker, are you?"

With that, Ziggy slowly enters the kitchen, tail between his back legs, and sneaks across to his brimming food bowl. He gets stuck in, knowing they'll soon be off for their morning chores, involving exercise for him around the property.

John stands to leave the table and turns to Katherine. "I reckon I'll go and have a look over by Mckenzie's bridge. There was a noise coming from there last night. Did you not hear it?"

He heads for the door, before quickly returning to take his empty bowl over to the sink and cleaning it, mindful of the earful of abuse he'd cop if he'd left it on the table, or in the sink for her to wash. "If there's nothing there, I'll come back and clean out the fireplace. The nights are getting colder. I should get some fresh logs for the fire tonight too." He puts his rifle over his shoulder, like he's done every morning for the thirty odd years they've been living there.

He kisses his wife on the cheek, and grabs her on the bum, before collecting a bag of rubbish to put in the bin on his way to the river. He whistles to Ziggy to join him on the journey across the field, then to the river and bridges a few hundred meters away. Ziggy jumps up, knowing they're off somewhere more interesting than the kitchen.

"Forgotten something?" Katherine asks, looking him up and down.

He returns her cursory examination and realises, to his amusement, what was missing, saying, "Whose gunna care that I'm is still naked?"

She gives him a look, and disgruntled, he props the rifle against the table and goes to the bedroom to get dressed.

Once dressed, he then strolls across the field, Ziggy at

his side, bounding here and there with all the energy of a recently acquired freedom.

John notices the last wisps of the slow burning fog, disappearing with the early morning sun. By the time he reaches the river, it will be gone completely, and he'll be able investigate what he heard last night, if anything.

The ground on the other side of the fence is coming into view, when John stops suddenly. He thinks he's heard the sound of a cow mooing. Ziggy's ears prick up and he growls softly. John calls him to heel, patting him, "Let's wait and see if we hear that again."

At that instant, the unmistakeable sounds of sheep and horses come from the same direction as the cow, bringing a frown to John's face. Ziggy tilts his head sideways, as if to say, *'what was that?'* John grins at his dog, wondering if he's ever heard these sorts of animal noises before.

Wondering where they've come from, he remembers the news on the radio last night about the flooding of the abattoir. He wonders how many animals there are. He stands up slowly, as his bones creak and crack. He moves slowly to the wooden fence and is shocked to find so many animals scattered around and in the river.

Something catches his attention... a piece of red cloth hanging on the horn of one of the bulls on the opposite bank.

Ziggy is making strange whining noises.

As he nears the bridge, he notices its timbers leaning at an odd angle. The remains of what looks like a major accident are scattered around and, just as he's taking this in, he sees a group of people sitting at the river's edge at the bottom of the bank. He is about to call out to them when he hears more voices coming from the other side of the river.

Someone yells, "Don't shoot, please, don't shoot."

John walks quietly along the fence line towards the bridge, stepping over broken timbers while making sure Ziggy stays close by.

He walks onto the remains of the bridge, coming to where a truck has gone through the side barrier, and down over the edge. He still can't make out what's going on with the group of people, and stands still for a moment, listening hard.

As he nears the end of the bridge, he hears a voice speaking with what sounds like a foreign accent. The voice is telling someone in broken English, "Boss didn't like you killing nephew, sent me to take care. For this... you must die. Come here, I put you from your misery. Sit down. Look other way. Don't need to see your face when I shoot."

Upon hearing this, John slowly walks towards the voice, and is shocked to see a larger than life monster before him. John thinks to himself, *'This guy must be at least...seven feet tall. Have I got any ammo in the rifle?'* John stops dead in his tracks, unsure of his next move when someone outside the group screams, "Shoot him!"

Awkwardly Milo swings around, stumbling and catching John off guard. Seizing her opportunity, Jo-Anne twists out of the grip Milo still has on her, and drops to the ground.

Milo is about to put a bullet into John before the farmer has a chance to use his rifle, when Milo senses something in his groin area. His head recoils backwards, screaming in pain as the sensation intensifies. He then looks down numbly and sees Ziggy in mid-air, hanging off a large chunk of his trousers and what's inside them. John accidently falls backwards and consequently fires the rifle, hitting Milo in the stomach. The shot just misses Ziggy's head as the giant topples backwards, Ziggy still hanging grimly on.

Milo is slumped on the ground unconscious, from either the rifle wound or hitting his head.

John orders Ziggy to let go and return to his side as Jo-Anne bends down to pat him. Scotty approaches John, asking him if he's okay and taking charge of his rifle. As the remainder of the group crowds around, emergency vehicles speed down the dirt track, with dust flying everywhere, to Mckenzie's bridge, their sirens wailing.

As the police sergeant climbs out of his car and approaches him with a bemused look on his weathered face, Scotty says, "I'll explain over a drink later, okay Sarg?"

48

(I THINK I'LL GO FOR A WALK)

Some women have problems after giving birth. It can last for weeks, perhaps even months, and they have no control over their emotions, because of stuff going on inside their body.

You can almost understand why some blokes don't like to hang around while their wives are experiencing these emotional feelings. Both parents should have some education as to the consequences of a difficult birth. Post-natal depression is no picnic.

NOW THAT THE emergency services have arrived and everyone is busy doing their jobs, Billy decides to go for a walk along the river. He doesn't bother telling anyone, even Scotty, because that's the way Billy is. He is motivated to leave after overhearing discussion about a missing baby called Stephen. He likes babies and doesn't think they should be alone with all these animals, or with ginormous trees and men with guns.

Walking along the edge of the riverbed, he finds it

surprisingly low, given the amount of rain Scotty has told him has fallen in the area in the last couple of days, especially overnight. He whistles to himself, he is pleased to be reunited with his copper mate.

He continues to walk carefully along the river, looking for any signs that might lead him to a lost baby, although he has no idea of what those signs could be. He is enjoying the tranquil surroundings, even if the number of dead bodies of the animals he's spotting is a bit disturbing. Some have their bloody insides and guts exposed already, as ravenous birds are enjoying the bonus early morning tucker. Billy has never seen anything like this before, except on television, or in a movie.

The constant squawking from above attracts his attention. It's coming from various birds hovering in the sky or trees, waiting to pounce once he disappears. Soon his stomach starts making those all too familiar rumbling noises. All this eating he's witnessing is making him hungry.

He notices a vehicle up ahead on the edge of the bank with a branch sticking out of its roof. Billy is confused by what he's seeing, and as he approaches the vehicle, he's startled by a large black bird flying up out of the hole in the car's roof.

He jumps backwards in fright and is frozen for a few moments, then says to him-self, "No bird scares me even if it does have a lump of what looks like flesh in its beak."

He hesitates before poking his head over the hole in the roof. There's not much to see, so he goes around the vehicle, peering through the windows, wiping away the storm's accumulation of debris for a better look.

He walks around to the back of the vehicle and stares through the rear window, accidentally bumping his head on it as he tries to see through the gloom of the vehicle. This brings a noise from within, a noise that sounds like the unmistakeable cry of a baby.

He tries to open the back door, but it's locked, so he walks round to the driver's side. He is about to open the front door when he trips over something on the ground. He stands up, checking his head for blood from where he fell.

It's then he realises he has tripped over the body of a man. He steps backwards in fright and trips again, stepping this time into a piece of fresh cow dung. He regains his feet, wiping away the remnants of the cow dung, and checks the body. The increasingly loud and incessant screaming from inside the vehicle makes him aware that the needs of the living take precedence over those of the dead. Wondering why they haven't found the baby before when it was so close by, he removes the key from the ignition and uses it to open the back door.

As he does so, the screaming becomes louder, resonating through the morning stillness. It's loud enough to be heard by the group back at Mckenzie's bridge, and Billy hears a scream, "MY BABY."

It's Pearl, and she can't quite work out where the cries are coming from. So she panics and starts moving around first in one direction, then another, while looking in several directions at the same time.

Billy has had little experience of infants, but he knows enough to realise he should pick this one up and try to comfort it. He leans forward and takes the baby out of the insert of the capsule, wedged into its current location by the force of the accident.

It has become stuck behind the esky bearing its nappies and other belongings, in a position invisible from anywhere else inside the car.

When the car went over the edge of the bridge, after

hitting the semi-trailer, the force of impact released the inner section of Stephen's capsule from its outer shell. Tiffany's unwitting release of the restraining seatbelt allowed the inner section, still carrying Stephen, to fly through the air, before Stephen was released up and out of the inner section. He was momentarily pinned to the roof, before the subsequent gravitational forces inside the vehicle allowed him to fall down into the outer shell, which eventually came to rest, and to be hidden miraculously behind the esky. Before they'd left her father's house, Pearl had given Stephen a sedative to help him sleep during the journey home, and throughout the rest of the night.

This must have left him out to the world, both during and in the aftermath of the accident.

A number of those standing at Mckenzie's bridge attempt to calm Pearl, but she becomes even more frantic waiting for Stephen's crying to start up again. But it doesn't, because Billy has him cradled in his arms. *'Beginner's luck'* thinks Billy and begins rocking Stephen to and fro like he has seen mothers doing. Then a particularly rank smell assails Billy's nostrils. Stephen is clearly in need of an urgent nappy change. *Definitely something for an expert*, he thinks.

Forgetting temporarily about the body, Billy turns and walks back towards the others. The change of rhythm starts Stephen crying again, a wonderful sound for Pearl, and it's getting closer.

Scotty looks around bewildered and is then the first to realise Billy's absence, and he runs in the direction of the crying, with Pearl scampering after him.

The rest of the large group, including the emergency workers who are unsure of quite what is happening, watch in evident delight. Tiffany and Rhys are rooted to the spot until Dianne urges them to join the joyous reunion. Forgetting their customary hostilities, they run to catch up to Pearl, helping her over the difficult terrain.

Just about everybody, particularly Luke, had accepted Stephen had drowned, and had been washed miles away down the river.

As the rest of the group catches up with Pearl and Scotty, they see Billy clutching Stephen in his arms while navigating the riverbed under the partly demolished bridge.

He yells out to Pearl, "Please stay where you are. I'll come to you. It's not safe ground here."

Pearl is in no state to be told to wait, and she races towards Billy, stumbling over a rock and landing on her knees in the riverbed. Scotty tells her to stay where she is and wait for Billy to come to her. Pearl cries out for Stephen and continues to stumble towards him on her knees, with Tiffany and Rhys struggling to hold her back.

Then in frustration, and exhaustion, Tiffany lashes out at her mother, "You speak words of frustration of not being able to get to your precious little baby Stephen, and having missed out on your precious time with him. What about me? Wanting from you and needing your help through this torment, I was going through, not to mention the continued arguments with Rhys. You speak words of hate not hours ago but now you weep, how the hell am I supposed to make sense of all this?" She started sobbing at the sudden loss of her father. "You make me sick and if I ever get out of this mess, I'm gone, you hear me, *gone*." And with that, Tiffany storms back to those that stayed behind.

Scotty says quietly to Billy, "Bring the baby here, mate, and let's reunite Stephen with his mother."

Billy walks forward cautiously, making sure he doesn't

trip, and finally gives the crying baby to Pearl. She hugs his little form to her bosom and croons, "There there, darling, you're back where you belong." She remembers to thank Scotty and Billy and points to the top of the riverbank, saying, "I'd like to go up there so I can breastfeed him. He must be famished, poor little thing, yes you are," she croons as she strokes his head.

Scotty and Billy help Pearl up the bank and find a secluded spot, where she sits down with Stephen in her lap.

Billy makes a comment without realising he could be heard by all those in the river, "this is hard work getting Pearl over here." Scotty apologises to Pearl.

Pearl replies to Billy, saying, "thank you for finding my baby. I'm not offended by your comment."

They arrive at the edge and Pearl is helped to sit down as she places him on her breast, much to Stephen's delight. Billy stands there and scratches his head, curious about what he's witnessing. Scotty grabs him away, telling him, "Listen, mate, I know you don't understand what just happened here. But what's going on is the most natural thing in the world, except that you're not allowed to watch."

They sit and wait for the feeding to finish before they head back to the others, where Scotty says, "I'm going to the vehicle where Billy found the baby. Someone needs to help Pearl and Stephen. Okay, Billy, come and show me where you found Stephen. Let's go."

Later, Scotty and Billy help the Emergency Services retrieve David's body from the river.

Luke continues to console Tiffany and Rhys, whose shock at realising their father is dead, is somehow mixed up with the joy of Stephen's rediscovery, and then they inadvertently come across the vehicle with Nick and Ryan in it.

Tiffany looks at his tattooed body but recognises the vehicle and the distinctive tattoo of a bird of prey, like a hawk, on his neck. All the memories of that fateful night come flooding back, and Tiffany breaks down in tears, and then over a couple of minutes, she tells all to Dianne, Rhys... and Luke.

To Dianne this now makes perfect sense and explains how Tiffany had been acting. Luke on the other hand is both shocked and not surprised that his vile older brother had done this, and is surprised that Tiffany would want anything to do with him. But he is reassured by the way she is clutching and hugging him now.

Tiffany is feeling better having told them about her ordeal of a couple of years ago. This brings a smile to her face and she continues to embrace Luke, and has no intentions of letting go. They all laugh in relief at having survived the night, especially Rhys, who is stunned by his sister's revelations and thinks about changing his attitude towards her, but that only lasts momentarily when he poses a thought from last night.

"When I saw stars in the night sky in between the rain and fog. I was wishing you were gone, but you're still here," he says, with a big smile on his face, as everyone laughs awkwardly.

Ron and the girls embrace each other, while looking around the now clear daylight scene of destruction.

The ambulance and the S.E.S. treat Milo as they scratch their heads at his enormous size.

Not long after that, one of the Emergency Services people goes to tend to the SUV with Nick and Ryan's remains in it. Not far away is Brian's body on the riverbank.

Katherine arrives to comfort her badly shaken husband.

Despite his familiarity with firearms, John doesn't shoot humans every day.

Jo-Anne sits in the police car and is still in shock, while all around them others tend to the dead humans and animals.

As Luke stands, taking it all in, especially Tiffany, a stretcher goes past him and as he turns to see who is on it. He is somewhat surprised and emotional. He now realises they had found the one brother he thought, would have supported him through his family turmoil over the years. It was not to be, but given the remorseful expression on Rick's face, and the gesture of a handshake he could not refuse, things might be looking better for the two remaining brothers after all.

Rick is about to be placed into the back of an ambulance on a stretcher as he passes Luke. He raises an arm in a gesture of apology and hope. Luke feels the tears start to flow, as the intense emotions of the past twenty-four hours hit home.

He nods at Rick and says, "I'll see you soon."

As the doors of the ambulance close, everyone gathers around Luke as a final gesture of thanks, and he receives a kiss on the cheek from Tiffany.

Luke looks across the sundrenched flooded landscape before him, and wonders what the future will bring...

EPILOGUE

After most of the dead and injured had been taken away, Luke is enjoying some quiet time with Tiffany, talking about the events of the evening. He turns, looking at her directly, and with compassion in his voice, says, "from your affection for me... which I return equally to you, I am a little bit troubled as to how to... or whether I should suggest to you about reconciling with your..."

However, before he has a chance to finish what he wants to convey to her with only genuine affection, she purses her lips in frustration and grits her teeth as she lets go of his hands, and begins to back away from him.

"I don't want anything to do with her, especially after last night, so if you really have any thoughts for me and what might happen to us after today, then don't go there, please."

Although Luke can see a determination not only in her manner but her expression as well, similar to last night, he also senses maybe there might be a glimmer of remorse somewhere in the far reaches of her mind, to at least listen to reason about what her mother is possibly going through.

"Can I at least ask her to come over and maybe you could both apologise to each other, so you and your mother can move on from this ordeal... please."

His warming smile and expression is too much for Tiffany to ignore, and she purses her lips again but in a more accepting gesture, as Luke says, "thank you, you won't regret this." He turns around and walks over to Pearl, who is quite relaxed as she cradles and dotes over Stephen.

Pearl sees a form of a shadow at her feet, and looks up to see a smiling Luke. Perplexed and somewhat happy to see someone, she is still psychologically in such a state, that she is remiss as to who it is standing before her.

Luke is about to talk when Pearl asks, 'who are you again?"

Luke replies and asks if he could bring her daughter over to chat about last night, hoping recent outbursts are far removed from Pearl's mind, and that Stephen is more at the front of her thoughts.

Luke turns to Tiffany, who is standing a few feet away, and as Pearl begins to stand with Luke's help, Tiffany somehow realises her mother has probably been through her worst night as well, and puts her arms around Pearl in a loving and apologetic embrace, as does Pearl, and the tears start to flow.

Both mumble apologies to each other as Luke looks on, pleased for both of them.

He takes Tiffany's hand and they embrace. Tiffany thanks him for everything and plants one firmly, and this time Luke responds in kind and doesn't let go.

Pearl is looking on, wondering when did this happen,

when Scotty comes over and also stands at her feet to get her attention.

Pearl turns and looks into his eyes and is still not sure who is who, with all these people around, and without blinking, but recognising the police uniform, just not his name, she asks, "Who are you... and what have you done with my husband?"

49

THE STEERING TIMES

There are criminals who in some way assume they are above the law.

Mario Sculini (alias The Boss) was one of those who is now dead, after years of ruling his chosen territory in the underworld. Last night, during a shootout between members of the Federal Crime Task Force, The Boss and a number of his bodyguards, a single bullet ended Sculini's reign.

A young girl, believed to be a family member, was found in a wine cellar with a young male. Police are releasing neither of their identities at this stage.

A tip off as to the whereabouts of The Boss was received by the Task Force after an alleged attempted murder in a small North Western Country town called Steering, about five hours drive northwest of Melbourne near Mildura, a few days ago.

A man of Russian descent was captured by police while holding a journalist and a policeman at gunpoint on the outskirts of the town. Reports are unclear at present, however I have been able to ascertain that it all stems from the journalists investigation into underworld dealings. But the senior constable, who had been under threat from the Russian, spoke of the heroic efforts of a farmer and his dog, which together disarmed their assailant, allowing the officer to handcuff him.

The accused was reported to be a huge man, well over 200cms (over seven feet tall) and weighing about130 kilos.

It has also been revealed that a serious accident occurred that night at the scene of the arrest. It is unclear whether the two incidents are related.

50

CORONIAL INVESTIGATION

ictim 1

DAVID LOCKWOOD WAS DRIVING a 2011 Mercedes (4WD) on the 3rd of February 2011. His wife, Pearl, was a passenger, along with their three children, Tiffany seventeen, Rhys fifteen and Stephen, six months.

The point of collision was at Mackenzie's bridge carrying a single lane in each direction. The Lockwood family entered the bridge outside the town of Steering around 7.30pm. The roads were wet from heavy rain that began two hours earlier and was still intense at the time of the accident.

At the same time a Kenworth prime mover carrying the owner/driver, Ron Williams 40, his wife Dianne 38, and their two twin children, Bridgette and Stephanie 8, was pulling a cattle trailer, and approaching from the opposite direction.

The prime mover crossed onto the westbound lane and

was not seen by Mr. Lockwood until it was too late for him to take evasive action, due to the intense rain.

A collision occurred between the front passenger side of the prime mover and Mr. Lockwood's 4WD, causing the latter to crash through the bridge's railing and into the river approximately ten meters below. None of the surviving occupants suffered serious injuries except for mild concussion, from which they all recovered later in the evening.

Unfortunately, Mr. Lockwood died during the night from snakebite to the neck.

The snake had reportedly followed the family into their car where they were sheltering from the fierce storm. He also suffered a broken arm.

Victim 2 and 3

After the initial collision, a SUV, driven by Mr. Nick McKenzie, and included his brothers; Rick, Brian, Ryan and Luke, arrived on the scene and collided with the trailer of the prime mover.

In circumstances described later, Nick, Ryan and Brian all met their deaths in a most violent manner, from being gorged to death by a terrorising bull. Rick was seriously injured. He is badly concussed and sporting a serious shiner on his right eye, and some minor cuts and abrasions on his chest and back. Luke McKenzie escaped virtually unscathed and was instrumental in the provision of assistance for remaining survivors.

The Crash Unit Forensics investigated the circumstances of the crash.

The prime mover was the subject of a mechanical inspection, and the opinion produced was that it was in good condition, with efficient braking systems. There were no suspension faults in the trailer.

The Road Transport Authority (RTA) also prepared a detailed report concerning the surface friction of the bridge at the scene, as well a safety analysis of the suitability of the bridge. Concerns in relation to both of these matters were expressed.

Mrs. Lockwood requested that an inquest be held as at the time of the accident she was in no state to comprehend what had happened. Given there were some considerable uncertainties in relation to a number of issues, a decision was made to hold an inquest.

THE ISSUES TO BE ESTABLISHED:

1. The identity of the deceased persons. When, where and how they died, what caused their deaths, and the circumstances leading to their deaths?

2. Conduct of the prime mover driver involved in the collision, and mechanical condition of the prime mover.

3. The condition, layout, and engineering of the bridge and road surface at, and near the site of the collision.

4. Whether similar deaths at the site can be prevented from occurring in the future.

. . .

THE SCOPE of an inquest goes beyond merely establishing the medical cause of death. An inquest is not a trial between opposing parties, but an inquiry into the cause of death or deaths. The focus is on discovering what happened, not on ascribing guilt, attributing blame or apportioning liability.

The purpose is to inform the family and the public of how the deaths occurred, with a view to reducing the likelihood of similar deaths.

As a result, the Act authorises a Coroner to make preventive recommendations concerning public health or safety.

A Coroner must not include in the findings any comments, recommendations or statements that a person is, or may be, guilty of an offence, or is, or may be, civilly liable.

AUTOPSY RESULTS

An autopsy examination found multiple, traumatic injuries suffered by Nick and Ryan McKenzie in the front seats of the SUV. These included crash injuries to the chest with multiple rib fractures and ruptured diaphragm. An extensively ruptured liver; multiple face and arm fractures and a non-displaced cervical spine fracture.

THE CAUSE of Nick McKenzie's death was due to the heart being pierced by the horn of a bull, which partially released itself from the crashed semi-trailer. The multiple rib fractures may have been caused as a result of the motor vehicle accident, with other injuries contributing. Pneumothorax, the presence of air or gas in the cavity between the lungs and the chest wall, causing the collapse of the lung, was also present.

Ryan and Brian McKenzie died from similar injuries, also attributed to attacks by one or more bulls.

Mr. David Lockwood died from the effects of snakebite. Significant quantities of the snake's venom were found in his system.

The Crash Unit Forensics (CUF) provided a report to the coroner, detailing the type of venom and it was requested the information not become public.

The lead investigator was Senior Constable Scott Taylor who was also the first response officer on the scene. SC Taylor had completed the basic Forensic Crash Unit training as well as having significant practical experience. Sergeant Bert Logan also assisted.

SC Taylor reported that the bridge has been rarely used since the decline of the local economy during the '80s.

CUF Report on Scene Observations and Conditions

It was estimated that Mr. Lockwood had less than a second to take evasive action. Having regard to the closing speeds between the two vehicles of about ten-twenty k.p.h. SC Taylor stated that realistically Mr. Lockwood had no opportunity or options to avoid the crash.

The truck driver and his passengers all suffered minor injuries. The unusual position and angle of the prime mover, which collided with Mr. Lockwood's vehicle, suggested to SC Taylor that the intense rain caused the crash.

The prime mover entered from the western side of the bridge, and its trailer was wedged against the light pole, after tumbling into the river and landing on top of Mr. Lockwood's car but not squashing it as the trailer was wedged against the bridge.

SC Taylor was able to confirm that the RTA Road Rules provide that it is legal for a motor vehicle to enter the bridge when it is occupied by another vehicle.

The investigation revealed that, as the bridge was rarely used by more than one vehicle at a time, this was a case of the three vehicles being in the wrong place, at the wrong time.

The driver of the prime mover submitted to a roadside breath test, which was negative for alcohol. There were no traces of drugs found either. Each of the three deceased brothers had blood readings over 0.10.

Senior Constable Taylor concluded there were four major contributing factors to the accident. In order of significance they were:

1. The intense rain, and suspect road surface.

2. The decayed condition of the bridge

3. The flushing by rain of the road surface

4. The lack of visibility for all involved

SC Taylor, in talks with the relevant authorities, has concluded there should be flashing lights set up at either end of the bridge to warn any approaching drivers that another vehicle is occupying the bridge, and to wait for this vehicle to exit before entering.

. . .

Conclusions

WHEN MR. LOCKWOOD saw the prime mover ahead of them, he had no opportunity to take any evasive action. There were a number of factors identified by the CUF investigations, which contributed to the accident.

It is difficult to apportion these factors in percentage terms, and I find they all contributed in some part.

Certainly the wooden bridge configuration combined with the slippery surface and decaying structure, played significant roles.

I will be recommending Luke McKenzie for a bravery award for his actions in helping rescue those involved in this terrible accident.

Mr John Meadows and his dog Ziggy will also receive my recommendations for recognition of their bravery in overcoming the assailant in the latter stages of this matter.

COMMENTS AND RECOMMENDATIONS

It is recommended, if not already being implemented, that the RTA proceed with the design and re-construction of the Mackenzie's bridge, and a flashing light system connected to the police station for regular monitoring.

I intend to provide information gained from the investigation and inquest to the relevant authorities forthwith.

I close the inquest.

State Coroner

25th February 2012.

Appendix

MOST ANIMALS SLAUGHTERED for food in Australia have had their throats cut open with a knife (referred to as "sticking") so that they can be bled out. Prior to this, they are typically meant to be unconscious (though as of 2011, abattoirs in Australia have permission from state governments to slit the throats of fully conscious animals, as part of the religious practices of "halal" and "kosher" slaughter). There are three main methods of 'stunning' intended to make animals unconscious before slaughter, captive bolt, electric, and gas chambers.

THE ART OF ROAD USE

Most drivers have a reasonable understanding of their approach to driving anywhere around the world, especially in trying conditions. However even the most dedicated and professional drivers, like me, will at times revert to the age-old saying "(I'm only human)." So knowing full well the ins and outs of driving in all weather conditions, as I have a reasonable grasp of the law, and how I understand the road rules.

I thought I would provide you with the following insight, that could best serve you while you are manoeuvring your way around, on the many and varied roads while on your journey from point A to B.

In anything we do in life, there is an inherent art or a developed skill that we have accumulated over time. Giving each of us the ability to do whatever we put our minds to. But sometimes these abilities can come undone for various reasons, as I will endeavour to explain in the following examples.

52

DRIVE TO THE CONDITIONS

I f you have been driving on dry roads for what seems an eternity, and there hasn't been any rain for a while. You might want to think about your abilities alongside the added risks involved, when driving in unfamiliar conditions. As you are confronted with more issues than you are used to, you should drive to the conditions, and plan your journey, especially if the road will take you through hills and fog-riddled valleys. In severe conditions it makes perfect sense to slow down, and take pride out of the equation. Remember you're only human, and you will eventually get too where you are going... alive.

53

OVERTAKING

Regardless as to whether it is day or night, you must be aware of a couple of things that will make your overtaking manoeuvre much safer, than just pulling out and planting it. First of all, you must be a reasonable distance behind the vehicle you are overtaking, plus be mindful if you're towing a trailer or caravan.

Once the road ahead levels out and your vision is good, and then make sure you are a minimum of fifty meters behind the vehicle in front of you. Then time your passing manoeuvre by slowly building up speed. As the oncoming vehicle passes you, you have a better and safer opportunity to pass unimpeded. And it takes less time than if you did not perform this manoeuvre properly.

Flash flooding and driving in water

Six inches of water under most family cars will cause the loss of control and stalling. Twelve inches of water will float many vehicles. Any more than two feet of water flowing fast or slow will move most vehicles, especially heavier ones like SUVS and Utes along with the current.

54

MIRROR-MIRROR INTIMIDATION

I f you continually look in your rear view mirror because there is a vehicle too close to you, then this driver has control over you, as you should be watching what happens in front of you, to control them.

What I've done is have the night vision on at all times during the day, so they can't see me looking at them. It's like your mobile phone, don't let anything distract your driving, focus on what's ahead, and stay in control. And take them out of the equation.

MOTION DISORIENTATION

I f you've been travelling at a high speed and then all of a sudden you have to slow down to half or a quarter of that speed, for school zones, roadworks etc. What happens here is that the brain tries to suddenly adjust. That will vary with every driver. Take your foot slightly off the accelerator and the rest will take care of itself. I do the same if I approach traffic lights, if I'm not prepared for a light change, especially if I'm towing or carrying a heavy load, like even a small trailer. Remember you're driving from point A to B and you must concentrate on that, not what you're doing at B.

BACK ROADS and dirt roads

Again drive to the conditions and take pride out of the equation and you'll get there eventually.

Back roads and dirt roads are narrower and treacherous at the best of times. And those with bitumen have wide or narrow dirt shoulders, and if faced with any oncoming vehicle, then the rule of thumb here is to slow down and pass each other at the same speed. If it's a larger vehicle then come to a stop. The stones in the dirt don't possibly hit your car or worse still, the windscreen.

With dirt only roads there are two thoughts here.

First, you have minimal control at the best of times. You should stay at best in the middle of the road, except when you are slowing down, or confronted with another oncoming vehicle. Secondly, braking suddenly provides you with absolutely no, none, nil grip whatsoever. So again, drive to the conditions.

56

LIGHT CHANGING

I f you're driving all night, like most interstate truckies do, you need a sleep/break, at sunup or sunset. Same goes if you're driving all day. And that's for ordinary motorists as well. It's a chemical reaction. Like when you're yawning or you're eyelids are starting to flutter, or close for periods longer than normal. That's basically telling you your body it's time to pull over, or change drivers. Especially if you're travelling interstate or long distance that you haven't done before. And with all these freeways being built around most countries, there's less hassle in stopping or going through smaller towns now, but you can always take a turnoff and visit one if you're tired or hungry, rather than stopping at one of the bigger truck stops.

It's becoming more attractive to drive, be it on your own or with others, and you can share the driving. You need sleep if you've been driving all night or all day. If you don't get even so much as a power nap, you'll nod off or have a microsleep, which can cause you to completely fall asleep at the wheel. That's why drivers often crash first thing in the morning, because they haven't slept all night, or have had too little sleep.

Most interstate and local truck drivers have fatigue management training nowadays, and are taught to have regular breaks. It is better policed than it used to be, so there's no excuse for trying to beat the system. Depending where you drive in this world, you might not have some or all of these regulations.

Nowadays you'll see trucks of all shapes and sizes parked on the side of the road, around lunch time. As it is now compulsory that truck drivers must have a regulated break, it's the law now, in Australia.

57

DRIVING IN SEVERE CONDITIONS

I continue on if I know the road, especially in conditions, like if there's fog. If you don't know the road, you should wait it out, or you should drive to the conditions, and take your time from point A to B.

Fog is claustrophobic at best, and to think you know better, means you are only asking for trouble. Depending on the various locations around the world, sleet, snow and whiteout conditions are even more treacherous. If planes don't fly in these conditions, then you shouldn't drive either, if you're not comfortable with what's in front of you.

Going through a tunnel for the first time

I spoke with a few people about going through a tunnel for the first time, and I was surprised how many were critical of road authorities, for failing to provide instruction on navigating the tunnel, regardless of where it is located.

Most professional drivers, including taxis, couriers and the like, who do it every day, we know how to... I guess... work the tunnel, as it's just second nature to us. But for the average motorist, be they in a car, van or towing something, my best advice is stay in the left lane, except in the single lane tunnels. Either way once you're in any tunnel, you're subject to the conditions, regardless of how you feel at the time. Then just go with the flow 'til you get more confident.

Apart from the morning and afternoon peak times, it will always seem like a long trip due to the amount of traffic congestion. But there are those who feel claustrophobic in a tunnel, and are anxious to get out as quickly as possible, thus creating more congestion because of what they are doing. They try to go too fast or too slow, and end up causing accidents. Sometimes the run is quite short, but can feel like ages. However you can double or triple that in peak times.

After a few times, you will start to gain a bit more confidence as to knowing what to do, and eventually you might start to use another lane, or just decide to stay to the left.

Some valuable hints when entering and going through any tunnel are as follows.

Check and understand the signs above and on the roadway, and normal headlights and radio on for emergency announcements. Do you have plenty of fuel? Don't use sunglasses in the darkened tunnel. If you see there is a breakdown or accident that has just happened, or if you are stuck for a short time, put your hazards on until you can indicate to get passed if possible. Or you'll have to wait until you can proceed by someone authorised.

Use your car's Air Conditioning on low, only on very hot days as it can get much hotter inside the tunnel when congestion occurs. If the traffic is fast moving and you've been in an accident or broken down, stay in the vehicle. Unless a vehicle is about to catch fire, turn off the engine also, if stopped for any period longer than expected. Pull off to the side if you can. Note your vehicle's location. Assess your vehicle's operating problem.

Call the emergency number located in the tunnel and tell them your situation. Wait calmly for an incident vehicle to arrive. When you exit the tunnel, wait until you have adjusted to the change in light conditions, especially during sunny days, and if it is sunny, you can choose to turn off your headlights.

58

ROAD HOG

I know there are people who don't like trucks hogging the road and sitting in the fast lane. A lot of motorists don't realise if they cut in front of a truck, they can't slow down or stop as quickly as smaller vehicles can, especially if they're loaded. It can cause an accident, as well as slowing other vehicles that are following on behind the truck. Unfortunately this will not change as some drivers that believe the fast lane, is always the fastest lane... not.

MERGING

This is another interpreted unwritten law that also exists. When you come down or along the onramp to merge with traffic already on the freeway, or any road, then it's your responsibility to merge with them, not the other way round, regardless if you have on ramp signals or not. Vehicles already on the freeway have priority, so you should give way to them and merge with them, by looking earlier, rather than waiting until the last second. By then it's too late, and you could cause others behind you to have an accident. Unfortunately, peak times it is pretty much everyone for themselves, as with the amount of vehicles in peak times and under-developed roads, there is no quick fix.

OBEYING SPEED LIMITS AND AT ALL
ROADWORK'S

S peed limits are a good thing generally, and on the odd occasion, you will get protests about a certain speed. Like recently in a suburb near me, parents forced the roads authority to reduce the speed limit near a school, and won, so there's a good outcome for all concerned.

As for roadwork speed limits, the problem here is lack of uniformity from the road authorities, regardless of where you live. And just as much intolerance from motorists, especially when there are no workmen around. Or there are signs that were left on the side of the road, forgotten after the works were completed. Workers are entitled to protection at all times. But sometimes there is no cohesion from both sides as to whether all the protocols have been implemented for their safety.

This is an annoying and common practice and it will only get worse due to the ever-increasing population, with not only new roads, but increasing lanes on current ones. There is a simple reason for these limits. But not a lot of thought has gone into the dynamic of the real time effect for continued flow of vehicles, and more importantly the safety of its workers.

61

SO THERE IS A NEED FOR...

One thing drivers don't realise is that you could be caught at any time flouting the law. But most drivers have become used to not being caught, so they continue on as if they are doing nothing wrong. And the same can be said about using mobile phones while driving, and it's only going to get worse. Especially with technology with more mobile phones, in every vehicle people are texting or talking with someone.

62

CYCLIST'S V DRIVERS, WHO IS AT FAULT?

I f you're following another vehicle and you are too close to them, as you do not want other drivers to push in front of you, then you are missing vehicles on the side of the road, more importantly a cyclist. Also if there are cyclists taking up most, or the entire lane, and they are continually doing every day, and you believe this should not be allowed, then you have the right to complain to the relevant authorities. Before you think about what inconvenience it is causing to others like you, you might not get the result you were looking for. Think about the inconvenience it's causing you, or are you not paying attention like you should be?

Driving a truck, bus/coach, what's the height?

IS THERE a need to check if there are any bridges that you need to go under on your way to point B. unfortunately most if not all apps do not have any information regarding bridges or the height? So I would urge all companies to have their drivers measure their truck, but, and most importantly, the height of their load. Also just before a bridge and at the bridge itself are well positioned signs telling drivers what the height limit is. So you should ask yourself, why you hit the bridge.

How to deal with big trucks in city and country areas

Like most things in life, trucks are a necessary evil, and there will only be more of them in the future. But there is one thing that is paramount, to you not getting anxious about these massive mobile monoliths. Treat them the same as any other vehicle around you and don't ever cut in front of them, even if you think there is a space for you. Simply put, they cannot stop on a small coin like a car can, and if they are loaded then their stopping distance is quantified by their speed and load.

Example, if it's travelling at sixty kph a loaded truck will take at least one hundred meters to stop safely, whereas a car can stop in less than fifteen meters. So respect the trucks, go with the flow of traffic and you'll get to point B in about the same time. As I said trucks are a necessary evil. The next time you go shopping for whatever you need, consider the ramifications with our bursting populations, as to how you would survive. Bees for example are a perfect analogy of how things in nature work. Truck drivers are the worker bees that are a required element, to allowing society to function as a whole. Somebody has to do it so we shouldn't be victimized like we are. A little bit of understanding and knowledge on your part would go a long way in bridging the gap?

Damaged roads who to contact, and road funding. Who's responsible?

CONTACT your local council and they should tell you if it is their road, or the road authority in your state.

63

WHAT'S APP

Regardless of the app you're using, there is no quick fix as to knowing if the time you're given to go from point A to B, will be within what it is saying. Accidents and road hazards are common practice these days, and as I have said on numerous occasions already, nothing is what it seems. However there are exceptions to this no matter what app or where you're driving. So what I do is expect double on most of my journeys to counter the unexpected, **in all peak times.**

It doesn't matter if it is day or night, City or Country, as you are guaranteed like the nose on your face that "shit happens." Good luck.

64

KILLING A HUMAN V AN ANIMAL

F irst and foremost, it's better to hit the animal rather than swerving or braking hard to avoid it. Most people have no wish to kill a live animal, but a human life is always more valuable. Missing a human and killing an animal is socially acceptable, but killing a human just to miss killing an animal, is not.

Distanced travelled with your eyes off the road

THERE IS a simple way to figure out how far you've travelled, while you're driving along any road. But nowadays a lot of drivers are practically doing exactly that, using mobile phones when they should be watching the road.

They don't understand the distance their vehicle travels while their attention is diverted. Every second their eyes are off the road, they're moving closer to disaster, like running of the road or hitting and killing someone.

Distances travelled at any speed are easily calculated at twenty five percent of the speed you are travelling at. For example, at one hundred kilometres per hour, you travel twenty-five meters in one second, that's the length of a b-double semi-trailer. A slower speed of sixty kilometres per hour, you will travel fifteen meters, that's the length of a normal semi-trailer, believing that it's okay to look away for what is only a second. In reality, someone could be dead by the time you read this sentence now.

HOPEFULLY MOST PEOPLE will listen to reason and think about what I've said, and who knows, some might realise what it would be like if us guys stopped for a week. There'd be riots with no food, milk, bread and so on, so maybe people should be a little bit more thoughtful about their driving habits.

65

DRIVE SMARTER NOT FASTER

Thoughts from the Author

As a driver for over forty years and being in the transport industry for about two thirds of that time, I have seen enough in my lifetime, to facilitate the above story. You either have your head in the sand, or you cannot avoid hearing or seeing, the many and varied incidents that I've witnessed on our roads over that time, some of the most shocking nature.

Speaking of nature, we are all in some way driven (excuse the cliché), but in some profound way we as in humans, animals and the weather, are all inextricably linked to our own destiny.

It's my belief that we all evolve every five-ten years, as we grow older. It's the life skills that determine our future.

In the environment of people we socialise with, it brings us into a place where your life skills transform you into something you have never seen or faced before. I've seen things most people my age could not even imagine, but it has to be in person. Seeing stuff on T.V. or in a movie just doesn't cut it, especially if you haven't been to a war zone.

Experience beats youth hands down, because as we get older, taking risks takes a back seat, and I can vouch for that.

ABOUT THE AUTHOR

My life skills were learnt, not taught. We all have our own way of digesting what we see and do in our lives.

Driving and working in many other occupations over my lifetime, and doing what I've been doing for so long, has taught me that you learn a lot about yourself, as well as others. Your life skills become your friend, and you pick them up as you do things like I have in driving and gardening. I had to learn about the weather so I could be in control of my work commitments, especially over the last twenty years.

Unfortunately, within a couple of months after getting out of my gardening business, our house was destroyed by fire, at 5am on a windy Sunday morning, gone in just seven minutes.

But driving around most of the country has also taught me a lot about being resilient, when the weather has been, how you say, horrible. Heavy rain, fog, wind, snow, narrow bridges, farms, city traffic and the list goes on. Not to mention dealing with all kinds of people and animals. Worst of all is the long journey Cyclone Yasi took from Mission Beach in North Queensland, until it left Victoria a few days later.

This is how I came up with this fictional story, and it is based on actual events over my trucking life.